CHARIOT

CHARIOT

CHARLES GRANT

A Tom Doherty Associates Book New York

CHARIOT

Copyright © 1998 by Charles Grant

This book is printed on acid-free paper.

A Forge Book
Published by Tom Doherty Associates, Inc.
175 Fifth Avenue
New York, NY 10010

Forge® is a registered trademark of Tom Doherty Associates, Inc.

Library of Congress Cataloging-in-Publication Data

Grant, Charles L.
    Chariot / Charles Grant.—1st ed.
      p. cm.
    "A Tom Doherty Associates book."
    ISBN 0-312-86278-4
    I. Title.
PS3557.R265C47   1998   98-35301
813'.54—dc21   CIP

First Edition: November 1998

Printed in the United States of America

0 9 8 7 6 5 4 3 2 1

For Minerva C. Grant,
with pride and love,
and a chocolate whipped cream cake.

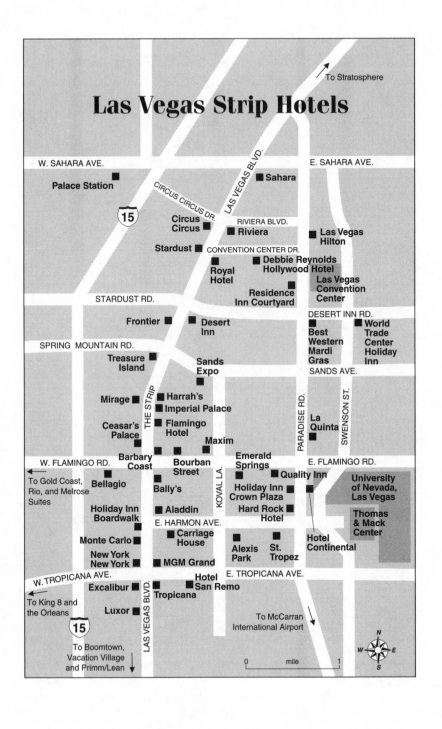

Las Vegas Strip Hotels

To Stratosphere

W. SAHARA AVE.

E. SAHARA AVE.

Palace Station

■ Sahara

CIRCUS CIRCUS DR.

LAS VEGAS BLVD.

15

Circus
Circus ■

RIVIERA BLVD.

■ Riviera

■ Las Vegas
Hilton

Stardust ■ CONVENTION CENTER DR.

■ Debbie Reynolds
Hollywood Hotel

Royal
Hotel

Las Vegas
Convention
Center

Residence
Inn Courtyard

STARDUST RD.

Frontier ■ ■ Desert
Inn

DESERT INN RD.

■ ■ World
Trade
Center
Holiday
Inn

SPRING MOUNTAIN RD.

Best
Western
Mardi
Gras

Treasure ■
Island

Sands
Expo

SANDS AVE.

THE STRIP

Mirage ■ ■ Harrah's
■ Imperial Palace

PARADISE RD.

SWENSON ST.

Ceasar's
Palace

■ Flamingo
Hotel

■ La
Quinta

Maxim
■

Barbary
Coast

Emerald
Springs

W. FLAMINGO RD.

■ Bourban
Street

KOVAL LA.

■ Quality Inn

E. FLAMINGO RD.

To Gold Coast,
Rio, and Melrose
Suites

Bellagio

Bally's

Holiday Inn
Crown Plaza

University
of Nevada,
Las Vegas

Holiday Inn
Boardwalk

■ Aladdin

Hard Rock ■
Hotel

Thomas
& Mack
Center

Monte Carlo ■

E. HARMON AVE.

New York
New York ■

■ Carriage
House

Hotel
Continental

■ MGM Grand

Alexis
Park

St.
Tropez

W. TROPICANA AVE.

Hotel
San Remo

E. TROPICANA AVE.

■ Excalibur ■

LAS VEGAS BLVD.

Tropicana

To King 8 and
the Orleans

Luxor ■

15

To McCarran
International Airport

To Boomtown,
Vacation Village
and Primm/Lean

N
W E
S

0   mile   1

Part 1

DREAMED LAST NIGHT . . .

1

1

The dragon lay in the middle of the desert. Sleeping. Always sleeping. A mirage, for those who believed in ghosts; a metaphor, for those who believed only in seeing. And what they saw, ghosts or not, were eyes and scales that glowed in Joseph's glorious colors as soon as the sun went down, bright enough to drive the stars back behind the mountains that formed the broad and long desert valley, almost bright enough to kill the moon.

Blinding without pain.

The dragon didn't care.

It never stirred; it only breathed.

And every sunrise it vanished, only the heat of its fire left behind, colors fading to bland.

The man who stood on the small porch of his small home knew it was a fanciful, even a gaudy notion—dragons and ghosts and scales and breathing fire—but it helped explain the way the city, smack dab in the middle of what used to be nowhere, had taken over the desert when the desert wasn't looking. He didn't much care for the dragon. He didn't much care for the desert, either, but there were times when he had no choice but to visit both.

He grunted a humorless laugh.

Visit?

Not likely.

Nobody really visits Las Vegas. It's a place people use as an excuse to die.

He grunted again, not liking his mood. It was dangerous, feeling like this, but he couldn't help it. Couldn't stop it. Couldn't figure it out.

He stretched, yawned loudly, and scratched the back of his neck vigorously. A glance at the white wood lawn chair beside the door, and he decided to stand. A day like today, it would be too easy just to have a seat and doze the evening away.

He was a medium-size man who managed to look taller through no effort of his own. Hair that brushed over his ears, thick and richly auburn, a smattering of silver he'd stopped bothering to hide. Eyes that squinted more often than not, even in the dark. A slight hook to his nose. Hands that looked rough and arms that looked thick; more than once he'd been mistaken for a laborer of some kind, especially since he seldom wore suits, and hardly ever a tie. He never visited a gym, or a spa, or had equipment at home, but a strong man nonetheless, naturally so.

The usual uniform tonight: a pair of polished brown boots, clean black jeans, an untucked white shirt that hung over his belt, not quite loose enough to hide completely the slow birth of a paunch. Sleeves rolled up one fold shy of his elbows. A pack of cigarettes in the breast pocket.

He stretched again, yawned again, and rubbed the side of his nose, hard, squinting against the glare of the fast-setting sun off the windows of the house across and up the street.

Y'know, he thought, left hand slipping under the shirt so the thumb could hook under the belt; y'know, maybe you ought to skip it tonight, y'know? Maybe you should just let the damn critter alone just this once.

A nice idea, very tempting; unfortunately, not an option.

The refrigerator needed filling, the rent needed paying, and he couldn't shake the feeling that his wallet needed, desperately needed, feeding.

That made him uneasy, because he didn't know why.

He knew it wasn't the news; he'd stopped watching that a long time ago. The explosive violence that had ignited across the country had calmed; the famine that had created lines for bread and eggs and simple pleasures like ice cream had been relieved when last year's spring rains had mercifully returned and farmers once again took to their plows, herds were replenished, and slowly, very slowly, the lines began to disappear.

That was the good news.

The bad news was the young woman, name unknown to him, who had staggered out of Notre Dame cathedral seven months ago, in Paris, in October, and collapsed on the steps. Fever burned her, eruptions pocked her, and no one wanted to admit that what had once been believed eliminated had returned.

With a vengeance.

The young woman had been the first.

She was far from the last.

He had no idea how many had the Sickness now, only knew that the fear he felt whenever he heard the latest rumors, whenever he inadvertently saw a headline out of the corner of his eye, wasn't entirely due to the horrors of the dead and the dying.

There was something else, and it gave him occasional nightmares, all bleeding colors and no substance.

A sudden gust of hot wind made him turn his head away from the grit and sand that hissed past him. He spat automatically, though none had gotten into his mouth, and wiped his lips with the back of a hand.

"Shouldn't spit, Trey," a little girl's voice scolded playfully. "Momma says that's impolite and rude and unsanitary."

The child who belonged to the voice stood in the unpaved street. A T-shirt, beat-up jeans, and thick-soled sandals. Long hair parted in the middle and hanging over her shoulders in braids. A pug nose he wanted to kiss each time he saw it. A dimple in her chin, just like her mother.

"Evening, Moonbow," he said, leaning a shoulder against the porch post, folding his arms across his chest. "Do you even know what unsanitary means?"

She nodded solemnly. "Sure. It means you can't eat the food you drop on the floor or you'll get icky germs."

He frowned. "That's funny. I do it all the time, and I don't get sick."

Her eyes widened. "Really? Will you call me the next time? I want to watch."

He laughed without a sound, pushed away from the post and stepped lightly off the porch. He inhaled slowly, filling his lungs, exhaled slowly with a long and exaggerated sigh of contentment.

"I think," he announced, "I am going to build a castle."

Moonbow giggled, and he shrugged.

Why not? It wasn't like anyone would notice, except maybe a couple of bored lizards and a buzzard or two.

He and those left of his neighbors lived as deep into the desert as they possibly could while still taking advantage of the city's services. A development that had gone so far as to lay out streets, mark acre-size plots with little stakes flying little red flags, lay in water and electricity, and erect a billboard that told the public they couldn't possibly do better than to live in Emerald City.

It was supposed to have been a showcase.

Expensive houses all over the place. Low-slung, sprawling affairs with, according to the artist's renditions in the slick brochures he had seen, walls and gardens and fountains and for God's sake trees that hadn't been seen west of the Mississippi in a good eon or two.

When the development company went bust some nine years ago and the city took over, the plots became magnets for those who wanted so desperately to live in the desert by the dragon that they didn't much care about what the city eventually built to recoup some of its losses—small four-room-with-bath stucco-façade houses with fake California-tile roofs, casement windows, and central air-conditioning units that growled like lost bears. One to an acre, most of the land in back. The rooms were small, function over comfort. When someone threw a party—a birthday, an anniversary, a thank God I'm moving out—everyone always ended up outside just so they could breathe.

No landscaping at all.

The yards, front and back, were sharp-bladed tufts of desert grass, sandy soil, a cactus here and there, and here and there a garden that usually required more tending than a sick baby. A shrub or two. Joshua trees.

And almost everything died by the middle of July.

Thanks to Moonbow's suggestion one night late last summer, he now had an invisible hedge that bordered the street. Together they trimmed it with equally invisible tools, made sure no one walked through it and damaged the branches, and had been thinking about turning some of it into a topiary after she'd seen one in a gardening book.

"You know, kid," he'd said one afternoon in November, "sometimes you're as loony as your mother."

She didn't speak to him for five days.

The dragon beat him senseless every night until she forgave him.

What she didn't understand, what he thought he truly understood, was that you really did have to be loony to live out here. Only one long street, no streetlights, no curbs, no paving, no sidewalks, no nothing.

Over the years, the place had picked up a reputation, and now the only ones who would live here were people like him. And Moonbow's mother.

Still, the city didn't seem to mind; it collected its due and left them pretty much alone, except for the occasional visit by a town or state official who wandered around the area, wondering what in hell had happened out here. The cops didn't care; they patrolled once in a great while, mainly just to see if anyone was still dumb enough to stick around. There was seldom any trouble. Nobody killed anybody; nobody robbed anybody else. And those who came out to do just that were actively discouraged from ever coming back.

The wind blew again, and he looked up at the sky running blood behind the sun almost gone.

He shook his head.

Stay home, the wind told him; do yourself a favor and stay the hell home.

And what if I don't?

No problem; you're going to die.

Quickly he turned back to the house, for no reason at all thinking he'd seen hunting cabins bigger than this, for crying out loud, and reached for the post with his left hand. He patted its rough sides, ran a palm along them slowly, and stepped back.

Nope.

He wouldn't die tonight. The house was still waiting.

"Trey?"

Yet the apprehension wouldn't leave. He checked the sky again, just to be sure there wasn't a storm on the way, and blinked when he finally figured out what was wrong—or part of it, anyway:

It wasn't the news; it wasn't the nightmares. It was, for the time being, more important than that—he had passed a milestone without realizing it.

"Two years," he whispered in quiet amazement. "Son of a bitch. Two years two months, this month."

"Cursing is bad for you," Moonbow scolded, coming up behind him.

"Germs?" he asked, not turning around.

"No. It makes you all ugly and disgusting inside. Like an icky gnome."

He hunched over, hooked his fingers into claws, twisted one side of his mouth, bulged his right eye, and whirled to face her. "Like *this,* little mistress?"

She studied him carefully. "I don't think so. I don't think you can drool inside."

He stared as she took a tissue from her hip pocket and gently pat-dried the side of his mouth. "Thank you."

"You're welcome."

They shook hands and moved to the gap in the invisible hedge. Stood side by side. Waiting for the sun to die behind them.

His house was the first on the right, the first in the development, and the only one with no blocking structure across the street. This allowed him to mark when the dragon's scales began to glow, a man-made borealis that put the rest of the city's lights to shame.

"How old are you, Moonbow?" Spoken softly, in the twilight.

"Ten. Next Thursday." She sounded disappointed he hadn't re-membered.

He nodded. "So what special present would you like?"

"Momma says it isn't right I should ask for anything. She said that would be . . ." She concentrated before saying, ". . . materi-alistic."

"I see."

"That means—"

"I know what it means, Moonbow. And no offense, but your mother's a loon." He stiffened, scolding himself for speaking without thinking.

"I know," the child answered, a little sadly, but grinning nonetheless.

"Good. Then I'll get you something anyway."

"A necklace," she suggested immediately, enthusiastically. "I'd like to have a necklace." Without looking up, she took his hand.

"Okay." He made a show of concentrating. "I think I can manage that. Emeralds or diamonds?"

"Pearls."

"Man. Didn't waste any time, did you?"

"I like pearls. They're pretty. Starshine says diamonds are tacky, though."

She would, he thought. Sister Starshine, two years older by the calendar, much older than that otherwise. At least she liked to pretend she was. Sometimes it worked. Trey thought she was spooky.

He glanced up the street. "Where is she?"

Moonbow shrugged. "Home, I guess. Momma won't let her out until she does her homework. I already did mine. It was easy. Starshine hates school, you know. She thinks it's a waste of time. She says everybody's going to be dead soon, so there isn't any point."

"Not true, kid."

"But—"

He squeezed her hand briefly. "So when was the last time we had a case here, huh?"

Moonbow frowned. "I don't know. Never?"

"Never, that's right. Not one. Ever. Las Vegas is as pure as the driven snow. Not even a pimple."

She giggled. "Starshine has pimples. One right on the top of her nose. She steals Momma's makeup to hide it."

"And you don't get them, right?"

"Nope. That's 'cause I wash my face every day. That's 'cause I stay clean."

"Good for you."

Twilight deepened.

A stereo up the block showered the street with soft violins.

"Trey?"

"Hmmm?"

"Are you going to be here? For my birthday, I mean?"

"I guess I am," he answered, sounding surprised. "You know, I guess I am."

Two years; two years and change without leaving.

Without—

"Good. I don't like it when you're not here."

He wasn't at all sure he felt the same. Yet, when he wasn't here . . .

He shuddered.

Not tonight; you *are* here, and that's what matters.

Up the street a light clicked on at the corner of someone's porch roof. Seconds later, another light, hooded and carefully aimed at the street so those who walked at night wouldn't be blinded. Every night, rotating equally among all the renters except him, they replaced the absent streetlamps.

Moonbow tugged his hand. "You gonna fight the dragon tonight?"

He nodded.

She whispered, "You're supposed to have a princess, you know."

"I have one," he answered, and squeezed her hand again.

A long minute, standing in the twilight, until she said, "Thank you."

And he said, "You're welcome."

2

His real name was Wallace Thackery Falkirk, and he hated it, never used it, and was, in retrospect, grateful his mother had been a card player and had nicknamed him Trey, because he was the third child, and the three was her favorite, lucky card. It didn't matter what the suit was; it was the number that counted.

It must have been lucky.

His brother had died shortly after birth; his sister was murdered by an addict in Chicago, breaking into her apartment, looking for something to steal, finding her in bed, and strangling her with the telephone cord while she called the police.

Biology demanded he have a father, but he never knew him, didn't miss him, and once he'd gotten into college, never once felt compelled to find him.

For the longest time after graduation, however, he couldn't shake the belief that he was too much like him.

Not much good for anything but taking up space.

An English major and a music minor did not, in the general scheme of things, lend themselves to positions of authority and lucrative salaries. The plan to get his Masters in one or the other so he could teach was sidetracked when his mother keeled over during an after-hours poker game in San Diego, dead before her face hit the table. It would have been poetic had she held aces and eights, but she'd been bluffing and her hand had been worthless.

No insurance, no property, no bank accounts, no inheritance.

Out into the world, and the world didn't smile.

But there were jobs out there, and if his mother had taught him anything, it was not to be too proud to mop floors for a living until you found something better.

So he did.

Eventually working in a doughnut shop in Sacramento, the only job he could get, bored to midnight-in-bed tears because the register didn't even trust him to record the correct prices, all he had to do was press the little pictures; quoting Tennyson and Sandburg with every sale, mystifying the customers, screwing up the inventory, sitting on a stool in back while the manager, a good five years younger than he, scolded him for not putting his mind to his work; mopping the floor less than twenty minutes to closing when a kid came in, waving a gun, yelling at the girl behind the counter, screaming at the old man huddled at the corner table, turning when Trey swung the mop, knocking the gun loose, but not before it fired wildly and the bullet went through the old man and the window, and everyone said they were sorry, and not one of them believed it.

When he couldn't find another job, his landlord threw him out, called him an idiot for acting before thinking, calling him a killer, sending him to the streets until his money ran out and his sanity became questionable and a thumb out on the highway brought him to the dragon for the first time, where he fought without half trying, and went back into the world, enough green in his pocket to feed him for a while and get him a tiny room not much bigger than his dreams.

3

"Hey! Hey, you guys, hey!"

He released Moonbow's hand and watched Starshine pelt down the street toward them, arms pumping, knees high. No braids, but a ponytail; shorts, not jeans; sneakers, not sandals; but the same pug nose and the same dimpled chin and the same slightly slanted eyes, this pair accentuated with a different kind of makeup every day.

Their mother must have been looking in a mirror when she had them. At least according to the photograph he'd seen.

"What?" Moonbow snapped.

Oh, great, he thought; wonderful.

Starshine, grinning like a maniac, skipped to a halt in front of them, panting, wiping her forehead with a bare tanned arm. "Nothing."

"You do your homework?"

The older girl lifted a shoulder. "Most of it. I've got time, brat, don't worry."

Moonbow scowled. "I'm not doing it for you."

"Nobody said you had to."

"Well, I'm not."

"Big deal."

"Creep."

"Brat."

"Pimples."

Uh-oh, he thought; low blow.

Starshine stuck out her tongue, looked at Trey for the first time, and said, "Momma wants to know if you'll stop at the 7-Eleven and pick up some bread on your way back."

"Sure. Hi."

Puzzled, she looked at him sideways.

"It's what you say when you see someone you know. You know? Hi? Hello? How are you? Nice to see you? How you doing? Nice weather we're having? Think it's gonna rain? Looks like snow to me, unless we have an earthquake and end up living in the center of the Earth with little guys who live in the dirt walls and have worms for Thanksgiving."

Moonbow giggled.

"You're weird," her sister said.

"Not me, kid. And sure, I'll get the bread."

Starshine nodded a thanks, kicked lightly at a pebble, looked up the street. "Mr. Freneau's getting drunk again." Quietly. Angrily.

The violins were replaced by singing, too muffled to understand, but there was a pounding beat behind it, and what sounded like clapping.

Trey wasn't sure what he was supposed to say. He knew the girls had an agenda—get their mother married and out of this place into someplace more reasonable, more civilized . . . more normal.

Since last October their quest had become more intense, even frantic, because the city, last October, decided it was time to try again. Land was too dear to waste on the likes of them. A new developer had been contacted, elaborate new plans drawn and near approval, and everyone in the neighborhood recognized the hand-writing in the sand.

Already, most of the seventeen so-called houses were empty, and the leases for the rest would be up at the end of the year. Renewal, this time, was a word in a foreign language.

From the girls' point of view, it was time to speed things up.

Roger Freneau had been Starshine's latest target. An associate professor at UNLV. Respectable and respected. Upright. Reasonably good-looking in a stuffy sort of way. Claiming to be a distant relative of a famed Revolutionary War poet and satirist. And lately, good friends with anything that had malt or hops in it, poetic or not. Trey had the feeling the man had been told he wasn't long for his job. He knew the look well. He'd seen it himself too many damn times.

Moonbow's target, on the other hand, was obvious; her methods, however, were a lot more subtle.

Trey was just over forty; he believed he had gotten pretty good at dodging.

"He's a pain," Starshine said, shaking her head.

"He's creepy," Moonbow added.

"Not creepy, just a pain."

"Maybe. I guess."

"He'll be better, though."

"Right."

"Momma says he's just going through a bad patch."

"Like on my jeans?"

"Not funny, brat. He—not funny."

Trey reached out, brushed the backs of his fingers across Starshine's shoulder to get her attention. When she looked, he could see tiny diamonds in the corners of her eyes.

He knew that look, too.

"Sometimes," he said, "it gets too much, you know? Different people handle it different ways. Sometimes it takes them a while to figure out what's the best way."

There was a moment, no longer than that, when her eyes softened. Then: "At least he doesn't leave." Shock, fingers splayed to her lips, and she looked to Moonbow for help, but her sister was too stunned to speak.

Trey smiled easily, his hide grown much too thick to be punctured by a wild dart from a kid. "It's okay, don't worry about it." He slipped his hands into his pockets, wrinkled his nose at the sky. "When you think about it, it's actually pretty much the truth."

"Used to be," Moonbow corrected loyally, with an if-looks-could-kill glare at her sister.

He agreed. "Used to be, right. A little money in my tuxedo, a spring in my step, and I'm gone. Outta here. Once again making my way through the corridors of economic power out in the vast canyons of the largest cities in the world. Scared the hell out of them, I did, in the old days. They chased me away every time. Pitchforks, torches, shotguns, tar and feathers, the whole nine yards. They couldn't stand the incandescent brilliance of myself."

Starshine grinned in spite of herself. "You're weird."

"Thank you."

"Seriously weird."

"Such praise," he admitted, spreading his arms, bowing grandly, "deserves riches beyond compare. Would that I had riches beyond compare to share with you, my dear Miss Levin, but such riches as I have are reserved for greater, more noble things, no offense, like getting that bread for your mother."

"And the casinos."

No one spoke.

The wind gusted again, too hot for April.

Trey was used to being the neighborhood anomaly. Most loyal citizens of the city in the middle of the desert didn't bother much with the casinos. Once in a while, maybe, but they had more important things to do. Like making a living. Many did, at the hotels; many more did, at the stores and schools and scores of other ordinary businesses the outside world didn't believe existed because all they saw were the lights and the magicians and the showgirls and the wheels.

In the neighborhood, they spoke only of his dragon.

Casino was a word few ever used.

Starshine had broken a golden rule.

She cleared her throat and swiped at an invisible insect. Swiped again, and looked for another pebble to kick, almost sighing aloud in relief when a car pulled up beside them, an old Oldsmobile long enough to be a cruise liner.

"Hey," she said to the woman in the passenger seat.

"Hey yourself."

"Going to work?"

"No," Trey said. "Mrs. Olin has hijacked her husband, and they're heading for Texas to raise miniature cattle somewhere south of Austin."

"He's weird," Starshine said, leaning down to wave at the man behind the steering wheel. "Hey, Cable."

"Yeah." More a grunt than a word.

As far as Trey knew, the man seldom said more than three or four words at a time in public, and only when he was feeling expansive. God only knew what it was like at home. Stephanie, on the other hand, would talk a politician to death if given half a chance. Her ambition was to be a singer; her current job was a showgirl at the Tropicana. He had made it a point, once having met her, never to see her on stage. She was lovely enough as it was; he didn't need to know how she looked without half her clothes on.

Besides, Cable would tear his head off.

"You going in, Trey?" she asked. A small high voice, long dark hair twisted over one shoulder, her figure hidden in a bulky sweatshirt and matching sweatpants. Legs long enough that Cable had to push the seat back, forcing him to drive virtually straight-arm. "Give you a lift."

He shook his head. "No, thanks. But thanks."

"I'll go," Starshine said eagerly.

Stephanie smiled. "I don't think so, hon. Your mother would scalp me."

"Dope," Moonbow muttered.

Cable gunned the engine, glaring at the windshield. His complexion was Mediterranean dark, a thick mustache to match wavy dark hair that spread from beneath a baseball cap. He worked at Treasure Island, sweeping up after the gamblers. He took the late shift so he wouldn't be tempted to watch Stephanie, and the men who tried nightly to pick her up. He trusted her; he didn't trust his temper.

That was the line.

Trey knew better.

It was his face that kept him under the cap and in the dark. One of the early Sickness victims, lucky to survive but leaving his skin severely pocked and scarred. There were lots of Cables in Las Vegas. Hiding. Judith Levin said it was akin to survivor's syndrome—guilt they hadn't died with all the others, and because of the tracks the virus left behind, unable to blend in with those who still lived.

"Come on," Cable growled. "We're gonna be late." He pulled away quickly, Stephanie waggling her fingers in a hasty farewell wave, forcing the others to turn away from the dust the wind scattered a moment later.

"I," Starshine announced, patting the dust from her T-shirt, "am going to be like her some day."

Moonbow scoffed silently.

"Well, I am! I'm going to make a lot of money, wear nice clothes, and . . ." She turned away. "And get out of here as quick as I can."

"What about Professor Freneau?" her sister asked, so sweetly it was almost unbearably nasty.

"He's a drunk. Screw him."

Moonbow wouldn't let it go. "But 'Shine, I thought you liked him."

"Screw him."

"But—"

Trey rapped her spine with a knuckle, making her yelp and turn. "Enough," he told her.

"But—"

"Enough." A chill walked his arms, and he rubbed them vigorously. The sky was clear, but he felt a storm just the same. "Your sister wants to walk around half-naked all the time, that's her business."

Starshine's eyes widened. "What do you mean, half-naked?"

He gave her a half-smile. "Come on, kid, you ever see Steph's costume? What there is of it?"

"Well . . ."

Too dark now, but he could have sworn she blushed.

The music grew. Singing, clapping, old-time gospel with a rambunctious choir that dared the world to end.

Moonbow grimaced. "I hate that stuff."

27

Starshine agreed. "She deaf or something?"

"Makes you feel good," he said, mildly scolding, a playful cuff aimed at their heads. "Besides, the woman's a star, remember? That's probably her singing. I wish there was more of it."

Starshine made a face. "Gross." She rubbed her stomach. "I'm hungry. Come on, brat, let's eat. Momma's gonna be mad if we're late. I'll take your plate if you don't hurry."

"In a while, okay? Besides, you'll get fat and won't be able to go around half-naked."

Starshine took a half-hearted swipe at her sister's head and ran off, no good-bye, no wave, slipping in and out of the dark places the porch lights couldn't reach.

Trey watched until she was gone, listened to the music, didn't move when Moonbow sidled over and took his head again.

"She's not your princess, right?" she asked hopefully.

"No," he answered. "She's the jester."

She laughed. "And Momma? What's she?"

"My executioner, if you don't get home for supper, kid."

The wrong answer; he could feel it through her hand.

She wanted him to say his queen.

But queens didn't marry, or even live with, men like him.

one who walks into a school in more cities than he can count, putting on the drab coloration of a janitor's uniform, sweeping floors, washing windows, washing blackboards, washing walls, talking with students until someone gets nervous and he's shown the door, politely, because liability was something administrations couldn't really afford;

never more than three or four months at a time, living in pay-by-night hotels and cardboard boxes and under bridges and in alleys until he can't stand it anymore and makes his way back to the dragon;

builds a stake;

runs back to the world;

and finds himself increasingly the target of those who think he's an easy mark, a bum with a few bucks who didn't deserve them; beaten, once stabbed, once just for the hell of it thrown from a bridge into the Allegheny River; learning to fight, learning to survive, trying to keep in mind that the plagues that have battered them give them no outlets for their frustration; and thinking at last while he lay in the intensive care ward of a hospital in the so-called City of Brotherly Love that it's all a crock, that he's just making excuses for people who are just plain rotten.

This time the beating hasn't been just for kicks; this time whoever it was had been trying to kill him.

After Philadelphia, he makes his way south, into the mountains of West Virginia, eventually into Martinsburg on the interstate, where he meets a young couple, Cora and Reed, nudging at twenty and looking a decade older. He spends three days there, bulky cast on his left arm, hunting a ride west, and in that three days he listens to them talking fretfully, hopefully, about finding a preacher who was supposed to be dead but didn't die because he was different.

"How?" Trey asked over the mouth of his longneck, through a mouthful of beer. Their treat, just like the dinner he'd just finished.

Cora shrugged. "Different, that's all."

"Like you," Reed told him with a grin.

Trey snorted. "Yeah, sure. What, he's a drunk?"

"No," Cora said. "He was the first."

"The first what?"

She didn't answer, and neither did the boy. They told him, that last night, of a place not even big enough to be a village, one of those communities that had exploded in the violence that had blown up two years back. Cora and Reed had escaped, hadn't looked back, and finally decided they had to find the preacher, Casey Chisholm.

"Crazy," he had told them. "All the crap that's gone on since, and you're looking for a guy who's probably dead? You're nuts."

When he wakes up the next morning, they're gone, not even a note to say good-bye. But there's money in his jacket pocket, enough to get home with if that's what he wanted.

By then he's so tired all he wants to do is sleep. Find a cave, an empty house, an empty shop, an empty town, and sleep until it was over.

Whatever *it* was.

Nevertheless he decides to keep moving. It's better than sitting, better than trying to find another job. In Martinsburg there's nothing. The first wave of famine had reached the Appalachians, hit them hard, and the town had decided to shut down. No visitors. No strangers. They had barely enough to feed their own. A cop, for some reason believing Trey wasn't as bad as he looked and ignoring the dirty cast, the healing bruises and slashes across his face, drives him to the interstate, flags down a westbound semi, and helps him into the cab.

"Thanks," Trey had said.

"No problem." Then he reached into his breast pocket and pulled out a folded sheet of notepaper. "You know a kid named Cora?"

Damn, he thought, but he'd nodded cautiously just the same.

The cop handed the paper over, waved the truck on, and it was nightfall before he decided to see what was there.

We forgot to tell you, Cora said, *that Reed thinks you're special. That's what he meant when he said you're like Reverend Chisholm. I think he's nuts, but he made me tell you anyway. Get a life, mister. Stay alive.*

He laughed so hard the driver nearly threw him out.

He returned to the dragon, and the house in the desert, deciding there was no sense leaving again. It had taken nearly twenty years, but he finally took the hint.

And queens never looked twice at men like him.

4

The time, when it came, came without words.

Moonbow released his hand and watched as he stretched in several directions, yawned wide enough to make his jaw pop, and scrubbed his palms over his hair, then used them to flatten it into a semblance of neatness.

He grinned at her.

She grinned back.

He waved up the street, knowing that her mother was watching through her living room window, knowing she disapproved of his somewhat curious profession, knowing she didn't mind that her daughters enjoyed his company. For the past seven months they had been the only children on the block, and while the others fussed kindly over Moonbow in particular, he seemed to be the only one who treated either one of them like a person, not some kind of fragile, pathetic doll.

He sucked in his stomach, tucked his shirt in and hitched up his belt.

Moonbow examined him, one eye closed, and pronounced her approval with a sharp nod.

Starshine, a month shy of being a freshly minted teen with all the posture that went with it, would have suggested he at least shave if he insisted on looking like that. Whatever, in her eyes, *that* was.

He touched his cheeks and was tempted. But not tempted enough. There were no other plans tonight. He figured he looked decent enough.

He reached into his jeans and pulled out a thin packet of money, folded over, small bills on top, and counted it carefully. With any luck, along with any of whatever it was that made him what he was, the amount would nearly double before the morning got too old.

Pay the bills, feed the fridge, put a little aside in the metal strong-box under the bed for the time when he was forced to find other accommodations.

"You're stalling," the girl accused.

"Yep."

"Don't."

"Okay."

"Will I be up when you get home?"

"Not if you don't want your mother to shoot you."

"You going to buy my present tonight, too?"

He reached out and yanked a braid. "Don't be greedy, kid. It doesn't suit you."

She shrugged as if she didn't much care.

He rolled his shoulders and strode across his excuse for a front yard, heading for the carport.

"Coat," she called after him. "You'll freeze if you don't, you know."

He almost ignored her, then realized the truth in it. Being the end of April, there was supposed to be warmth, not midsummer heat. Nevertheless there had been heat lately. But at night, the desert floor not yet ready to hold it all back, the heat left and the chill returned with the stars. His shirt wasn't thin, but the girl was right, so he veered to the porch, opened the door, reached inside, and grabbed a beaten leather jacket off the peg on the wall next to the jamb.

He didn't need it right now, but later, win or lose, he would. One more regret if he left it behind.

Stop it, he ordered. Regrets belonged to memories that didn't have to be.

Yet they were what they were, and unless he discovered the secret of time travel, it was a waste of time wishing they were something else.

Beggars and horses, he reminded himself; beggars and horses.

Under the sagging carport roof was a pickup whose time had come and gone, its previous owner having extended the already spacious cab to allow for a narrow benchseat in back, if whoever sat there didn't mind sitting with his knees in his mouth. Its paint gleamed because Trey had redone it only a couple of years before and made sure it stayed clean. And polished. Black as the gaps between the stars. Capturing the slightest light and sliding it across the hood and roof, glimpses of quicksilver fish swimming in dark water.

He patted the hood.

He looked in the bed to be sure no demons or stray cats had taken advantage.

He got in, tossed the jacket onto the passenger seat, took the keys from his other pocket, and shook them twice before inserting one into the ignition, asked silent permission to be able to ride safely tonight, and turned it.

The engine woke instantly, growling softly to itself, pulling at the handbrake until he released it, sighed relief all seemed well, and coasted into the street.

"Hey," she called.

He braked and waited.

Her head ducked, her foot toed the ground. "I'm glad you're smiling again." So soft he barely heard it.

He wasn't quite sure what to say. "That bad, huh?"

She nodded.

"That long?"

She nodded again.

"Sorry."

" 's okay."

He took his foot off the brake, turned left, and let the pickup take its own speed. As if, he thought, the engine were stretching its muscles first, before working up to speed.

A long time ago, when Moonbow first learned about his battles with the dragon, she told him he had to have a steed, like they did in the movies and the picture books, and the steed was not, by any means, black, and it sure didn't look like any truck she ever saw.

"No steed," he had informed her solemnly. "This boy rides a chariot."

He never told her why.

She had looked it up herself, but it took a while before she saw the chariot he owned, not the truck. When she did, she claimed it made sense. Open in back, all the horses up front, room for one, maybe two others beside the driver. Not exactly smooth even on a smooth road. The more she talked about it, the more sense she said it made and refused to allow him to give it a name, because horses had names and chariots didn't.

Maybe it did make sense, maybe it didn't, but it was the chariot that took him slowly down the street, left hand waving out the window, dust cloud spinning lazily away from the tires, headlamps dividing the night ahead into shifting blacks and greys.

At the end of the street he stopped and checked the rearview mirror. Moonbow was gone. Settling dust hung in the porch lights' glare, and staring at it too long created shapes that grew eyes and watched him.

"Man," he whispered, shook himself, and turned left onto a barely paved narrow road not much wider than a driveway, no center or shoulder lines at all, lights just behind and lights far ahead, but nothing in between but the glowing eyes of a couple of startled critters on the verge, which, when he checked again, turned out to be shards of broken beer bottles, nothing dramatic or wondrous at all.

"What," he demanded quietly of the dashboard, "is the matter with you, boy?"

Wrong again; not the realization of the time he had spent here, but something different. Certainly not the urge to leave, to try his luck with a real job yet again, because he knew that if he did that, some town's ICU would have the last bed he'd ever lie in.

Philadelphia, and all the places before, had taught him that, if nothing else.

And it wasn't the feeling that a late storm brewed beyond the ridge line horizon.

Something else.

He tapped a finger on the steering wheel, waiting for inspiration to bring him an answer. A shrug, then; what the hell. Probably prebattle nerves. Pulling back his hand as it reached for the radio.

No; no noise.

Not now.

This was the most silent part of the ride, and because of the silence, it was also the longest. This was when he truly made up his mind whether to fight or not, and there had been times, were always times, three or four times a month, when his hands began to tremble and his neck muscles began to tighten and no matter how hard he tried, he couldn't work up a decent spit.

That's when he turned around and ran for home.

That's when he began to wonder if maybe it wasn't time to head on out again, give the outside world another shot, prove to the family ghosts around him that he hadn't wasted his life, his schooling, his mind, his soul.

That the next beating wouldn't kill him.

Two years, a couple of months, a handful of days, but who's counting.

The road climbed abruptly.

The magic time. A convergence of illusions that had reinforced the dragon image.

Far ahead was an interstate overpass, some trees, some darkened warehouses. At the top of the rise, they cut off the regular city lights, just for a moment, hardly more than a second or two, and left only the glow of the dragon's scales. The first time he'd noticed it, he had stopped and stared, amazed that he could, even from here, pick out the different colors that blended into the glow that stretched for nearly a mile through the city's heart. Shimmering. Shifting. Once in a while changing shade and hue, but never their strength.

For no reason he could think of at the time, he thought of a dragon's scales, probably the memory of a magazine cover, or a child's book illustration. It didn't matter. The image struck, and stuck.

He liked it.

It fit.

Trey Falkirk in his chariot, riding hellbent to fight the dragon.

Trey Falkirk in his old pickup, heading for the reasons Las Vegas still existed.

It wasn't much to brag about, but hell, it was a living.

An airplane rumbled overhead, gliding into MaCarran. Sickness there may be, but that hadn't stopped the tourists.

He could hear, but couldn't see, a fighter squadron either heading into or away from Nellis. Or maybe, he thought with a sardonic grin, Area 51, hot on the trail of the latest batch of invading UFOs.

When the road eventually intersected with the highway that led into town, he switched on the radio, searching for some music to get his blood and anticipation flowing. Sometimes it was rock, sometimes the twang of real country; tonight, skipping rapidly over the news so his mood wouldn't slip away, he found a station that beamed in from Arizona, and it made him laugh and shake his head: good, old-fashioned, foot-stomping, hand-clapping, soul-dancing, eyes raised to heaven and feet moving like wind gospel. Nothing less would do.

A sign, because it was the last thing he had heard leaving the ridiculously named Emerald City. The kids may not like it, and he may not believe its message, but there was no denying the infectious good feeling it engendered.

He absolutely knew it was a sign when the first song he heard was an up-tempo, full choir, honky-tonk piano and guitars and fiddles version of "Good News, The Chariot's Comin'." He had never heard it that way before, most of the time it sounded to him like a plodding, by the numbers, not much of anything song, and by the time it was done, he never wanted to hear the old way again.

Screw the real world.

Praise the Lord and pass the ammunition.

He was on his way to fight the dragon.

2

1

Muriel Carmody stood at her living room window and watched that bum hold that poor little girl's hand. He was no good. She knew it. He was one of those child molesters. She knew it. She could tell. She wasn't the smartest woman in the world, that was a fact, but she read enough books and she watched enough TV to know about what they called the profiles of such monsters, and that bum fit them. All of them. She knew it. She could tell.

Thank God the other one had run away.

What she didn't know was why their mother put up with that bum, letting him spend so much time with the girls without adult supervision. Parental neglect, no question about it. The woman was a flake anyway. What kind of mother called her child Moonbow? Or Starshine, for God's sake? What kind of names were they? Stupid ones, that's what, and Muriel would bet her life that as soon as those children could, they'd change their names to something more respectable, more normal.

If she hadn't felt so off-kilter, she would have gone out there and told the bum off, told him to leave the children alone. She coughed lightly into a fist, swallowed hard, and whispered a quick prayer that it was only her usual spring cold.

Of course, it could be the storm on its way. Her head felt banded in iron, her sinuses plugged with cotton. That always happened when a storm was on its way. It made no difference if the weatherman's map didn't show any clouds. *She* knew. She could feel the fool thing.

"Muriel?"

She rolled her eyes, but she didn't leave the window. She wanted to make sure the child was all right. She wouldn't sleep if she left now.

"Muriel!"

"I'm in here," she said, and snorted. My God, you couldn't sneeze in these houses without someone hearing you up the street, so why the hell did Lillian insist on calling when all she had to do was poke her head out of the fool kitchen and look. But that would mean she'd have to get up. God forbid Lillian would ever get up unless she absolutely had to. God forbid she did anything unless she absolutely had to.

What was she going to do when they had to move, wait around for someone to carry her, for God's sake?

And that damn music was driving her crazy.

Whenever Eula was home next door, she played it louder than Gabriel's trumpet, slipping through the windows and walls as if they weren't there. Every fool night, most nights of the week. Didn't the woman have any other kinds? Something nice? Something classical?

Gone for days at a time, being a bigshot, then back in that house and blasting the street with that . . . that music.

It made her yearn for the old days, not all that long ago, when the street was quiet. Peaceful, except for a party now and then, or somebody gets drunk or mad or miserable and starts screaming. But that hardly ever happened. In fact, the more she thought about it, the more she recalled complaining how dull it was out here.

Please, Lord, she thought, please make it dull again.

And Eula, what kind of name was that anyway? Moonbow, Starshine, Eula, it was like living in the middle of a damn hippie commune or something.

God knew she wasn't a bigot, but sometimes she wondered about people like that. The world's going to hell in a handbasket, and all they do is sing and clap their hands and make like the Lord doesn't know what's going on. Their whole lives in church without a clue what's happening in the real world.

"Muriel, what are you doing?"

"What do you think I'm doing?"

"Oh, for heaven's sake, leave the poor man alone. He's not hurting anybody."

"He's a bum."

Dragging footsteps behind the thump of two crutches.

A miracle: Lillian was actually leaving the kitchen when she didn't have to.

When a lamp switched on, Muriel jumped away from the window, scowling. "What the hell are you doing?"

"I can't see in the dark, you know."

"But he can see me!"

Lillian lowered herself gingerly onto the couch, sighed the sigh even God must be weary of, slipped her arms out of the crutch sleeves and let them lean against her baggy-jeans legs. "You're impossible."

Muriel didn't answer. She dragged her favorite chair—a Boston rocker with padding she'd made herself—to the side of the window and sat so she could keep an eye on the bum and still look at her daughter.

"They're holding hands," she said in disgust.

"She likes him. Good Lord, Muriel, what's wrong with that? He's like, I don't know, a father figure or something. Poor thing doesn't have a father, you know. Mr. Falkirk is the substitute figure."

Muriel snorted again. "Substitute figure? Where'd you get something stupid like that? One of those TV shows? He's a bum, Lillian. And one of these days he's going to hurt one of those girls. If you know what I mean."

Lillian didn't say anything. Her thin lips were pursed in almost silent humming, and she tapped her feet in time to whatever music it was.

Movement across the street caught Muriel's attention. As she watched, Ricardo Hicaya stepped onto his porch, scratching his bare hairy belly as he looked up and down the street. The man was a bum. Even though he always wore a suit when he left the street in his not-so-new car, when he was here, he was a bum. Scratching himself, belching as loud as he could, making rude comments to every woman he saw. A bum. Good-looking in that kind of dark Spanish-Mexican-Indian sort of way, kind of skinny with muscles like rope, except for that left hand that looked like a bird's claw, but he was still a bum.

"No," Lillian said with a laugh in her voice, "he's not."

Muriel blinked. "You reading my mind now?"

"I don't have to. There isn't a man on this street who isn't a bum to you."

"You live on this street, you *are* a bum."

"Which makes us . . . what?"

Muriel couldn't keep her lips from twitching. "Bumettes, my dear Mrs. Tarque. That makes us bumettes."

Lillian laughed so hard the crutches slipped to the floor, and that made her laugh louder, harder, until the tears came, quickly followed by spasms of hiccups. Muriel only chuckled, about as close to a full laugh as she ever got these days.

What a pair, she thought; what a pair.

Twenty-six-year-old Lillian, thin as a European model, face like an angel, movie star hair bright as fire, walking with crutches because they had to replace her right knee after she'd fallen from the horse, the other leg useless now, they had to fuse it stiff; and Muriel, a year shy of twice her age, who had stopped calling herself big-boned a long time ago. Pleasantly plump was a fond memory. Reasonably heavy was the order of description these days. Nowhere near obese, but large enough to make walking hard, and to keep the men away. Most of them, anyway. Fat, but not rolling. No folds, thank God, no sagging tires around her waist and thighs, and the fat under her arms didn't swing when she moved them.

Full-bodied.

That's what that bum, Ricardo, had called her once, at someone's party a while back.

As much as she hated to admit it, she kind of liked that. Like a good wine. What did they call it . . . robust? Something. It didn't matter. She still liked it.

Ricardo left his porch, punching his way awkwardly into a T-shirt, and sauntered up the street, whistling. Bad hand in his pocket. Once he was out of sight, she checked on the little girl again, and scowled.

Still there.

With the bum.

"Muriel," Lillian said wearily, "stop it."

Muriel ignored her.

Coughed again, harder this time.

"That does it," Lillian said. "Tomorrow you're going in to get that flu shot."

"No."

43

The bum let go of the girl's hand and walked around the side of his house. Getting that awful truck, she supposed. Getting ready to waste his money.

"Muriel—"

"I'll get the shot," she said, keeping her eye on the truck as it left the carport, "suppose I get sick? Some people do, you know, they have a reaction. Who's going to take care of you, I want to know?"

"I'm not a cripple."

"Don't pout." The truck pulled into the street, flashed its red brake lights, and drove away slowly. "You're too old to pout."

"Yes, *Mother*."

The little girl waved once and ran for her house. Poor thing. Probably scared to death.

"Don't call me that."

Lillian laughed, a short and bitter bark. Then she retrieved her crutches, grunted to her feet, and thumped her way the front door.

"And where do you think you're going?"

"I'm going to ask Eula to turn the stereo down a little, then sit with her a while." Lillian opened the door. "Have a drink, have a cigarette." She looked at Muriel. "Maybe get converted." She grinned then, and winked. "Besides, I'm dying for a cigarette. Unlike some people I could mention, Eula doesn't care."

Muriel said nothing. She didn't offer to help, only watched as her bastard, widowed daughter clumped across the yard and out of sight.

The street was empty.

Muriel coughed and wondered if maybe she ought to get that shot. It couldn't hurt.

2

Ricardo had no idea where the hell he was going. He had planned to amble down toward the mailboxes at the end of the street, but once he'd seen the gambler's truck, he changed his mind. It wasn't that he didn't like the guy, but . . . okay, so he didn't like the guy. Doesn't have a job, doesn't work out and still looks like he could break a man in half, and keeps to himself like he's some kind of special. Only time he mixes is when somebody *else* throws a party. It was crazy, this bad feeling, but he couldn't help it. And for some reason, Eula's music only made it worse.

So when he saw the truck, he didn't think twice, he swung right instead of left and started walking. The trouble was, there wasn't anything up this end of the street but a handful of empty houses the desert had already begun to wear down. Still, he didn't want to meet Trey and make phony small talk, and he knew he was being watched, and he figured it would drive Muriel out of her mind, trying to figure out what he was up to now. So maybe he'd walk around for a few minutes, take in the early night air, listen to the wind, then get on home, and get dressed for work. Or maybe he'd get dressed, call in sick, and pay a visit to his across-the-street neighbor. That would drive her crazy, too, wondering what he was up to. So maybe he'd bring her some flowers. Just a couple. Drive her up the wall because she wouldn't believe for a second he had any real interest in her at all. But she'd be tempted. He'd seen the way she looked at him when she thought he wasn't looking, and even though she was a couple of years older, she was still a fine-looking lady. Her daughter wasn't ugly, but she was much too skinny, especially after that terrible operation, and she didn't seem to have any interest in men at all.

But Muriel . . . a lot of woman there to explore.

Flowers.

He grinned.

Flowers, and maybe an invitation to dinner at one of the hotels. Not the all-you-can-eat junk. A real restaurant. Force her to dress up a little.

That would drive her nuts.

He laughed aloud, told himself he was a terrible person, she didn't deserve it, but she was so easy to taunt, to tease, to flatter. At the party last month, the going-away party for the family whose name he no longer remembered, he remembered calling her full-bodied when she'd said something stupid about being too fat to dance, and she had actually blushed. A woman her age, blushing.

He hadn't forgotten it.

He thought about it every night.

That some women reacted to him that way wasn't his fault. Not deliberately, anyway. Not all the time.

Because of his looks—the hair, the skin, the cast of his face—they assumed he was Spanish, or something more exotic, like an Indian, an Apache. They also assumed he had a command of the language. Romantic. Hinting of romance. And while it was true he affected an accent sometimes, when he was reasonably sure he wouldn't get caught, it was as false as his airs. As his name. Richard was dull; Ricardo had panache. Only once, years ago, did guilt compel him to confess—to a woman long faded in memory—that his family had been in America since long before the Civil War, and that each succeeding generation had been adamant about diving headfirst into the melting pot.

The last one to speak Spanish with any fluency at all had been his great-grandmother, and what little Ricardo knew he had learned from the movies and one year in high school.

One of his brothers had once claimed a dead Scot could roll his Rs better.

He hadn't argued.

Nevertheless, the ladies still came in spite of the hand, and he still kept the pose, and still snuck off twice a month to learn how to tango. A great way, his teacher claimed, to guide a woman into bed.

Perhaps Muriel . . . he laughed, shook his head at the fantasy, and walked on. Wrinkling his nose at a faint smell. A familiar smell. He squinted westward toward the mountains. No clouds, but something was on its way. He hoped it wasn't another sandstorm. The valley rarely had them, but this year, and last, there'd been something like eight or nine. Just like they were living in the middle of the Sahara.

Took him days to clean all the sand and grit out of the house.

His hair had looked like hell.

Rain, he prayed; just let it rain, okay?

When the houses finally stopped and the street stopped and the desert stretched into the dark toward nothing at all but more dark, he turned around, whispered a prayer of thanks that Eula had finally turned down that damn music of hers, he hated that stuff, and thought for a minute before nodding sharply.

Flowers.

Invitation to dinner.

If Muriel accepted, fine.

If she didn't, which she probably wouldn't, not the first time anyway, he'd try again tomorrow. And the next day. And the day after that.

She may not give in ever, but it would really drive her nuts.

3

During the drive into town, Stephanie said, "Cable, don't you think we should have told Trey about that man?"

"Nope."

"Maybe he's in trouble, you know? Trey, I mean. You know, with some criminal or something."

"Not our business."

"Well, I still think it was a mistake."

"You worry too much. And the guy's a creep."

"What? What's the matter with him?"

"Don't like him. He looks at you funny."

"Cable. Please. How many times—"

"Forget it, Steph. And forget that old man. Whatever Falkirk's into ain't our business."

"But we lied, Cable. If that guy finds out we really do know him, maybe—"

"Steph, you worry too much."

"You don't worry at all."

"No sense in it. A waste of time."

"I mean . . . like the Sickness, it—"

"Steph."

"But—"

"It ain't here, Steph. We don't got it. We get it, we probably die. You don't worry what you can't do nothing about."

"Well, we can do something about that man."

"Steph."

"What?"

"Shut up."

4

The most difficult thing about being a drunk, Roger discovered, was the awful stuff you had to drink to achieve that unchartered state of blessed oblivion. Liquor wasn't so bad when it was tempered with other things. Orange juice, tomato juice, tabasco, pineapple juice, water, club soda, salt, pepper, celery stalks, other liquors—all of it was preferable to drinking straight from a bottle. But having no facility for mixing cocktails either popular or of his own concoction had left him with no choice but the bottle.

Being a drunk, for reasons he could not bring to mind at the moment, had seemed to be, evidently, a good idea at the time, whatever time that had been when he'd started being a drunk.

But then, so had accepting the position at the university.

He grunted a bitter laugh.

University. Las Vegas. A hell of a combination, or so he had once believed.

What he hadn't counted on was the city beyond the Strip. Which had turned out to be about as mundane as a city could get without being buried in the Midwest. What he hadn't counted on was how utterly, horrifically boring life was once the neon and the billboards and the constant music, the constant noise had eroded excitement's edges to something less sharp than a butter knife.

What he hadn't counted on was the reaction:

"You work at UNLV?"

"That's right."

"Say, what's with the Running Rebels anyway? They let Wyoming whale the tar out of them again, it's getting to be a bad habit."

"I—"

"Never used to be that way, you know, nosir. Number One, that's what we were. Number One. Nobody could touch us. Nobody."

"Well—"

"Disgrace, that's what it is. A goddamn disgrace. What kind of school you got there anyway, letting them slip like that?"

Basketball was not his sport. As far as he was concerned, it shouldn't be anyone's sport. It had nothing to do with the fact that he was slightly shorter than average and therefore completely dwarfed by any third-string freshman; it had everything to do with the fact that running-and-dunking for however long it took a clutch of ungainly young giants to run-and-dunk, all night long, was . . . boring.

Yet, as a faculty member he was expected to be a basketball expert, a basketball fanatic, a rabid follower of the, for crying out loud, Running Rebels, give me a break, I need another drink.

What he hadn't counted on was living in a place like this, a has-been development soon to be yanked out from under him, populated by people who didn't seem to want to read, didn't seem to want to think beyond how to survive from one dismal paycheck to the next, didn't seem to care that the world was falling apart around their ears.

They lived their lives, moved in, moved out, listened to music loud enough to deafen him, and didn't have the vaguest idea what a decent, intelligent conversation was like.

They didn't care about the world outside what Trey once called the dragon's valley; they didn't care, perhaps didn't even think about, all the hospitals overflowing, the clinics filled to the gills, the . . . ah, the hell with it.

He took another drink.

But he couldn't stop thinking.

Those who hadn't fully recovered from last year's famine had been the first to succumb, too weak to fight against the virus that should have been, had in fact been declared to have been eradicated years ago.

The rest had little more than a fifty-fifty chance of surviving the fever, the dehydration, the debilitation.

They called it the Sickness because no one wanted to say small-pox. No one wanted to admit that it was back, and it had changed.

Not that it mattered; they died anyway.

He sat on a lawn chair behind his house, facing the mountains he could no longer see. His only clothing a T-shirt and bright green boxer shorts. A bottle of Dewars. Gooseflesh breaking out along his arms and legs. His free hand made a futile pass through thick, shoulder-length wavy hair, then tugged at a neatly trimmed beard kept short to minimize the appearances of the occasional grey.

He took another drink, immediately spat it out, and said, "Christ, Rog, you're pathetic."

He then slid to the ground to his hands and knees, crawled ten feet away, and threw up.

Wept.

Threw up again.

Wept again.

Jesus, he couldn't even make a good drunk.

He rocked clumsily back onto his heels, gulped for a breath that didn't make his stomach queasy, and stood. Blinked heavily. Side-swiped the ground with one bare foot to cover the mess. The stench and movement made him gag, and he turned away hastily, clamped a hand to his stomach and gulped air again. Only when he was positive nothing else would come up did he stagger toward the con-crete back stoop and the kitchen door. As he passed the chair, he glared at the bottle, not at all tempted to take it with him.

One step up, and he paused, shuddering at a sudden chill that reached his skin from the inside, as if streaming from his marrow.

A second step up, and he paused, swallowing hard to bear the stench of himself. The imagined stench.

The top of the stoop—no welcome mat, just weather stains and food stains and liquor stains. And cool beneath his soles.

He reached for the screen door, tugged, and after a long second let his hand slip away.

He looked at the stars.

"Well . . . *shit!*"

One more time, just to be sure, before he scratched through his hair, his beard, across his chest, and put his hands on his hips. He looked at his feet, wriggled his toes, and grinned.

"You are in your skivvies, my boy," he said, sniffed, and hiccupped. Swayed. "You are a little drunk, you are locked out, and you are in your skivvies. Now what have we learned from this? Aside from the fact that you're an idiot, that is."

He was fairly certain the front door was still unlocked. All he had to do was walk around the house without killing himself. Use the walls as a crutch and not fall into his cactus garden. Make sure no one was out there to see him—please, God, don't let Judith be on her porch—and sneak in. No one any the wiser. An embarrassment only to him and his shadow.

An extraordinarily simple, straightforward plan, which he implemented before he had even finished thinking about it. He only wished he hadn't left all the damn lights on, blasting out of the windows like Eula's awful music. There was no dark here, nothing to hide in, nothing to conceal the way his legs, every few steps, decided to go their own way and had to be fought back into position. Nothing to keep the others from watching him fall on his ass four times before he reached the front corner.

Anger at himself gave way to the giggles.

"Hey, Señor Prof, you okay?"

What he hadn't counted on was every damn human being on the planet calling him "Prof" just because he taught at a university.

Thank God he hated sports; otherwise they'd probably call him "Coach."

He squinted, barely made out Hicaya in the street, and waved grandly. "Just making my way back home, Rick," he said, grabbed the porch post and hauled himself up.

"How come you're not dressed?"

Using his left hand to keep from falling, he took small steps toward the door. "It's a professor thing," he explained, and covered his mouth and tried to fake a cough to hide a belch he couldn't stop. "It keeps my brain from . . ." He blinked rapidly. "Fogging up."

"Ah. You eat yet?"

He found the door, found the knob, prayed, turned it, and sighed when the door opened. "No."

"Next time, then, when you drink, Señor Prof, eat something first. It don't hit you so hard, then."

Roger stared as the man laughed and headed on down the street, shaking his head. He tried to think of something to say, something witty, something so far over the jerk's head he'd get whiplash trying to catch up, then stumbled over the threshold, closed the door, and turned the lock in the fake brass knob. Anger born of humiliation made him grind his teeth.

"Bastard," he whispered, suddenly thought of the perfect retort, and hurried back to the porch, slamming the door behind him.

"Hey, Rick," he called, but Hicaya only waved a hand over his shoulder without looking back.

Roger opened his mouth to shout it anyway, and froze.

"Well," he muttered, "shit."

He didn't have to turn around.

He knew the door was locked.

Which probably wouldn't have been so bad if he hadn't seen Lillian across the street, sitting on Eula's front step, smoking a cigarette, and grinning.

"Nice shorts," she called, and laughed so hard she began to choke, all the while weakly waving her cigarette hand in a not terribly sincere apology.

He hugged himself, feeling the night's chill inside and out, and pressed his knees together when he realized how full, and how eager to be emptied, was his bladder. To make matters worse, Lillian flicked her cigarette into the street, grabbed her crutches, and stood.

"No," he said automatically. "It's all right, Lil, honest."

She ignored him.

He belched, groaned, and leaned against the jamb. Not wanting to watch and unable to stop watching as she hauled herself toward him, the breeze that began to freeze him slipping her hair in and out of her eyes. She nearly fell once, and he finally closed his eyes, snapped them open instantly when all the lights behind his lids began to swirl like a tornado filled with sparks.

"No key, huh?" she said as she climbed the steps.

He shook his head, not daring to speak.

"You don't keep a spare out here somewhere?"

"No."

Her expression took a moment to register, and he still wasn't sure if it was pity or disgust or isn't that just like a man.

"Some woman dump you?" she asked idly as she examined the lock as if actually planning to pick it.

"Me?" His laugh was quick and hoarse. "No, not me."

"So why do you drink, then?" She backed away from the door. "You don't seem like the type."

He didn't want to answer. It was none of her business. "The city," he said anyway, "my job, the world, my life, take your pick."

"I see." She scanned the porch floor. "You have renters' insurance?"

"No."

"Too bad." She raised one of the crutches and smashed the front window with a single sharp blow.

He was too astonished to react, didn't even flinch when she patted his cheek as she headed for the stairs. "I'm not climbing in," she told him. "You'll have to do that yourself."

She was halfway down the walk before he looked at the glass-littered porch, looked to her and said, "My . . . my feet are bare."

"Tough," she answered without looking back. "It's the end of the world, Rog, or hadn't you noticed? A couple of lousy cuts here and there aren't going to make a bit of difference either way."

"You're crazy," he said, but not loud enough for her to hear. Then he looked at the glass, at the shattered window, and couldn't decide which to do first—throw up or cry.

He did neither.

Rage overwhelmed him, and he kicked the door viciously with the sole of his right foot, lost his balance and fell on his back, and watched helplessly as the door swung slowly inward.

He would have screamed, but he heard Lillian's voice, high and sweet, singing one of Eula's godawful gospel songs as loud as she could.

When his eyes closed, the sparking tornado returned, and he couldn't really tell as he passed out if he were crying, or throwing up.

5

She had gotten used to the pain.

She had gotten used to the crutches.

She had gotten used to the physical therapist who came out three times a week to torture her good leg and scold her for not doing the exercises on her own, what was she thinking of, did she want to use the damn crutches for the rest of her life?

She had even gotten used to the way people looked at her, either when they thought she wasn't looking, or with those sideways glances that tried in a split second to figure out what was wrong.

She would never get used to not riding again.

Never.

Oh, they told her she'd eventually be able to do trails if she was careful; they told her she could hang around corrals on the back of some old nag that could barely put one leg in front of the other.

That didn't count.

The important thing was, she would never be able to really *ride* again. Take that animal around the ring at speed, bareback, doing backflips and side jumps and handstands and headstands while over five hundred people twice a day screamed their lungs out, pounded their tables, and cheered and whistled when she was finished.

She would never again wear the Hollywood-style medieval clothes with the ruffles and frills and billowing sleeves and rawhide fringe and sequins and rhinestones that flared in the laser light that flashed across the arena; she would never again watch from behind the curtain the hokey King Arthur show, knights jousting and swordfighting and ax-fighting and just plain fighting while the crowd did what the crowd was urged to do—scream and cheer and yell and boo, all while eating a halfway decent meal with their fingers.

Over a year, now.

Over a year.

She had tried to kill herself, twice, and had told no one about it— she didn't need a rubber-wall room to go with the crutches.

Then Eula had moved into the neighborhood, driving everyone nuts with her loud music, and at the same time making most everyone feel just a little better about how things were. Lillian didn't know how the woman did it, but she did. There was no preaching, no proselytizing, no New Age bromides, no Bible quotations, no phony sympathy, no manufactured empathy. She just talked, and played her music, and Lillian just listened.

"Child," Eula had said last month, "you don't have to be that way, you know," pointing to the crutches.

That's all.

Nothing else.

Just: "You don't have to be that way."

Tonight, she had answered, "Show me."

And Eula had said, "You think about it first, dear. Think about it hard. Ain't no free ride in this world."

Lillian had grinned. "Pay the piper, huh?"

"Something like that."

That's all.

Nothing else.

The acres between Eula's house and hers, on a good night, seemed like a mile. Now it seemed like ten.

Ride; never ride.

If it had been anybody else—doctors, shrinks, nurses, therapists, letters from nuts who promised miracle cures—she would have laughed. Somehow, though, Eula was different. Others recognized it too, so she knew she wasn't imagining things that weren't there. A special something, a special caring, a special way of checking out the world to find the right places to be at the right times . . . with the right words.

She had only said something about it once to Muriel, who had rolled her eyes and said, "What's she going to do, Lillian, cast a voodoo spell on you? Make you bathe in some kind of stinky herbs and mud?" Her voice had softened. "Lillian, this is real, not a dream. Do what the doctors tell you, and you'll soon enough get as good as you'll ever be. Not like you were, you know that, but as close as you can get. No shortcuts, Lil. There are no shortcuts."

Lillian hated it when her mother was right. She knew there were no shortcuts, no spells, no magical herbs. She knew that. But then, Muriel had never sat long enough with Eula to listen to that voice. Really listen to it.

Different; something different.

Ride; never ride.

What, she wondered, did she have to lose?

If it didn't work . . . well, they say the third time's the charm.

6

The Levin sisters sat on rickety lawn chairs on the concrete slab that was their front porch. Paper plates in their laps held sandwiches; paper cups on the floor held milk. Paper napkins lay unused next to the cups; it was easier to swipe a palm over a knee or thigh than bend over.

Starshine chewed as if she were eating steak. "You think he's coming back?"

"Sure. Why not?"

"Momma says it's like waiting for the other shoe to drop."

"What's that supposed to mean?"

"It means," said Judith Levin from behind the screen door, "that there's always a next time."

Moonbow jumped, scowling at her sister for not warning her. "He's staying."

Her mother's voice, a soft rasping: "How do you know?"

The girl waved vaguely. "They're getting sick out there, and they're not sick here. He won't take the chance."

Starshine snickered for what her sister didn't say, and yelped and almost dropped her plate when the screen door opened slightly and a hand reached out to whack her lightly across the top of her head.

"Don't laugh. It never hurts to have faith."

Moonbow looked up the empty street. Lillian had long since gone inside, and Ricardo had long since driven away to his fancy waiter's job on the Strip. The music was over. Early evening, not yet eight o'clock, and it felt as though she should have been in bed hours ago.

"What do you have faith in, Momma?"

Her mother's shadow, stretched thin across the porch, shifted as if the woman had turned away.

"Momma?"

Starshine pinched her thigh, warning her to shut up.

"Come on, Momma, fair's fair."

A quiet chuckle. "You're right."

"You can come out, Momma," Starshine said over her shoulder. "Nobody's around."

The door remained closed.

"Lillian," Judith said, "had faith in her horse until it threw her. She doesn't really believe she'll ever walk without crutches again. Who knows, maybe she's right."

A distant high roar and a flare of red as a fighter climbed over the mountains.

"Muriel won't diet anymore, she doesn't think she'll ever lose weight again. I even offered to do it with her, but she said no, she was happy the way she was. A walking heart attack begging for a stroke. And Ricardo wears a glove to keep people from staring at his hand. Six operations, I think it's six, and it still looks the same. He won't have another."

Grumbling this time, an invisible jet liner heading for the airport.

When that faded, an outsider would have said the neighborhood was quiet, unable to hear the whisper of the wind across the sand in the yards, in the street.

"Boy," Starshine said into the silence, "that's pretty gloomy, Momma."

Her mother laughed. "Yes, I guess it is."

A glint of light distracted Moonbow. She looked down toward the end of the road and saw headlights approaching slowly, as if the driver didn't know where he was. "Company."

A moment later she heard a table drawer open, and she knew Momma had taken out the gun. Every house but Trey's had one. Everyone on the block knew how to use one.

Most of the time it was someone lost. They'd stop at the first house with lights, ask directions, and get out a whole lot faster than when they came in. Once in a great while it was someone who heard something about Emerald City and came looking for stuff to steal. They never expected the way the people who were left knew what was up; they sure never expected to look at a gun. They never came up slow.

Starshine thought it was exciting, better than television.

Moonbow usually hid in the kitchen until it was over.

Carefully she placed her plate on the floor and stood, dusting her hands on her jeans, reaching around to scratch her back.

The headlights softened, curls of dust rising through the beams.

"Moonbow."

"It's okay, Momma." She deepened her voice, tried to imitate Southern syrup, the way Eula did. "They just be lost travelers, lookin' for a way out."

Starshine snorted, then cursed as milk shot out of her nostrils. "Aw, gross."

"Use the napkin," her mother told her, laughing. "I'll get some paper towels."

Moonbow stepped down to the walk, making sure the driver saw her. Now *this* was exciting. Strangers. Maybe they were millionaires looking for Wayne Newton's ranch, or some bigshot Mafia guy who took a wrong turn, or a movie star thinking maybe this would be where she would make her next film.

When it was close enough, when the headlight glare no longer obscured it, she sighed a little. An ordinary car, rental plates. A tourist who didn't realize how big the night was.

A shrug, and she moved down to the absent curb, one hand fiddling with a braid, smiling politely as the car pulled abreast.

A woman in the driver's seat, wavy hair and bangs, kind of a small nose. As Moonbow bent down to ask what she could do to help, the passenger door opened and a man got out.

"Holy shit," she heard Starshine whisper from the porch, and heard a harder whack and a louder yelp.

Still, her sister wasn't far from wrong.

The man was old. Really old. Not very tall, and dressed in a white suit with dark piping on the lapels and yoke like country singers wore. A white straw cowboy hat with a red band. A bolo tie. He walked around the front of the car, smiling, wiping his hands with a handkerchief, and she almost said, "Holy shit," herself when she saw the silver snakeskin boots.

"Good evening, child," he said.

She gaped.

There weren't many wrinkles on his face, and when he took off his hat, there wasn't much hair up there either. Combed straight back, most of what was there a glittery silver. He squinted as he examined the house, looked up and down the street, and she had the definite feeling that he could look down his nose at a giant without lifting his head.

"You're English," she blurted.

His smile widened. "As indeed I am, child. Indeed I am."

The voice. Momma made them watch Shakespeare on PBS all the time, and most of the time the actors were English. It sounded weird unless they were.

This man looked and sounded just like every one of them. Except for the hat. And the stupid boots.

"Sir John," the driver said impatiently.

Moonbow backed up a step.

Sir John?

"You a king or something?" Starshine asked.

Moonbow whirled, nearly colliding with her sister who was right behind her.

"No, child," he said, still smiling. "Tonight I am just a tourist. Looking for someone."

"Yeah? Who?"

"Starshine!" Moonbow snapped. "Be nice."

61

"Starshine?" The man held out his hand. "So very pleased to meet a young woman with such a lovely name."

It wasn't the words; it was the way he said them.

Moonbow gaped again when her sister really, no kidding, blushed and shook the man's hand. For a moment there, she thought the creep would actually curtsy.

"And you, my dear?" he asked.

"Moonbow," she answered shyly, softly, and took the offered hand, and shook it. Lightly. The way she thought a real lady would.

"Delightful," he exclaimed. "Did you hear that, Beatrice? Starshine and Moonbow. Lovely. Absolutely lovely. What a marvelous imagination their mother must have."

The driver only scowled, fingers tapping the steering wheel. "Sir John, it's getting late, and—"

"Yes, of course." He looked at the street again. "My dear young ladies, I am searching for a man I used to know a very long time ago. I . . ." He inhaled slowly, deeply. "I thought to surprise him, but he is a very difficult man to find."

Moonbow watched his hands, the long fingers and the way they folded the handkerchief into a perfect square with a tail thing on top, then tucked it into his jacket pocket and patted the part that stayed on the outside. All without looking at it once.

The entire display hadn't taken more than a couple of seconds, but it made her acutely aware of how she and Starshine were dressed. His clothes were kind of silly, especially with that accent; nevertheless, she suddenly felt as if they were dressed in rags.

"Sir John," the driver warned.

Startled, Moonbow looked at her. She could only see the woman's profile, but it, and her voice, was enough to let her know that she was scared.

That made her frown.

"In good time," the man told her, as if he had all the time in the world. "All in good time."

That smile, those never-all-the-way-open eyes, those long elegant fingers . . . Moonbow felt dizzy and grabbed her sister's hand, hoping she'd say something, even if it wasn't very polite.

But Starshine had gone mute.

Finally, Moonbow, fearing her voice would crack and make her sound like a little kid, said, "We'll help if we can, sir."

Sir?

She never, ever called a man *sir*.

"Splendid," he said. A raised finger. "A surprise, remember? It must be a surprise, or I—we will have traveled quite far in vain."

The girls nodded mutely.

"Splendid. Wonderful." He looked at the house, then at the girls. "I'm looking for Mr. Wallace Falkirk. I believe he's called Trey by his friends. I've tried to call but—"

"He doesn't have a phone anymore," Moonbow said in what sounded to her like an apology.

"Really? You don't say."

"He pulled it out of the wall a couple of months ago. He never got it fixed."

"Is that so. How interesting." A glance to the driver. "Well, that explains quite a bit, wouldn't you say, Beatrice?" He looked back to Moonbow. "And where, then, did you say I might find him?"

"He—" Starshine yanked her arm sharply. "He's not here."

The man nodded. "Ah. Too bad. Uncrossed paths yet again." He lifted his chin slightly and scratched idly at his neck. "Do we know where we can find him at this time of the evening?"

"Nope," Starshine answered instantly.

Moonbow shook her head.

"Now!" the driver insisted. "Now, Sir John, before—"

"It's all right, Beatrice," he said calmly. Sniffed. Replaced his hat. Touched the handkerchief again. "I would offer you an inducement to tell me where he is, my dears, but I think that would insult you."

"Damn right," Starshine said, her old self again.

The man laughed silently, nodded, and looked right at Moonbow. "I suspect, child, he is a special friend of yours. Would you tell an old man where he might be?"

It came out before Moonbow could stop it: "He went to fight the dragon."

The man didn't blink. "The . . . dragon, you say."

"That's right," Starshine said.

"I . . . see."

Starshine half-turned toward the house, pulling Moonbow with her. "We gotta go, mister. We got homework to do. It's a school night, you know."

"Of course, of course," he said, and rounded to his car door. "You go right ahead. I'm terribly sorry to have bothered you. Have a wonderful evening, and do give my best to your wonderful mother."

Moonbow didn't look back until Starshine had practically dragged her onto the porch.

Momma wasn't at the door.

When she heard the car start, she pulled free and turned around, just in time to see the man hurry up the walk toward them. Starshine called to their mother, but Moonbow stood there, waiting.

"My dear child," he said, puffing a little, "when you see our mutual friend again, you will give him a message for me, won't you?"

"I . . . sure, I guess so."

The man lowered his voice. "Wonderful. How kind of you." He touched a finger to the side of his nose. "Tell him for me, if you will, that I am looking for him. That I must speak to him of urgent business. Can you remember that?"

She nodded.

Starshine, sounding panicked, called for her mother again.

"And tell him one more thing," he said as he turned to go. The voice deepened. The shadows beneath the hat brim hid his eyes. "Tell him he can't run anymore."

"What?"

"Tell him he can't hide anymore." The man raised a finger, a reminder to remember. "Tell him, dear child, that his dragon is dying."

3

1

Trey had never told anyone how nervous he was, the nights he chose to leave the house, fight the dragon. The display for the girls was nothing more than bravado. And as soon as the music had ended, the fear returned—what if this was the night the streak ended, the luck ran out, the dream was over and he woke up with no way to protect himself anymore.

What if it was all over.

He sat in the parking lot behind the Excalibur, taking deep breaths, searching for calm.

Fear or not, he'd never know until he made the first move; until he left the chariot behind.

Sort of.

Just before he opened the door, he touched the center of his chest, feeling beneath the shirt a small gold casino chip his mother had given him when he was nineteen. On its face had been etched a chariot drawn by rearing horses. Nothing fancy. It hung from a piece of high-test fishing line because he'd gotten tired of all the broken strings he'd had. For years he believed she'd bought it for him in some Las Vegas or Reno souvenir shop, but one night, after a particularly good session, she told him some guy had given it to her, she couldn't remember his name. A good luck piece. A warding off of evil spirits. Protection against whatever she wanted protection against.

A nut, she'd said, laughing when she hung it around Trey's neck; lost a bundle and he still gives me this.

Gamblers are nuts, kid, she told him; don't ever forget it. They're just plain nuts.

A one-sided smile, a swallow, a pat for the gold chip, and he opened the door, grabbed his jacket from the front seat and put it on so he wouldn't have to carry it. Above him the hotel poked at the night with fairy-tale towers topped with pennants and flags, much larger at night because spotlights made it so, in storybook colors.

Onward, he thought, and made for the entrance.

The routine seldom varied.

A ritual to calm him, bring him balance and confidence, keep his hands and knees from shaking, and his stomach from throwing up what wasn't there because he never dared eat before he made the first move.

Once through the sliding-door entrance, he moved quickly across a small, high-ceiling lobby toward a broad, carpeted ramp that led up to the casino proper. Walls that looked made of large stone blocks. Heraldic flags hanging from the ceiling. Crossed swords and shields and crossed lances just out of reach. On either side, on the flat before the ramp, entrances to the towers that housed the guests; no chairs, no benches, no place to rest.

At the top he paused, letting his eyes adjust to the light, while the sound of lost-and-found money struck him as if he had never heard it before.

CHARIOT

Incessant bells to signal tiny victories, coins and tokens rattling into metal trays to make those victories seem much greater than they were; electronic beeps and whistles, electronic snippets of unrecognizable tunes; voices of the dealers, voices of the players, voices of those who stand and watch and encourage and laugh and cheer and commiserate and urge friends and strangers to give it another shot; roulette balls and table dice and the slide and slap of cards from a hand or boot. Waitresses trolling, coins jingling in pockets, music from a lounge open to the floor.

It didn't take long for it all to become white noise.

For it all to become silence.

Only when it did, did he move on, around the perimeter to avoid walking through the crooked aisles that separated the slot machine rows. That would come later; right now he had to keep moving. Strolling, really, pausing at the roulette tables to wonder how it would be to put one fifty-dollar chip on one number and win; pausing at the craps tables and trying to figure out how three or four men and women could keep track of dozens of bets and dozens of combinations and not go crazy by the end of their shift; passing right by the blackjack stands because these people were too solemn, too busy trying to read the dealer's mind; ignoring the sucker variations of the wheel of fortune; fascinated in but not tempted by the newer games, most of which claimed to be Oriental, some with cards, some with tiles and cards, all with too much movement, too little joy.

An hour, not much more.

Noting, as he always did, how this casino, like all the others, was arranged so you couldn't get from one part of the hotel to the next, or to any of the exits or the attractions, without passing through the games; noting the staircase and elevators that led to the second level, to shops and eateries and a long passageway that led to the black pyramid of the Luxor; noting that his stomach wasn't jumping anymore.

Walking until he couldn't stall any longer.

Until the ritual was over.

A deep breath, an adjustment of the windbreaker's collar, and he made straight for the nearest change booth, got himself fifty dollars in quarters and a fat plastic cup, and began to wander through the islands of slot machines, their aisles never straight, never leading directly to anyplace else but another aisle.

No one looking up, noticing his meandering. His own eye picking out a drugstore surgical mask now and then on someone who still couldn't, or wouldn't, believe Las Vegas was free of the Sickness. But the odd thing was, no one stared at either the mask or the wearer. It was much too common; just another article of clothing.

So far the city had been lucky; no one predicted that would last forever.

He moved on, searching.

He never played the dollar or larger slots; that would bring too much attention to himself, and it would make him too nervous.

He never played the nickel slots because he'd be here all week and never get what he needed.

He looked for a row which few, if any, people used, sat on a padded stool, and examined the machine.

It made no difference what theme it had, how many ways it offered to take his quarters and multiply them into dollars; he never looked at the running total of jackpots hanging above in blinding lights, winking at him, suggesting that if, just this once, he varied the routine, he could win tens of thousands, not just a paltry few hundred, or a sports car or an RV or an automobile that looked twice as big as his house.

"Hi," he said. He didn't care that he spoke aloud. People did it all the time, even to the video games. "How you doing tonight?"

He leaned forward and patted the side of the machine, ran a palm down the cool smooth metal, and leaned back.

Damn; no good.

Not this one.

Sometimes it took him more than a dozen machines; sometimes it took him only two or three; sometimes there wasn't one that wanted to talk back and he'd head for another casino, begin the ritual again.

Tonight, as if aware he was on the brink of something he didn't understand, he couldn't find a thing. Another hour wasted, his fingers snapping unconsciously, his tongue licking at his lips until he stopped it by clenching his teeth. Finally he gave himself one more shot, and if it was wrong, he'd move up the Strip. It happened once in a while. It was near to ten-thirty before he found the one he wanted.

He said, "Hi, how you doing?" He patted its side, he used his palm, and it was *right*.

No vibrations, no imagined voice, no tingling, no sparks.

He only knew it was *right*.

He pushed his sleeves, shirt and jacket, up as far as he could to expose his forearms, set the cup in the gap between his machine and the one on his right, took a cigarette from the pack in his breast pocket, placed it in the deep plastic ashtray beside the cup, and smiled.

Time, gentlemen; start your engines.

He put in the first quarter, never more than one or two at a time, and pulled the handle. He hated the buttons. Pressing a button was too much like working a remote control. One-arm bandits demanded the arms were used, otherwise what was the point?

The cylinders rolled, beeps and chimes, and two quarters landed in the tray at his knees.

He grinned.

A hand brushed over his shoulder in greeting.

"Evening, Mr. Falkirk."

He didn't have to turn around. "Hey, Dodger. What're you up to?"

Dodger O'Cleary sat on the stool to Trey's left. He was an ordinary man who couldn't have looked more Irish if he tried. Tight wavy red hair sifted through with white and sand, a drinking man's nose, dark green eyes, fair freckled skin that had begun to sag into jowls, yet with a chin so sharp and square Trey figured it could probably cut through steel.

"Just hanging around, Mr. Falkirk, just hanging around." He nodded at Trey's machine. "You feeling lucky, huh?"

Trey scooped out the fifty cents with his right hand and showed it, and the palm, to him. "Gonna buy my mansion in Kentucky, Dodger."

They laughed easily, not quite friends, not true adversaries either.

After all these years, Trey was well aware that the casinos knew who he was, by sight if not by name. Every so often they would send a man or woman like Dodger to have a polite chat, pass the time of day, comment on the state of the world, maybe make an offer of a free lunch or cheap dinner, and at the same time make double-damn sure he wasn't using some kind of special spooky electronic equipment. Dodger was easier than most. He didn't much care, not really, even though it was his job. He genuinely liked Trey, and they frequently met in one of the hotel bars for a drink after the night's playing was over.

On the other hand, Trey wasn't stupid. He also knew Dodger would make short work of him if he ever discovered how Trey did it.

Assuming, that is, Trey ever found out himself.

"Haven't seen you in a while, Mr. Falkirk."

Another quarter, lost when the stars and bars didn't match.

"You scare me, Dodger."

O'Cleary grinned, lips thinning to the point of vanishing. He knew that Trey deliberately spread himself around, up the Strip and down Fremont Street, out to the fringe hotels that tried to draw the Strip toward them. Trey had told him once that he didn't want to bruise his luck sticking too long in one place; the man understood. Win consistently, the way Trey did, in the same place every night, and there would be more questions than there already were. Possibly even a blackball.

O'Cleary sniffed hard, took out a handkerchief and blew his nose. "The damn air-conditioning," he explained. "In and out all day, I'm lucky I don't catch pneumonia."

A quarter, three back.

A quarter, five back.

Two quarters, nothing.

The man shifted, and Trey looked at him sideways, frowning. "Got a problem?"

"Not with you, Mr. Falkirk, nope." He shrugged. "Things, that's all."

Trey stared blindly at his machine—quarter in, five out—and nodded. "Gonna be starving when I'm done. Your shift is over when, at midnight? How about a sandwich or something? I'll be crawling by then if I don't get something to eat."

O'Cleary slapped his knee lightly. "Date." He rose, patted Trey in a friendly fashion on both upper arms, and left.

Quarter in, ten out.

Never, ever, taking more than fifty or sixty dollars in one session in one place. Ever. And if he didn't keep track and ended up with a lot more, he changed coin into bills, went to the nearest roulette table and lost it. A little at a time, but he always managed to trim the excess. Which he knew drove the men who watched the security monitors crazy.

One of the perks.

Just one of the perks.

Like Dodger O'Cleary. A genuinely nice guy whose job it was to protect the casino's edge, yet wasn't a fanatic about it. He was good, very good, at nabbing the cons and the pickpockets and the idiots who thought the cameras weren't watching them.

Trey had become a challenge, but evidently not one he lay awake nights trying to solve.

Two hours and sixty-seven dollars later, he picked up the unsmoked cigarette and tucked it behind his ear, grabbed the plastic cup, and went to the cashier's window at the floor's outer wall. When the bills were in hand, he folded them over, stuffed them into his jeans pocket, and made his way up the escalator to the second level. He avoided the line to the all-you-can-eat buffet hall, swinging instead around a small bar to one of the quietest places in the building—the Sherwood Forest coffee shop, so named, he supposed, because of the really godawful phony fat tree in the middle, its branches cut short by the low ceiling. It was out of the direct flow of visitors and guests, and the bar itself made no noise at all.

O'Cleary sat at one of the tables in back, behind the tree. His hands were cupped around a mug of coffee, while a burning cigarette was propped in a plastic ashtray. Hangdog, and somehow rumpled in a perfectly pressed suit.

Trey almost didn't go in right away.

The feeling touched him again.

Not quite oppression, not quite caution.

Even inside, there was something in the air.

He ordered himself a sandwich and a soda at the counter, took his number, and made a show of pulling out a chair, taking off his jacket, and sitting with a great, thank God it's done for tonight sigh.

O'Cleary looked up with a wan smile.

"So," Trey said, "what's up?"

The older man shrugged. "You know how it is. You get a little tired sometimes."

Dodger's wife, Eileen, had been taken by the Sickness just after Christmas. Perfectly healthy, not a sick day in her life. One trip to San Francisco was all it had taken. The damnable part was, as far as the medical teams were concerned, she had probably been the last case there before the Sickness moved on.

Trey knew how he felt, but didn't want to assume that was the problem. A reprieve when a server called his number, and he went to fetch his meal, such as it was.

"The thing is," O'Cleary said when he returned, staring at the steam rising from the mug, "I'm thinking maybe it's our turn, you know?" He glanced up. "We've been lucky so far."

Trey nodded as he picked up his sandwich. His stomach grumbled, and they grinned at each other.

"What you need is a wife," the man told him, only half-joking. "You probably forget to eat half the time, right? Right. Don't know how you stay fit, eating the way you do."

"It is," Trey said, "the blessing that is myself, my friend. I do what I can to run myself down, but everything I touch turns to nutrition. I drive doctors up the wall. Maybe that's my calling."

"You're an odd one, Mr. Falkirk, you know that?"

Trey laughed. "You're not the first one who's told me that today."

They ate in silence for a few minutes. Blessed silence. Voices on their way downstairs to the casino or on their way to the store-lined passageway that led to the Luxor, were muted and, at this time of night, less prone to excitement. A juggler strolled past, six fluffy red balls in the air while his female companion tried to adjust his jester's cap, giggling so hard she nearly pulled it off. During the day, he would be trailed by a swarming gaggle of kids; now he was alone and seemed smaller for it.

Midnight in the land of make-believe.

O'Cleary emptied his mug and went to get a refill. Trey watched him pass some time with the clerk, and chewed thoughtfully without tasting bread or filling. When the man returned, Trey braced his elbows on the table, made a fist with both hands, and pressed it lightly against his lips.

"Okay," he said, "what else?"

O'Cleary blew his nose, sipped his coffee, fussed with his plastic utensils, rolled his eyes when the juggler passed in the other direction.

"Dodger."

"Could be nothing."

"Could be something."

"Yeah. Could be."

"So . . . what? Damn, O'Cleary, are you supposed to give me my walking papers or something? Sixty bucks once a week or so and I'm banned?"

"No," O'Cleary answered. "It's a man."

"A man?" He leaned back. "What man?"

"I don't know him, but he's looking for you."

Someone comes looking, the first thing you wonder is who you might have ticked off for some offense or other. You don't automatically think it might be good news, great news, fantastic and life-changing news that might, if nothing else, get you a decent suit of clothes. You don't think it's an angel or a genie or a leprechaun with wishes. You don't think it's a someone you used to know, used to work for, 'way back, who's decided the company can't do without you anymore, name your price, we want you back.

You don't think this because you stopped thinking this, dreaming this, once in a blue moon praying for this a long, long time ago.

So long ago, in fact, you sometimes wonder if you've dreamt it all.

Someone comes looking in the place where you're positive you're finally safe, and something with cold wings begins to flutter in your stomach, and for a moment all the noise comes back, waves of it that deafen you until you catch your breath and there's silence again.

Broken arms and busted ribs, a split lip and a blurry eye, snow that slips through the grime-stained cracked window of your cracked plaster and mildewed room, shadows that scurry ahead of you in an alley, voices that growl like animals when you're spotted . . . nothing frightens you as much as *he's looking for you*.

And the scariest part is, you haven't a clue why.

So the first thing you say is—

"You sure it's me he wants?"

O'Cleary nodded. "Knew your name and everything. You have any relatives who might be trying to find you?"

Trey stared at his empty paper plate, pushed at a crumb with a finger. "I have none, Dodger, you know that."

"Maybe it's your old man."

Trey looked at him so hard, O'Cleary blinked and looked away, a mumbled apology making his lips quiver. "No relatives. None. Not even a cousin."

O'Cleary shrugged. "Okay."

"Maybe . . ." He emptied his glass, took a tiny ice cube between his teeth and crunched it slowly. "Maybe I made the mistake of hitting on a Mafia princess and didn't know it."

O'Cleary grinned. "Trey, you know there ain't no Mafia out here anymore. Where've you been? There sure aren't any Mafia princesses. And when was the last time you ever hit on anybody anyway?"

Trey lifted a hand. "Hey, I'm just thinking out loud here, okay? Just thinking out loud. So tell me about him."

O'Cleary lit a cigarette, blew a wobbly smoke ring at the tree, and did.

Trey lit his own and said, "A Brit? Are you sure?"

"I'm not deaf. I've heard more accents than the goddamn United Nations coming through here. I know what I know, and this guy is a Brit, and he's class. So far up he's probably on a first name basis with the goddamn Queen."

"Crazy." Trey blew smoke toward the ceiling. "Dodger, I do not know anybody from England. I do not know anybody from Scotland or Northern Ireland or . . . or . . ."

"Wales," O'Cleary finished. "Everybody always forgets Wales, the poor jerks."

"Whatever. I don't know him."

"Well, he sure as hell knows you. He even offered me money to tell him when I saw you again."

"Jesus." Trey almost left the chair. "He's staying here?"

"No. But he's come in every day this week. I swear to God, he must've charmed the skins right off the snakes for the boots he's wearing, he's that good. I almost took the money."

Trey's eyes widened. "An old man, an old Englishman with snakeskin boots?"

"Silver."

"Silver snakeskin boots?"

"And the lady with him kept calling him 'Sir.' "

Trey felt a giggle rise in his throat. "Sir as in yes sir, no sir?"

"Nope. Sir as in Your Lordship kind of thing."

Trey leaned forward again. "Dodger, April Fool's Day was three weeks ago. This is not funny."

O'Cleary's thick eyebrows rose. "You don't think so? Man, you should see him, then you'd think it's funny."

Neither man laughed.

Trey scratched his head. "If he knows who I am, wants to see me so badly, why hasn't he come out to my place instead of bothering you here?"

O'Cleary shrugged, pushed his plate away, picked up his cigarette, and stared at the tip.

Trey felt it then, the change in the air; he saw the change in the man's expression. Not friends now; this was business.

Even so, it took a moment before O'Cleary said, "Trey, who do you owe?"

"Huh? I don't . . . what do you mean?"

"Who do you owe, Trey?" O'Cleary looked up. "You play these places long enough, you know, sooner or later you're in over your head. You forget where the odds lie, and the next thing you know you're drowning. You hock what you can, sell what you can, sooner or later you get desperate enough to ask around, you meet some people, and . . ." He shrugged broadly. "Who do you owe? I don't care, you understand, but maybe—"

"Nobody."

"Okay."

Heat wrapped around his neck. "I *said* I don't owe anybody, Dodger."

"And I said okay. Jesus, Falkirk." O'Cleary shook his head, put the cigarette out, and pushed away from the table. "I gotta go home. I'm falling asleep on my feet here, and I ain't as young as I used to be."

Trey didn't stand. He stiffened when O'Cleary walked behind him, gripped his shoulders, and leaned down.

"You're a good guy, Falkirk, don't get me wrong." He pressed down, hard, when Trey tried to squirm away. "But this old guy, he wants you pretty bad, all right? God knows why, but he does. So you find him, okay? Talk to him, find out what he wants, maybe you're the long-lost Duke of Something, who the hell knows?" He lowered his voice to a whisper. "Who cares? But I don't want him in my casino anymore, you understand what I'm saying? Tell you the truth, he spooks the guests, he spooks me, and I don't like being spooked. Take care of it, you hear me? Take care of it. Now."

2

Trey didn't watch O'Cleary leave; he watched his hands instead, white-knuckled where they gripped the edge of the table. Then slowly, very slowly, they slid into his lap.

Staring at the empty plate, not seeing a thing.

Not thinking; barely breathing.

Finally pushing away from the table and standing, one hand on the back of the chair to keep himself from falling because suddenly his balance wasn't working very well.

He should have said, "Look, Dodger, I told you I don't know any old man, I don't know why he wants to see me, but he isn't my problem, he's yours. You want someone to take care of it, do it yourself."

He should have said, "Go to hell, O'Cleary, I've got more important things to do than chase around after some old nut in a stupid cowboy hat."

He should have said, "What do you want me to do, stand in the middle of the casino and shout here I am, you old fart, come and get me? Is that what you want?"

He should have said . . . something.

The change in O'Cleary had taken him by surprise, and the none-too-subtle warning had startled him into a temper he didn't dare give a voice.

But he should have said . . . something.

He took a step and nearly fell, grabbed the chair again and dropped into it heavily, blinking, wiping a trembling hand across his eyes. Paying no attention to the handful of other customers who undoubtedly figured he was close enough to drunk that the security guy had to give him a quiet talking-to. A sideways glance in his direction; a smirk; a whisper.

He reached for the glass of soda, gripped it tightly without lifting it because his hand shook too hard, and he wasn't sure he wouldn't drop it. A swallow, an inhalation, and the trembling eased.

someone comes looking

God damn, he thought, and drank quickly and deeply, taking some of the tiny hollow ice cubes into his mouth. Crunching them between his teeth. Shuddering at the cold, hearing the sound of the chewing resonate in his skull, reminding him oddly of steady footsteps in a snow-covered field.

someone comes looking

Another drink emptied the glass, and he reached into it, pinched an ice cube between thumb and forefinger and pressed it against his brow, holding it there with his palm until it melted. Drying the numb skin with the back of his hand. Wiping the back of his hand across his thigh.

This, he thought, is ridiculous.

No; it's past ridiculous into ludicrous.

Some outlandish old man is looking for him, for whatever damn reason, so O'Cleary overreacts and gets bent out of shape, for whatever damn reason, and now he feels as if a battalion of geese has marched over his grave.

For whatever damn reason.

You *do* know what it is, he told himself.

"Right," he muttered. "Right."

He stood again, waited, then made his way out of the coffee shop. Slowly. Carefully. Walking as if he'd just been released after six months in a hospital bed, the fearful anticipation of falling, keeping his head down, his stride short.

He wasn't quite sure what to do next. He didn't feel up to taking on another casino and adding to the slight heft he felt his pocket needed, and he damn sure wasn't about to search for that old guy, no matter what O'Cleary wanted. He supposed he'd kind of like to know what the big deal was, but right now he had more important things to worry about, like, for example, finding a new place to live before they shut Emerald City down.

He told himself that one more time, and gave up because he didn't believe it.

someone comes looking and you're angry at yourself and you're angry at the old man

At the escalators/staircase, he moved to one side and looked down and out over the casino. It was quiet down there now, normal world quiet. Most of the tables had been shut down, most of the players were concentrated mostly at the slots and around one roulette wheel. In the limited area he could see he counted less than two dozen people, a few still with air-filter masks, but not one of them wearing a straw cowboy hat.

No voices now, just the occasional clatter of coins and the tinny electronic music.

Too many lights for shadows.

The hell with it, he thought, took the staircase down, and made his way toward the exit, every so often turning to walk backward a few steps. Just in case.

When he wasn't stopped or hailed, he zipped up his jacket and went outside, shivering at the natural chill in the air. By the time he reached the pickup, almost the only vehicle remaining in the huge lot, the goose-and-grave dread had slipped away, leaving him with a grin because once again he had won another few dollars for his old-age fund. Not bad; not bad at all for a guy who can't do anything else with his life.

The engine rumbled softly.

CHARIOT

He waited a few moments, watching the exit, watching a great white limousine pull up to the canopy, watching a half-dozen people in evening clothes climb out, laughing, holding on to each other, looking small beneath the high towers of Excalibur. They were still there when the limo slipped away, and he wondered why they didn't go in. Enjoying the evening, probably; they didn't want it to end.

Then one of them accidentally triggered the automated doors, and with one last look at the sky, they all bundled reluctantly inside, arms around each other, still laughing, still chattering, but not quite as loudly, the excitement slowly draining, leaving bittersweet exhaustion behind.

He grunted.

One of these days, he promised himself as he switched on the headlamps, he would take some of that stash under the bed, buy himself a tux, and do the town right. A reward, not an indulgence. Something to think about; why the hell not.

But he didn't move.

His hands on the steering wheel, palms slipping around the rim, down and up, down and up again.

Waiting for the old man to appear in the doorway.

"Jesus," he whispered.

But he still didn't move.

Down and up, and down and up again.

The engine rumbled softly, patiently, and the heater warmed the cab. Without taking his gaze from the hotel, he reached over to switch on the radio, turn the volume down, blinking stupidly at it when he heard

dreamed last night

His lips moved

i was on the boat to heaven

and his left heel tapped the beat through a prolonged burst of static

. . . and the people all said

and his hands slipped around the steering wheel rim, down and up

sit down

down and up again.

Funny thing about the desert this time of year, all that sun during the day, all that ice at night. Funny thing, how you ought to be singing at the top of your voice, you know this song, your mother used to sing it all the time, but your lips move without sound and your heel taps without sound and that thing in your gut still has cold wings.

Down and up.

sit down

Tires and brakes shrieked out on Tropicana Avenue, and he started, stiffened, bracing for the sound of shattering glass and crumpled metal because you remember

a night the summer after you first arrived to stay for good, a night when you stood on the sidewalk outside the Mirage, the red-water volcano erupting loudly behind you every fifteen minutes, traffic on the boulevard slowing down to watch the display, and one driver loses concentration and jumps the curb and should have crushed you between the fender and the low wall that marks the hotel grounds. But it didn't happen. You were bumped, nothing more, and it took half an hour to calm the driver down because he kept telling you over and over that you should have been dead

and even now he can't help wincing at the memory, recalling that at the time he thought the man was right.

The only one he ever told was Jude Levin, and the best she could do by way of explanation was, "One of those things, Trey, just one of those things. If you start looking for something else, you'll drive yourself crazy."

She was right, of course, and he had indeed chalked it up to one of life's wondrous miracles, with maybe a little help from his mother's gold chip, but somehow he couldn't bring himself to tell the story again. It was, he had decided, one of those "you had to be there" times, because the telling couldn't come close to the terror he had felt as the car bore down on him and he hadn't been able to move.

sit down you're rockin' the boat

The song ended abruptly, swamped by more static, louder, almost rhythmic, and as he reached out to shut the radio off, a dark figure stepped through the open doors. He leaned forward, staring intently, holding his breath, finally rolling his eyes when he recognized the security uniform. It was one of the guards who checked the keys of those who wanted to get to their tower rooms. Sneaking a cigarette while on duty, it looked like, and Trey grinned, released the hand brake, and headed for home.

Halfway there, after finding another station to fill the cab with noise, he remembered the bread, groaned, considered feigning forgetfulness, and sighed surrender at an image of Moonbow's disappointed face.

He couldn't do it.

It took him twenty minutes to find a convenience store, bought the bread, a few things for himself, and drove the rest of the way home at speed. Humming to himself, unable to keep from looking in the rearview mirror to see if he was being followed.

3

There was a full moon over the desert, and a slow steady wind that slipped down from the mountains.

Trey stopped at the line of mailboxes hammered to a wood plank facing the only street in Emerald City. He tugged down the door of his, fumbled around inside, and pulled his hand back, empty. It didn't bother him. At least there weren't bills or bothersome sales brochures. At least there wasn't the official eviction notice that would send him back to the streets in the one place he didn't want them.

"You know," he said as he pulled the truck around, disgusted at the way his mood kept shifting, "you keep this up, pal, you're going to end up slitting your wrists or something."

He drove slowly, keeping the engine to a low grumbling, switching off the headlamps on a whim, to let the moon show the way. A young man's dare, but the moonlight left no color behind. All the porchlights were off, the windows all dark, and had he been a stranger he would have sworn there was no life here, none at all.

Something urged him to lean on the horn, just to see what would happen. He laughed silently, knowing full well the trouble he'd be in, except with the kids. A nice thought, but never mind. So he backed the truck into the carport, and sat for a few moments while the engine ticked down and the night's chill seeped in and gooseflesh traveled slowly along his arms.

Strange night, he thought; hell, a strange day.

But when he yawned so hard his jaw popped, he rubbed his eyes briskly and ordered himself to bed. He'd think about it in the morning, when his brain wasn't riding on fumes and, with luck, his moods would have finally settled.

He opened the door, winced at the slow squeal of a hinge demanding oil, and reached in to grab the plastic bag of groceries.

"Thanks," he said to the dashboard, to the truck, and dragged the bag toward him, straightening as he did, and whacked his head against the ceiling's metal edge. The impact wasn't hard, but it was hard enough, and he cursed as he backed away from the cab, rubbing his scalp gingerly with his free hand.

"I said thanks, for God's sake," he muttered sourly as he swung onto the porch. "Damn."

Someone had taped an envelope to the front door. He shook his head and pulled it free, shoved it unopened into his hip pocket. Moonbow, no doubt, with another drawing for the invisible topiary. The last one had been for a miniature Mt. Rushmore. This one was probably Hoover Dam. A sweet kid, but she didn't know when to quit. He'd read it when he got up, and figure out a way to let her down easy.

His left hand was on the doorknob, when he heard the footsteps.

He turned his head slowly to look up the street, thinking it was one of the girls, sneaking out to see how the battle had gone; it wouldn't be the first time. Then frowning as he remembered O'Cleary and the old Englishman.

It was neither.

And it wasn't footsteps.

He didn't realize he had opened the door until he felt it swing inward. He let it go and used the hand to pass roughly over his face.

Moonlight cast a different kind of shadow, and at first he wasn't sure there was anything out there at all, that what he thought he had seen was nothing more than a flurry of dust the wind had kicked up.

Movement changed his mind.

He eased away from the door, heading forward, squinting against the wind and the moon's unreliable illumination, nodding when he spotted the hind end of a horse as it walked toward the desert, braided tail swishing slowly side to side. On its back was Lillian Tarque; he'd know that hair anywhere.

Which, he immediately told himself, was impossible, because Lil could barely walk yet, much less get back in the saddle. Much less in the middle of the night.

A quick step to the edge of the porch, his mouth open to call her, ask her what was going on, but horse and rider had already moved out of sight.

He waited, heard nothing but the slow and even hoofbeats that faded, and were soon gone.

Not a sound, then.

Not a sound but the soft hiss of the wind coasting over the ground.

And there was no dust in the air where the animal had been.

You're dreaming, he thought, but he didn't move. Not for a long while. Not until the grocery bag gained weight and his vision began to blur and his head began to ache from staring so hard.

Still, he didn't move.

Tired as he was, as churned up as he was from O'Cleary and the casino, he was not, and never had been, prone to seeing things.

He waited, then set the grocery bag down and stepped off the side of the porch, hurried across the yard into the street, and walked slowly toward the end. He was no hunter, certainly no tracker, but he figured he'd be able to recognize a hoofprint when he saw it.

Just one was all he wanted.

He didn't find any.

By the time he reached the place where the street faded into the desert, he was shivering, and his back had begun to protest him bending over so much, but he sure wasn't about to go out *there*. He didn't much care for it in daylight; he sure wasn't going to traipse around there at night. Too many shapes he didn't recognize; too many ways to get himself in trouble.

So what did you see? he asked his shadow as he turned around. Wishful thinking? God knew, Lil deserved a break, and her stunt-riding job had been her life . . . until the accident. He had seen her a couple of times at the Excalibur arena, had been impressed by her skill and enthusiasm if not the venue, yet he could only imagine how she felt now. He liked her, so maybe wishful . . . not thinking, maybe hoping. Maybe that's what it was: wishful hoping.

Or maybe he was just plain nuts.

When he drew even with Eula's place on his right, the professor's on his left, he stopped, struck once again by how deserted the street felt. How utterly silent it had become. How small he seemed under the huge moon. A spaceship could come down, snatch him up, carry him off to Saturn or some damn place like that, and no one would ever know he'd been here tonight.

He took a step and looked at the ground behind him.

No print.

No one would know.

"Okay, that's it, stupid," he said to the pale shadow that pointed toward home. "It's getting a little deep here, and I don't have a shovel. In fact—"

you're rockin' the boat

He stopped again.

He had been talking primarily for the sound of his voice, to fill the silence. But he didn't like the faint echo he heard, as if he were walking through a small cavern. His imagination, of course, but he still didn't like it.

"Bed," he ordered.

No echo this time.

No wind.

Just the moon.

4

You sit in your dreamscape with the television on, remote in your hand, surfing the channels for something to watch, a beer on the table beside you, a cigarette hooked behind your left ear.

Outside, in the desert, wolves bay at the full moon.

Outside, in the desert, a woman weeps bitterly at the top of her voice.

Eventually, the bottle at your lips, you find something that looks interesting, until you look closer at the screen and see that the man on the street looks remarkably like you.

You smile a little sheepishly and glance around the empty room, hoping no one will recognize you; then you scoot the chair a little closer so you can see a little better because your eyes aren't quite the way they used to be when you and the world were younger.

It's an amazing show, an incredible achievement of sights and sounds and smells, as if you were really there. Ambling along on Fremont Street. A bit footsore and weary because you've been dragon-fighting all day, building the next stake to take you out of Nevada because you just don't learn, do you; you just don't learn.

And outside, in the desert, wolves bay at the full moon.

Inside, on the screen, you see a bandy-legged cowboy lurch out of a bar, blinking against the flood of neon, trying to focus on the crowds who sweep past him without looking. You're preoccupied with trying to figure out if your luck, or whatever it is, will stand one more try, so you don't hear the cowboy yelling right away.

When you do, you look back, and he's yelling at you.

In his left hand is a knife, its long serrated blade flaring neon as he waves it.

You look around at the others, who are moving away from the cowboy quickly, an uncertain smile on your lips, you can't be sure it's really you the drunken fool wants.

Something about running away with his wife.

Something about payback time.

Before you realize what's happening, he charges, and you're too stunned to move until it's too late, and all the dodging and ducking and throwing wild punches of your own doesn't stop the blade from slicing through your shirt, twisting, and taking out a good piece of your waist.

When you yell in pain, grab your waist with both hands, and drop to your knees, the drunk is so astonished by what he's nearly done that he immediately hands the knife over to the cop chugging up behind him and asks if he's the only one who saw the ghost in the leather jacket.

A man helps you to your feet, saying, "Where's the blood? Where's the blood?" over and over until you check your shirt, pulling open the gap, thinking it must be shock that you don't feel anything anymore.

When you can't find anything, you pull the shirt out of your belt, pull it practically up to your neck, and nearly bend yourself double trying to find the gash the knife left behind.

There isn't one.

Not a gash, not a cut, not a single drop of blood.

The cop tells you you're lucky, and you tell him you don't want to press charges, just make sure the cowboy gets on back to his damn ranch or wherever before he really does hurt someone.

Then you look right at the camera, look right through the screen, look right at yourself sitting on the couch with a bottle of beer in your hand, and you say, while the wolves outside howl at the moon, "You're supposed to be dead, you know. You're supposed to be dead."

Part 2

SIT DOWN, YOU'RE ROCKIN' THE BOAT

1

1

. . . and he says to tell you that the dragon is dying.

In T-shirt and jeans Trey stood on his porch, sunglasses on, hands in pockets, staring down the street as if daring that son-of-a-bitch old man to show himself again while he was actually around. Paying little attention, other than a perfunctory glance, to the high white clouds that soared over the valley, cutting the sun once in a while, but never the heat.

The air was still.

Emerald City was quiet.

Behind him, through the open door, he could hear local news anchors reading amazement at the storm that had blown through down in Boulder City earlier that morning. One called it a sandstorm, the other a duststorm, but the results were the same: cars scoured, windows pitted, a few helpless pedestrians cut up and admitted to area hospitals. Their tone, however, was meant to be calm, to be soothing, to make sure the tourists didn't panic because this was, after all, a very rare occurrence.

What they didn't say, what they meant was, be grateful it isn't the Sickness. We've been lucky so far, let's count our blessings.

He stepped off the porch, glaring now.

He had read Moonbow's note right after breakfast, too late to catch either girl before they'd left for school. He'd been tempted to drive over there, drag them out of class, and interrogate the hell out of them. Instead, he decided to be just angry, not stupid, and be thankful that the note had driven away the last of the shakes his nightmare had left behind.

He didn't much believe in dreams, not as much as his mother had, but that particular one had shaken him—because it had really happened, the cowboy and the knife. But in the dream, watching it as if it were a scene in a film, he realized, or admitted, for the first time that what had happened couldn't have happened.

you're supposed to be dead

A raucous used-car commercial blared through the front window, startling him, and he turned with a muttered curse, went inside, and shut the television down. A tap of his hand against his leg, and he was outside again. Off the porch, heading up the street, letting his anger flare once again.

The house next to his was empty, as was the one opposite it, but he looked anyway at the blind windows, the sand piling against the doorsills, trying to recall who had lived there and shaking his head when he couldn't. He wasn't sure, but he thought they had been empty when he'd returned to stay.

The next house on the right had all the shades down, Cable and Steph asleep for at least another four or five hours.

He angled left, not sure what he would say, right hand slapping his leg lightly to dispel the anger as much as he could, disperse some of the energy. By the time he reached the porch he was, if not calm, at least in control.

The inner door was open, the screen door locked. He could see straight through the front room into the kitchen, dimly, the back door little more than a rectangular glare. He knocked on the frame and stepped back, glancing up and down the street, pursing his lips in a silent whistle.

He was patient.

At last he smiled, because he knew she was watching.

"Hey," he called softly. "Come on, Jude, it's only me."

The back door's glare vanished as she moved out of the tiny back room where, in a better time, washers and dryers would have been; now she used it as her bedroom, little more than a nunnery cell.

He took another step back as she approached, the screen's mesh keeping her outline indistinct.

"Hey," he said.

"Hey yourself." Her voice was soft, faintly harsh as if speaking were difficult, and slightly muffled by the thin cloth mask that covered her face from below the eyes to her neck. This wasn't the kind of surgical mask he saw periodically in town, people from outside who weren't used to walking around without some kind of protection no matter how feeble. It was loose, thin, reminding him each time of an Arabian woman's veil.

"You coming out?" he said, another step back so he could lean against the post. "Nobody around, Jude. Get some air for a change."

He didn't push; it all depended on how the night had gone. No sleep, and she'd stay inside, a tall, slender ghost in a place too small to haunt. If she rested, and if there were no strangers, she might, only might, come out to join him.

He had learned fairly quickly, and painfully, not to push.

The door creaked as she unlocked it.

He grinned. "It walks."

"Funny," she said sourly, slipping onto the porch, reaching around to test the latch to be sure she could slip back in. Taller than he, what figure she had was cloaked by a long formless white dress with only the slightest scoop at the neck; no belt or sash, no trim. Long dark brown hair down to her waist, so straight he sometimes wondered if, like kids in the old days, she ironed it once in a while.

Large, round, amazing sable eyes.

"I like the Hollywood look," she said with a nod to his sunglasses. "Very you."

"My action star mode."

She grunted a laugh, then narrowed her eyes. "What's the matter? You didn't sleep well?"

A jerk of his head for a shrug. "Bad dream, no big deal. And . . ." He scratched under his nose with the flat of a finger. "I spooked myself, too."

"How nice."

"Not very. I thought I saw Lil riding up the street last night. On a horse. The whole deal—sight, sound, smell."

She didn't respond for a moment. Then: "Flashbacks, huh? Stuff you took in college?"

"Yeah," he said. "Right." He tapped his leg thoughtfully. "I would have sworn it then, Jude. You put a Bible in my hand last night, I would have sworn I'd really seen her."

But all she said was, "Strange days, action hero. Strange days."

Not, he thought, what I want to hear, lady.

They watched the empty street in comfortable silence, until she pushed at her hair and said, "You're going in today." Not a question; a faint whiff of condemnation.

"All day." He shifted to rest his back against the post, cross his feet at the ankles. Face down the street to catch anyone coming in. "You need anything else at the store?"

"You just said you'll be gone all day."

"I can come back, Jude. No big deal, you know that."

"Your karma thanks you."

He almost said, *my karma sucks big time in case you hadn't noticed*, but he only gave her a noncommittal nod. "Just let me know if you want something."

"What if you meet that man?"

He pushed a hand over his hair, thinking maybe, before the heat finally reached furnace levels, he'd get it trimmed. Buzz cut. Crew cut. Marine cut. Hell, maybe shave it all off and be done with it.

"Did you see him last night?"

She nodded, but offered nothing except, "He frightened the girls."

"Apparently," he said, feeling anger stir again, "he's been to at least one of the hotels a couple of times. Guy I know told me last night." He grunted. "He, the guy I know, was not very happy. He said . . ." He laughed shortly. "He said the old man was spooky."

"You don't know him?"

"Jude, I don't know anybody."

She didn't respond.

He laughed again. "I thought it was, you know, somebody connected. If you know what I mean. That maybe I'd ticked somebody off for some reason or other. You know, a contract, stuff like that."

Which, when he said it aloud, sounded awfully damn stupid.

"I doubt that," she said, humor in her voice. "You should have seen him, Trey—older than God, for crying out loud, a really bad rhinestone cowboy."

"With a British accent."

"Oh yeah." This time she laughed aloud. "With an English accent." A gesture with a long-fingered hand. "He was very polite, very upper class, but after a while Moonbow didn't like his vibes. I'm not sure why. Maybe it was that crack about the dragon. I—"

When she stopped herself, blinking rapidly in realization, he waited a moment before nodding. "I know. It didn't hit me right away either." He passed a finger lightly over his cheek. "So how does he know about the dragon?" A sweep of his hand to the street. "We're the only ones. Maybe not even all of them. You guys anyway."

Too quickly he turned to face her, and she started, automatically reaching for the latch. When she realized what she had done, she let the hand fall as she lifted a shoulder in an apologetic shrug. Habit. Flight was a habit, and not one she was about to break any time soon.

He had seen the face behind the veil only once, when a gust had caught it and flapped it up over her eyes and it clung to her hair. No matter how little she thought of how he made ends meet, he had become someone special when he hadn't blinked, hadn't flinched, hadn't made a sound. All he had done, before she could duck away, was brush the veil off her head to let it fall back into place.

She had changed it since then, weighted it, so the wind could ruffle it but never lift it.

"How does he know?" he wondered softly, looking back at the empty street rippling with cloud shadows. "How the hell does he know?"

"Wait around until he comes back, and find out."

"Can't."

Again she kept her silence.

"Anyway, if he wants me all that badly, he can damn well find me."

Nothing.

He lowered his sunglasses just enough and met her gaze over the tops, steady, without emotion. His thumb pushed the glasses up again, and he stepped off the porch.

"You're leaving, aren't you."

He didn't move, didn't look back.

"That's what this is all about, isn't it? Last night, all day today? You're getting ready to leave again, aren't you?"

Finally he shook his head, glanced over his shoulder. "Can't, Jude."

"Of course you can," she snapped as she yanked open the door. "You do it all the time."

"Nope. Not now. Can't."

A hesitation. Doubt. A painful clearing of her throat.

He half turned this time, a hand up to stop her from speaking, to save her voice. He opened his mouth, caught himself, and closed it. You don't know, he wanted to tell her; you don't know what it's like

when you step into your backyard a few days after you first rent the house almost four years ago, no plans to do anything with it, no grass or garden or even a chair and umbrella table. You just want to see what it's like back there with its tufts of grass that look more like spikes, and cacti whose names you'll eventually learn from a book one afternoon because you're monumentally bored, and a pair of half-dead Joshua trees way in the back.

You don't see the rattlesnake.

When you hear it, it's too late.

There's not much you remember because it happens too damn fast. One minute you're crouched by a cactus, wondering if those spines are really as sharp as they say, the next you're staring into this obscene, terrifying face, listening to rattles like thunder. You forget you're in a crouch when you start to back away, and you fall on your rump.

A frozen eternal second before you panic and scrabble backward as fast as you can, feet pushing and hands pulling, and the snake strikes and there's a sharp pain just above the top of your right boot and the panic trebles, you roll over, get to your feet, race back to the door, explode into the kitchen, slam the door, drop into the chair, and prop your leg on the table. Breathing so hard you almost pass out. Sweat blinding you, hands trembling violently, fingers scratching at your jeans to pull the leg up. You're dying; you know you're dying, and you can't remember what to do next, scenes from a million movies flash through your mind—cutting the wound, sucking out the poison—and it takes you a while before you notice there's only a small scratch on your calf, before you look closer and see the burr that latched onto your leg and stabbed you when you panicked.

Release and relief in a single yell, and it isn't until months later that you admit to yourself that the burr wasn't there until you retreated; and you retreated because the rattler bit you, and no one will ever know because you don't know yet yourself that

there's something about the city she'll never understand, and if you try to tell her, she'll think you're crazy.

"Trey?"

"Nothing," he said wearily. "Nothing. You're right. Not enough sleep." Then he straightened and gave her his best smile. "And I'm not leaving, Jude. Just racking up a few shekels for a rainy day."

A pointed look at the sky. "By then you'll be at least a billionaire."

"I wish."

She cleared her throat again, tilted her head to tell him she couldn't talk much longer. He gave her a *hey that's okay* wave and started across the yard.

"Be careful of the hedge," she said, actually giggling.

He stopped, turned his head slowly, and said, "What?"

"The girls decided we had to have a hedge, too."

Then, surprisingly, she blew him a quick kiss and ducked inside, the white of her dress fading behind the screen, another ghost.

That the girls weren't around didn't matter; he made a show of returning to what would have been the front walk if the builders or Jude had bothered to put one in, and went into the street, feeling inordinately giddy. A big grin on his face. For the hedge or the blown kiss he couldn't be sure, but that too didn't matter.

His mood had lifted, and he whistled his way back to his house, two-stepped inside, and took a quick and cool shower. Put on the uniform, laughed aloud when he was halfway to the door before remembering his jacket, and decided that if he ran into the old man, he wouldn't slug him first for upsetting his friends.

He would have sung, very loudly and very badly, several bars of the chariot song if he hadn't paused at the front door to make sure he had his keys, looked up, and saw Eula Korrey.

2

Green.

In the midst of the drab sand and drab houses, the lifeless grass and cacti waiting for one lousy drop of rain, the first thing Trey had noticed about her, the first thing anybody had noticed about her, was the green.

There had been other colors surely, but no one remembered them with any clarity.

It was green; always green.

Today was no exception.

The temperature, an hour shy of noon, had already begun to flirt with ninety, and Eula wore a green, light coat that reached to her knees, exposing the matching green dress beneath. A green felt hat, its brim rolled up, its crown low and round. A dark green purse whose strap was hooked over the arm she held beneath her breasts. Green shoes with solid low heels. Green linen gloves with dark green lace trim at the cuffs.

Freneau once called her the emerald in Emerald City.

She wasn't terribly short, but her bulk made her seem so, and she was the first one to let people know that she knew full well she was fat. Yet the way she walked, the way she held herself, the weight she carried seemed the perfect weight for her.

Trey stepped back from the open door, just in case she looked in his direction. Down at the end of the street a taxi waited. It was the way she always traveled, never asking for rides, never asking to borrow someone's car.

She certainly never asked him.

It was always a taxi, and it always waited at the end of the street.

And she always sang softly to herself as she walked to her ride. He could hear her now, words indistinct, hanging in the heat, but the rhythm and verve were there, her head bobbing slightly, her stride keeping time. As always. Practicing, no doubt, for her next engagement.

The driver scrambled out to open her door, and she nodded to him gratefully, graciously, giving him a huge broad smile. She paused before she got in and looked back suddenly. Trey started; although he knew she couldn't see him through the screen, he would have sworn she knew he was there. The smile broadened, she nodded absently at something the driver said, and backed in, green shoes last to disappear into the car.

The driver slammed the door shut, looked around, shook his head as if to wonder why a woman like that could live in a neighborhood like this, and took his place behind the wheel. He drove away slowly but dust rose anyway. Without a breeze to stir it, it just floated there.

Hanging in the heat.

When the sound of the engine faded, Trey stirred, reminding himself that he had more important things to concern himself with today than an old fat woman's inexplicable animosity. There was a stash to be added to—big time, if he could manage it—and the more immediate mystery of the old man and his companion.

Suddenly he laughed aloud.

"You know," he said as he hurried to the truck, "you drop dead today, you sure can't say your life has been dull."

She had moved in at the end of last summer, and for a while, everyone stepped lightly. She had certainly been friendly enough, always a smile and a pleasant greeting nod, yet only the kids didn't seem nervous around her. It never occurred to them to attempt to find out if she was militant or sensitive or political or apprehensive; all they cared about was the hard candy she kept in her purse, an endless supply always shared with a deep-throated laugh.

Finally, one afternoon in late September, Steph and a reluctant Cable threw a welcome to Emerald City, front yard barbecue which everyone attended. After a lot of milling around and trading well-worn gossip about the fate of their street, Steph, being Steph, asked her quite innocently how it was, growing up an African-American in the South.

Eula looked up at her, head slightly cocked, before lifting a hand in a dismissive wave. "Shoo, girl," she said, grinning, showing her teeth, "there's this little place in Alabama, you ain't never heard of it, a lot of old shacks and cabins, and that's where this old fat woman's from. Been through nigger and Negro, colored and black, I guess those politic boys mean well but I been here longer than God and a few angels." She shook her head, still grinning, and took Steph's arm. "Ebony is black, honey, and I'm damn sure tougher than that."

Her laughter coasted across the desert on the late afternoon's slow wind, and once she had been persuaded to sing them all a song, no one ever noticed the color again.

Except the green.

Jude thought it wonderful, all God's children living together and getting along.

Trey didn't pay her much mind since he wasn't around all that much, until shortly after they realized she had become, in finger-snap time, a star on the gospel radio circuit. Concerts in churches, auditoriums, high schools, wherever a sound system, a choir, and at least a solid piano could be found.

He had been on the porch, watching her head down the street toward the taxi, when a gust slammed the hat off her head. It arced like a boomerang, and without thinking he lunged into the yard and grabbed it before it hit the ground, stumbled a few steps, and came up grinning.

"Haven't moved like that since I was a kid," he said, handing it over.

She fussed with her hair, mostly white, then dusted off the hat and set it in place.

"Maybe you ought to tie it down," he had said, miming it flying loose again.

When she was done, everything in place, she looked up at him. Not smiling. Lips tight. Hands clasping her purse snug against her stomach.

"I think," she said at last, "I got nothing to say to you."

And walked away.

Leaving him in the street, watching her back, wondering what in hell line he had crossed.

That was no Big Star talking to a Little Person.

That was pure and simple personal.

A few questions to his neighbors over the next several days gave him no answers. Everybody loved her, and she loved everybody. Trey had obviously insulted her somehow, it was his fault, he was the one who had to make it up to her.

He never did because he never tried. Her problem, not his, and they never spoke again.

Jude, in December, had tried to intervene, but he didn't want any part of it. It was, he told her, no skin off his nose. She thought that a particularly cruel and cold sentiment, but the only response he could give her was a *whatever* shrug.

So the animosity remained.

Hanging in the heat.

3

The plan was simple: even though it was too early for O'Cleary's shift, he would avoid the Excalibur, in fact stay away from all the hotels at the bottom of the Strip just in case Dodger went wandering. The last thing he wanted today was a confrontation with a man who was almost a friend.

Instead, he would start midway along, either with Caesar's, or the much smaller Barbary Coast across Las Vegas Boulevard, and work his way up. Taking his time. No hurry at all. If the slots were well-disposed toward him, he might even visit the older casinos, the ones that hadn't been given over to families and fads, where the only themes were gambling and dining.

Usually he wouldn't do so much in one day; usually Jude didn't throw him a kiss.

Had the gesture been more studied, more elaborate, more grand, he would have known it to be mocking, almost scolding. It hadn't been. It had been quick, without thought. Not much to base a surprise on, but for him, for the time being, it was enough.

If the cherries, the bars, the sevens lined up right, it wouldn't be long before Moonbow would have more than a necklace for her birthday.

Then it wouldn't make a difference if queens didn't take to men like him.

4

His stomach betrayed him.

Anxious as he was to talk to his machines, his stomach launched a vigorous and noisy protest as soon as he had parked in his usual space behind the Excalibur. He hoped to ignore it, to get at least one decent session in before he had to appease it, but it gurgled so loudly that one or two people stared, and one or two laughed at the reminder he'd only eaten a slice of toast for breakfast.

Patience, he thought; patience, my boy, and some food.

Since there were still remnants of his good mood hanging loose over his shoulders, he decided to treat himself to Madame Song's, a small, decidedly non-fancy restaurant a block up the Strip from the MGM Grand, tucked into the middle of a handful of small shops that laid obvious traps for obvious tourists. It was associated with no hotel, had no slots in its small foyer, seemed in fact determined to ignore the bustle of the boulevard entirely. A large menu, inexpensive meals, and a willingness to permit its customers to linger made it a favorite among those who were weary of hotel food and prices.

Tinted glass in the large front window shielded the inside from the boulevard's glare; the air-conditioning was set permanently to "semi-Arctic," which taught Trey fast enough not to order hot meals he couldn't finish quickly; and the noise level was so low it was almost churchlike.

A place to think, to recoup energy, to brood over losses over a large cup of coffee at three in the morning; no one to hassle you, no one to ride your back if you've had one or two drinks too many, no one to provide false hope, false cheer.

The setup was ordinary: padded rounded booths against the walls and along the front window, bare darkwood tables in the middle, a short counter hardly anyone ever used. No taped music, Chinese or otherwise. Murals of Chinese landscapes in muted colors. A sign at the register facing the front door that warned potential customers that this was *not* a Chinese restaurant, get your moo shu pork somewhere else.

Trey sat in a booth for four near the entrance, his back to the door, chosen because he had long ago discovered it was one of the few places in the room where the air-conditioning ducts didn't blow straight on him, and his meal. With no effort at all he could see the sprawl of the Monte Carlo across the street, and Caesar's through the shimmering glare farther up. A little effort looking over his shoulder gave him the skyline-designed New York, New York one block down, and the Statue of Liberty and the Excalibur towers beyond that. Pedestrian traffic was light, street traffic moderate.

It was Friday; the crowds would turn out much later in the afternoon, seduced by the myth that the heat wouldn't be so bad once the sun headed for the Spring Mountain Range.

The waitress, a terminally bored young woman of the old-fashioned gum-chewing, pencil stuck behind the ear kind, brought his egg salad and iced tea and walked away, all without cracking a smile, speaking a word, or letting him know in any number of ways that he was an old and valued customer.

Her name was Rhonda, and she didn't give a damn as long as he didn't forget the tip.

Which, today, was exactly how he wanted it.

As he ate, taking his time, he tried to think of Jude throwing him the kiss, and an abrupt wash of sadness close to despair froze the sandwich halfway to his mouth.

You're a fool, he thought; you're building a vague dream on one small gesture. An out-of-character one, at that. You charmed her, you jerk. For one moment you charmed her with a smile and those dimples, that action hero crap, and she forgot, for that moment, who she was.

Who you are.

He chewed. He swallowed with some difficulty. He looked through the tinted glass and saw the dragon for what it was in sunlight—lifeless despite the activity, small despite the size. Harsh. Without the depth and magic that night and a million lights cast upon it.

He took a breath, took a bite, and watched a group of four couples stroll by. They were, as best he could tell, Japanese, two men and three of the women unselfconscious in their surgeon's masks, the stiff protruding kind that, here, were covered with tiny intricate designs to camouflage another kind of harshness, one that existed outside the valley. They carried cameras, they peered briefly through the tinted glass, they huddled with maps out and fingers pointing, as if the huge signs weren't maps enough.

Suddenly one of the women put a palm to her forehead and swayed. Trey watched in horrified amazement when, as she fell backward, the man with her sidestepped quickly to get out of the way. He didn't even lift a hand to try to catch her.

Trey almost heard the awful hollow sound when her skull hit the pavement, cursed when none of them moved even then, and bolted from the booth. Once outside he shoved two of the men aside roughly and went down on one knee beside her, hissing soundlessly when his hand touched the burning concrete.

She was young, almost painfully slender, black hair in even bangs, wearing a short-sleeve blouse with matching white shorts and knee-socks.

"What are you, nuts?" he snapped at the man who didn't help her. "Stupid bastard."

Carefully, aware that others had begun to stop and look, that the woman's friends were muttering to each other, he touched two fingers on her neck to get a pulse, then just as carefully gripped her chin and turned her just enough for his left hand to slide under her head.

He felt the dampness immediately, looked at his fingertips, and saw the blood.

"Jesus!"

On his feet again, he slammed open the restaurant door and pointed at the waitress behind the counter. "9–1–1, now!" and bellowed for Madame Song. He didn't wait, but returned to the woman's side, pulling off his shirt as he knelt again. He folded it into a pad and as gently as he could slipped it under her head, his good luck charm hanging over her chest.

"What's her name?" he asked harshly, without looking up.

No one answered.

He glared. "What the hell is her name, damnit?"

One of the women, eyes watery, whispered, "Yomiko."

A curt nod of thanks, and he tapped the fallen woman's cheeks lightly with a finger. "Hey, Yomiko," he said. "Come on, Yomiko, come on back."

"She . . ." The woman leaned over. "She sick?"

No, but she damn well needs to breathe, he thought.

"Knife," he said, looking at each of them in turn. "Do any of you have a knife?"

They just stared, and it was then that he realized he wasn't being crowded. Except for the one who told him the woman's name, the others stayed well away.

"Here," a man in the growing crowd said, and tossed him a small Swiss army knife.

Trey slid open a blade and sliced through the elastic cord that held her mask in place. "Hey, Yomiko," he whispered, letting the mask fall to one side, "come on, kid, don't get stupid on me here." He tapped her cheeks again. He glanced at his shirt and saw the red stain. "Yomiko, come on."

Her eyelids fluttered just as Madame Song bustled from the restaurant. She was an imposing six feet tall, as always wearing a blue silk Chinese dress covered by an immaculate apron. Her hair was in a large bun pierced by a gold comb, and however old she was, it did not leave a mark on her face.

She looked at Trey, looked at the others, and immediately launched into a series of questions, each of whose stammered, respectful answers made the next one more shrill.

Trey leaned closer to his charge's face. "Come on, Yomiko, you're not dead, you know. Come on, honey, wake up."

Madame Song yelled and waved her arms; the others cowered.

A siren.

Yomiko's eyelids jumped, fluttered, and opened.

Trey shaded her eyes with one hand, and smiled. "You feel okay?"

Dazed, she stared at him.

"I know. Stupid question. I'm the town expert, in case you're wondering."

Her lips, tiny and pale, twitched.

"You fainted, huh?"

Without warning she tried to sit up, gasped and groaned, and would have cracked her skull again had he not caught her. "Easy, kid, take it easy. You're going to have a lump back there the size of a baseball as it is."

Tears filled her eyes. One hand trembled across her face, and those eyes widened until he took her wrist and gently pulled the hand away.

"It's okay, it's okay, don't worry." He winked. "Best air in the West, I guarantee it. You'll be okay."

Her eyes closed.

"She be all right?" Madame Song asked over his shoulder.

"Yeah, I think so." Gently he brushed the bangs from her brow, using the side of his finger to sweep the sweat away. "The heat probably got to her, that's all."

Then, as both a police cruiser and an ambulance pulled into the curb at the same time, he made the mistake of telling her what had happened. That darkened her face and sent her spiraling into another shrill tirade, the tone of which he had heard a couple of times before, when her employees weren't doing what they had been told. He didn't need to understand Japanese, or how Madame Song knew it, to know that Yomiko's friends were being threatened by everything from curses to butcher knives, and by the gods, if they didn't do right by this young woman, she would hunt them down and take care of them herself.

He didn't dare check to see their expressions; this, he figured, was absolutely not the right time to laugh.

A moment later a hand tugged his shoulder, an "Okay, mister, thanks, we'll take over," and he was on his feet. Squinting in the glare. Not feeling all that terrific himself. There were questions, however, and lots of talk, lots of faces, but the only thing he remembered clearly was the sight of Yomiko on a stretcher being slipped through the ambulance's back doors.

And her hand, waving to him weakly.

Finally, the crowd dispersing at the urging of a uniformed cop, Madame Song grabbed his arm and pulled him toward the entrance. "You. Inside. You burn to a crisp, you practically naked."

He didn't argue. He let himself be brought back to his booth, where she ordered Rhonda to give him anything he wanted, and if she charged him for it, she'd be back walking the Strip with the rest of the scum.

And with that, the woman was gone.

A few seconds passed in blessed silence before he looked up and said, "You know, I don't know if I can eat anything, tell you the truth."

"Aw, come on, mister," Rhonda said, her accent pure East Coast. "If you don't—"

"You eat!" Madame Song yelled from the kitchen. "You eat, you don't die in my restaurant of starvation."

The waitress lifted a pencil eyebrow—*it's both our lives, mister, your choice.*

He rubbed his upper arms briskly, shivering slightly in the chilled air. Deliberately not looking outside at the few remaining stragglers peering in at him, he took the menu from his hand and began to ask about the specials.

"You get double burger, well done, all the trims," Madame Song yelled from the kitchen. "Don't push it."

He started to laugh, caught himself, and handed the menu back with a shrug. "How," he wanted to know, "does she do that?"

Rhonda rolled her eyes. "Chinese magic, for all I know. She does it all the time, spooky as hell." She snapped her gum for punctuation and added, "I'll see if I can find something back there for you before you freeze to death."

"Thanks."

"Don't thank me," she said as she walked off, hips in motion. "You so much as get the sniffles, my children'll be cursed cross-eyed."

He did laugh then, quickly, quietly. "Come on, you have kids?"

She didn't look back. "Nope. But I ain't taking no chances."

A shake of his head, the idea that this was going to make a beaut of a story to tell the girls, and he wondered what in hell those people had been thinking. That Yomiko had the Sickness? A slight cough was all he had noticed, and no wonder—if they weren't used to the desert, which they probably weren't, all that coming and going into and out of air-conditioned rooms would give anyone a cold.

The fact that the Sickness, the smallpox, often began with symptoms that resembled the flu, was no excuse. He hadn't lied to the poor woman—Las Vegas had yet to have a single case, even though, for a time, it had swept through Reno, leaving scores of dead behind.

And even if she did have it, did that mean those who cared for her had to desert her when she needed them most?

Damn.

And people wondered why he kept to himself.

Then a new, white cotton shirt, still in its package, dropped onto the table in front of him. He jumped, and looked over his shoulder just as a voice said, "My dear fellow, you look absolutely frigid. Do put it on before you catch your death."

5

He was as Jude and Dodger had described him.

With an apologetic smile, he slipped into the booth and set his white straw hat down on the table by the window. An immaculate white handkerchief mopped his dry brow. A long-fingered hand pushed back over his mostly white hair, while the other hand waggled to speed Trey into the shirt.

It fit perfectly.

"Much better," the old man said with a nod. "Can't have you getting ill, now can we?"

Trey buttoned the shirt, rolled the cuffs up twice, and leaned back, more than a little bemused as Rhonda suddenly appeared at the table, order pad at the ready, all but simpering as she took the man's order—cheese and lettuce sandwich, coffee, and if it wouldn't be too much trouble, my dear, would it be possible to have a small plate of honey and biscuits.

Trey waited.

Rhonda said, "No problem at all, sir, believe me, no problem at all."

He stared at the waitress in disbelief, his mouth working soundlessly as Madame Song burst through the swinging kitchen doors, apron gone, and fussed behind the counter. Not saying a word. But smiling.

Trey looked from her to the old man and said, "She never smiles, you know. In all the years I've been coming here, she's never smiled once."

"Yes, well . . ." He extended his hand. "Harp, Mr. Falkirk. John Harp."

Trey accepted the greeting without speaking, mildly surprised at the strong, dry grip.

Harp shook out his napkin and placed it on his lap, glanced around the table before fussing with his silverware. "It was a wonderful thing you did out there. That poor woman. A mild concussion, no more, I should think."

"Who are you?"

A small constant smile: "It's quite amazing, and a little sad, don't you think? How people in a perfectly neutral location can't seem to let go of their fears, even though there's nothing at all to fear."

Trey leaned back, wondering why all the nuts and losers in the world were so attracted to him.

A curse.

It was probably a curse.

"Nevertheless," Harp continued, "you didn't think twice about assisting that poor child. Remarkable. Quite remarkable."

"Who," Trey repeated carefully, "are you?"

The old man leaned back as well and folded his hands on the edge of the table. A glance out the window, a glance toward the counter, and he inhaled slowly. "Mr. Falkirk, I believe there are four far more important questions you ought to be asking." He lifted one finger. "Why, for example, do you suppose you are able to do the things you do? Why are you able to tell which slot machines will pay off for you, and which will not?"

Trey opened his mouth to demand an explanation, closed it when he decided it would do him no good. This man, this John Harp whoever the hell he was, was not accustomed to being pushed, or to being bullied by demands.

"Why is that, do you suppose?" Harp repeated mildly.

And Trey answered, without thinking, "I met a man."

I met a man once. It was about seven, eight years ago. I was in Reno, having no damn luck at all, down to my last couple of dollars, again, trying to get down here. I was walking, looking to find a ride, when I saw this guy with his head stuck under the hood of a pickup that should have been put out of its misery twenty years ago. I don't know anything about engines, but I figured maybe I could help anyway, so I walked over.

When I got close enough I could see he was pretty old, long white hair braided to beat the band. An Indian. I can't tell the difference, so I didn't know whether he was Navajo or Apache or what, but he was fiddling with some wires.

And he was either talking to the engine or to himself.

A couple of seconds later, he stood up and saw me.

You need a ride? he said.

Yeah. But I don't think I'm going to get it here.

He laughed as he slammed the hood down. Once in a while, he said, it gets stubborn. Like a horse that decides it doesn't want to work today. You have to work around it sometimes. Sometimes you have to trick him. Get in, get in.

My legs were sore, my feet were sore, my head was sore, I was pretty much at the end of my rope, so I figured I didn't have anything to lose. I got in. He asked me where I was headed, I told him, and he gave me the kind of look that made me want to apologize for everything I'd ever done wrong in my life.

Not a way to live, young fella, he said.

The only way I know how, I told him.

He shrugged, put the key in the ignition, and damned if he didn't ask the truck if it was okay to ride all the way to Las Vegas with a half-cracked white man inside who wanted to piss his life away at the gambling tables.

When the engine started, he shrugged again. I guess it's okay. You got money for gas?

I had three bucks.

Always me, he said to the dashboard. I always get the dumb ones.

I didn't say anything for a long time, just watched the mountains. After a while he started talking, not really saying anything in particular, but with a lot of hours ahead of us, I suppose he figured it was better than nothing since the radio wouldn't work.

We talked about the usual stuff—his family, what was left of my family—and I eventually asked him why he talked to the truck like he did. At first he didn't say anything, and I figured I'd put my foot in it. Not an unusual thing.

Then he said, I always ask permission to drive. It's the right thing to do. I get big trouble otherwise.

I guess I looked as if I was the one riding with the nut, because he kind of laughed and said, you know Indian stuff, right? You must have read about it, or seen it in the movies or on TV. Some Indian prays to the gods to help him fight the enemy, or show him where the food is, things like that? You must have. Well, it's like this— everything has a spirit. Trees, animals, rocks, rivers, they all have spirits, and if you're a good Indian, you talk to the spirits, ask them if it's okay to do whatever it is you have to do.

But this is a truck, I said.

The old guy said, So? If a rock can have a spirit, why can't a pickup? Once you figure out it's true . . . And he shrugged, laughed, and offered me a drink from a bottle he kept under the front seat.

We talked about all kinds of stuff after that, complaining, you know, about politicians and the weather and women and stuff like that, and it turns out he was a doctor. It was night by then, and I couldn't see his face very well, but just about when we could see Vegas in the distance, I asked him why he didn't ask the spirits to help his family with a hellish couple of years of fatal illnesses which, he had told me, had taken quite a few before it was over.

Because, he said, sometimes they just get pissed off, and there's nothing you can do about it.

He dropped me off a little after that, and I hitched another ride into town. Found a shelter and stayed the night. Went to a small casino the next afternoon, lost two of my three bucks, and figured what the hell, why not, I'm going to starve anyway, and asked the slot machine if it was okay to win a little so I could get a sandwich.

Didn't happen.

I couldn't find a job, ended up panhandling, made about five bucks, and tried the asking thing again.

Didn't happen.

A cop busted me for vagrancy when I hit the streets, but I guess he figured I wasn't into dope or robbing convenience stores, so he gave me ten bucks and a couple of hours to get out of town before he locked me up.

I took the money, got out of town in a hurry on the back of a truck hauling grain to Four Corners, and three months later I was back.

It took me six hotels and I couldn't begin to count the number of slots before one of them gave me the feeling it would be all right to play.

I won.

John Harp nodded as though he understood perfectly. Which was more than Trey did. Even now, talking about it with a stranger who knew too damn much about him, the whole thing seemed, if not improbable, then downright impossible.

But it worked.

Asking how or why wasn't going to change it.

Madame Song and Rhonda delivered the meals. They fussed, they waited until Harp had tasted his sandwich, sipped his coffee, and exclaimed over the size and light weight of the biscuits, before backing away.

Trey couldn't believe it.

They actually backed away.

Harp interrupted him: "What if I told you that your success has nothing to do with spirits in a machine?"

"You'll jinx me," he answered immediately, reaching for the catsup.

Harp laughed heartily, deeply, and shook his head. "My dear fellow, that's the perfect answer for now. I salute you." Which he did with his cup of coffee.

This, Trey thought, is nuts.

He couldn't figure out why he wasn't angry, why he didn't push a confrontation, why he simply didn't get up and leave. The answer to each was the same: He was curious. The man didn't seem to be a threat, certainly not physically, and there was something oddly engaging about him. As if he knew full well what a ridiculous figure he cut, with the hat and the suit and the boots all coupled with the aristocratic accent and bearing. As if he knew and didn't really give a damn.

Besides, he had bought the shirt, and he had somehow managed to tame Madame Song. That in itself was worth the price of waiting a while longer—at least until he'd finished the largest burger he'd ever seen.

Customers filled the booths and tables, the noise level rose, and a second waitress made the rounds with Rhonda. Madame Song retreated to her usual position in the kitchen, and each time one of the swinging doors opened, he could hear her scolding the cooks. Everyone could, and only those who weren't regulars paid any attention.

Business as usual, he thought as he watched Harp touch the corners of his mouth with his napkin each time he finished a bite; business as usual . . . sort of . . . and I think I've fallen into the rabbit hole here.

The initial surprise and curiosity began to give way slowly to a niggling apprehension. The room seemed unreal, the diners characters in a play. Not quite real. Not quite there. As if, if he looked hard enough, he would be able to see right through them.

The idea was unsettling, made him look outside, but the street, the sidewalk, was no more real. Cars and cabs, buses and the occasional limousine drifted by silently; pedestrians held conversations in mime.

Harp checked his watch and made an impatient clucking sound. His eyes narrowed, and he stared blindly at the sun, his lips pursed.

"Problem?" Trey asked.

Harp didn't answer. He reached for his hat, changed his mind with a nearly inaudible grunt, and slowly, very slowly, turned his head.

"Mr. Falkirk," he said softly, "second question: Have you ever wondered why you don't seem to be able to get hurt in Las Vegas?"

2

1

Emerald City was empty.

Jude could feel it.

For an hour after Trey left, she had fussed around the house, cleaning what didn't need to be cleaned, making a spare lunch of salad and tea, cleaning again, wandering always. When she couldn't stand it any longer, she went to the porch and hunted for a sign that would tell her she wasn't the last person on Earth.

But Emerald City was empty.

She knew that Muriel had taken Lil for her therapy, that Roger was in his office at the university; she suspected the others had taken off on errands which would keep them away for a while.

Safe, then; for the moment she was safe.

Nevertheless her hand trembled as it peeled off the veil, to allow her face to feel the air again.

There was no need for her fingers to probe the pink-and-flat white scar tissue that took the place of her cheeks, no need to trace what remained of her nose and lips, all in the hope that night had some-how rendered her whole.

Too many years had passed.

All she had left were her children, and the veil.

There weren't even any tears.

She drifted into the yard, the veil in her left hand, just in case. Just in case.

A dry wind slow-danced with her hair, rippled her formless dress around her hips and breasts. If she could have smiled, she would have at the sight of a flock of birds too distant to identify, darting and wheeling over the desert.

She wandered up the street, kicking at loose pebbles, softly hum-ming a song she had heard at Eula's last week. She didn't know the words, didn't know the title, but it had infected her to the point that she couldn't get it out of her head. And didn't want to.

When she reached the end of the street she hesitated before moving on, wishing there had been a shower at least so the cacti would be in brief stunning bloom. Still, the spare beauty of the land-scape caught her as it always did, making her wonder, as she always did, how anyone could think this place was harsh and barren.

One hundred yards later she reached the boulder Trey claimed marked the city limits out here. On it he had etched with the edge of a small sharp rock, the words now worn to grey and fading, *the chariot stops here,* and she grinned. Like all gamblers he was su-perstitious, and since he had moved back, evidently to stay, he had never ventured beyond this point. When she had asked why one night, all he'd said was, "The snakes kill out there," and wouldn't tell her what he meant.

You're a dope, she thought fondly; you're a dope, and I wish I could love you.

The wind stopped.

The flock was gone.

She was alone, and feeling small, and after brushing a thumb over the boulder for a vague kind of luck, she hurried back to the street, every so often kicking out a sandal to get rid of the sand.

I wish I could love you.

She paused in front of Eula's house, and didn't realize she'd held her breath until her chest began to ache. When she shuddered in air, too fast, too abruptly, she swayed with brief dizziness and stumbled back a pace.

"You know," Eula had told her not so long ago, when they met while Jude had been night-wandering the street, "that a pretty veil thing you got there, child, but you don't got to wear it."

"You don't know," Jude had answered stiffly.

"Oh, child, yes I do, I surely do."

A shooting star had streaked over the desert. Her eyes closed briefly, and Eula had laughed softly, without scorn.

"You making a wish?"

Jude nodded.

"It got something to do with that pretty veil?"

Jude hesitated before nodding again.

Eula lowered her voice then, and took light hold of her arm. "Listen to me, child—the song got it wrong, wishin' don't make it so, no, it don't." A step closer, so close Jude could smell the warmth of the woman, and something else, something familiar that she couldn't put a name to. "It don't have to be, Miss Judith Levin. It don't have to be."

Then she had walked away, humming, snapping her fingers, every few steps laughing aloud, filled with joy.

Jude hadn't moved until the old woman was gone, then she had looked up at the sky, saw another shooting star, and this time she didn't wish. That had frightened her without reason, so much so that she'd barely said two words to the woman since.

Now, staring at the house, wondering where Eula was today,

where she was singing, making others dance and clap, eyes raised to the rafters, she put the veil on, frowning a dare at the woman to come out and talk again.

When nothing happened, she blinked once, hard, and remembered the kiss she had blown to Trey that morning.

I wish I could love you.

She whispered, "Oh, God," and felt a chill centered around her heart.

Emerald City was empty, and it was suddenly too big, and she ran all the way home because she wasn't safe anymore.

2

The automobile was Rick Hicaya's pride and life. A blinding white convertible destined to attract all sorts of women to his side and to his bed, until, once in the passenger seat, they saw the glove on his hand and remembered too many eerie movies and begged off with headaches and appointments and get lost, you spic creep, I ain't into that kinky stuff.

He sat in it now, staring at the sun exploding off the hood, in the parking lot of the Boulder City hospital where, his local doctor had told him, they might be able to help if he was willing to spend the money. But after studying the charts and the histories and the hand itself, they told him birth defects like this didn't lend themselves to answers easy or otherwise . . . unless . . . unless . . . and after much consultation they had showed him a glossy book with a dark leather cover, and a locked glass cabinet, and in both he had seen the most frightening, horrifying, realistic prosthetics, and it hadn't taken him long to grasp the implication of what they would not dare say aloud, and with a pained smile and a formal thank you, he had grabbed the glove and left and had been sitting in the convertible with the top down, for an hour. Ignoring the heat. Trembling with anger, fear, humiliation, back to anger.

Tears of all sorts in his eyes, blinked away before they fell.

Prayers hadn't worked; healers hadn't worked; doctors couldn't work unless they maimed him; and a shrink in Arizona had told him that coming to terms with his disability was only the first step toward the healing.

But it wouldn't heal the hand.

Don't have to be that way, boy, you know it don't have to be that way.

I don't believe in voodoo, old woman.

Ain't nothing voodoo about it.

So . . . what? Potions? Spells? You got a direct line to God or something? You got some weird magic stuff from those swamps in Alabama or Mississippi or wherever the hell it is you come from? What are you talking about, huh? What are you bothering me for?

You just think about it, boy, just take your time and think about it. Don't have to be that way, you know. Don't have to be that way.

You're nuts.

Maybe, maybe not. But I'll tell you something for free—you do not want to know where I come from, boy. No sir, you most certainly do not.

He held the withered hand in front of his face, studying the way the glove made it seem as if it were whole. To him, anyway, if not to anyone else. Now the sons of bitches want to put something else in its place. Something plastic. With gears and wires that attached to his nerves and muscles. Like it was a puppet. Trapped in a glove.

He looked at the hospital, and he looked at the glove, and he said, "Screw it," and left the parking lot on a trail of acrid smoking rubber.

Tonight he would talk to Eula, and maybe tomorrow he'd ask big Muriel to dance.

3

Stephanie pushed her cart up and down the grocery store aisles. She barely knew what she picked off the shelves because her eyes kept tearing up and she couldn't read the labels. Cable couldn't help her because he was sitting in the car.

He always sat in the car.

It didn't matter that she didn't care if people stared at him; it didn't matter that the only important thing was that she loved him so much sometimes that her chest hurt and she couldn't breathe; it didn't matter to her, but it mattered to him, and not two hours ago it must have mattered to some asshole at the Mirage, because a guest had complained late last night about the creepy ugly guy sweeping the rugs and how he was ruining folks' vacations, and when Cable refused to wear something over his face, one of those masks or something, they had told him they really liked him and had no complaints about his work, but they had to let him go, you know how it is.

Then, just before she came into the store, he had told her he was seriously thinking of moving them out of Las Vegas. No place in mind yet, just out of the city. He didn't care about her career; he didn't care when she tried to explain that she was close, *this close,* to getting a chance to sing in a lounge up the Strip. She might not make it, there were lots of people who didn't, but she'd never know, would she, if she didn't give it a try. He didn't care. He just wanted out, and it was so damned unfair that she loved him and couldn't leave him and didn't want to miss what might be the only chance she'd ever have to prove she could do it, that she could sing with the best.

It was so damned unfair.

But damn it all to hell, she wasn't going to let the dream get away.

The tears dried.

The clerk at the register rang the tally and took her check and she lugged the bags to the car and loaded them in the backseat and sat beside Cable, took a deep breath, and said, "You listen to me, you sorry son of a bitch that I love more than anything in the world, you are going to stop feeling so goddamn sorry for yourself and you are going to let me take my shot, you understand? And if you think otherwise, you're twice as stupid as you look."

With his mouth half open he stared at her, swallowing.

"So tonight," she went on, "you and me are going to pay a visit up the street, and I don't give a shit if you think she's crazy, because I will not miss this chance, Cable. I swear to God, I will not miss it."

"You're drunk," he said.

"Go to hell, and drive."

4

Roger Freneau watched the last of his last morning class wander into the hallway, evidently unconcerned that finals and their future weren't all that far away. He scanned the empty desks, turned and stared at John Locke's name carefully printed on the blackboard, looked at the hallway again and said, "*Tabula rasa,* my ass, nothing sticks in their brains unless it's blowtorched there."

He picked up his briefcase, checked the desks again on the off chance someone left something behind, and tested his feet with a single step. Winced. Wished fervently he could just sit down for the rest of the day. He had been walking on the sides of his feet since he'd left home, because he had been too drunk last night to pay attention to what he was doing and had cut up his soles walking over that glass Lil had shattered on his porch. They weren't deep cuts, they were more like paper cuts—barely seen and stinging like all get-out. Plus, his legs ached too from walking funny like that.

Misery; nothing but misery.

All he wanted to do now was get to his car, get to the nearest bar, and spend his lunch hour numbing the pain. With any kind of luck, he wouldn't be able to make his one class this afternoon.

Trying to look as normal as possible, he stepped into the hall and pulled the door closed behind him. He hadn't had a chance to take more than one breath before a tall, lanky, bearded man hurried up, clipboard in hand.

"Rog, you got a minute?"

"Sure, Alf, what's up?"

Alf Davis was department chairman, never without his suit and school tie, never without a cigar in his jacket pocket. His teeth were yellowed, his breath was garlic foul, and Roger pretended he liked him because it was this man who had fought to bring him to the faculty.

Alf knew it too, and never let him forget it.

"I want you to sign this petition," Davis said, thrusting the clipboard into his free hand.

Frowning, Roger tried to read the small print at the top, but Alf snatched his briefcase away and put a pen in that hand.

"Just sign it, Freneau. I've got a million other people to see before the administration meeting this afternoon."

"But what . . . ?"

"Sign, will you? I haven't got all day."

Roger read it anyway. Read it again. "This," he said, "is a petition to get rid of—"

"The coach, that's right," Davis snapped. "Something has to be done, and no one else in this damn place seems to have the guts to do it."

Roger prodded at his ear as if he weren't hearing properly. "Let me get this straight—I haven't been able to order an up-to-date text in two years, but you want me—"

Davis glared him into silence. "Facts of life, Freneau. We don't have a successful basketball team, we don't get into the NCAA tournament next year, the alumni get pissy, they don't donate, we lose money, we have to start cutting corners. You can philosophize all you want about the role of sports in academia, but this is the real world, and you will sign that petition."

"No," he said, surprising himself. "This is really dumb, Alf. Really dumb. Besides, I don't know anything about sports, you know that."

Davis lifted his chin. "Freneau, maybe you're not getting the message here."

Jesus, Roger thought; I don't sign, I'm fired?

"And what the hell is the matter with your feet?" the chairman continued. "You're walking like a drunken sailor. Jesus Christ, Freneau, am I going to regret you for the rest of my life? Sign the petition."

Roger stood straight and welcomed the pain.

He dropped the pen, took the clipboard in both hands, and as hard as he could brought it down on Davis's head. The chairman staggered backward, screeching his pain like a child, covering his head with both hands even as the shock brought him hard to his knees.

Roger saw the blood on the man's forehead.

He saw a dozen or more students gaping at him from a distance.

Walking on his heels, he turned around and went back into the classroom, sat at his desk, and took off his shoes and socks. He estimated five or ten minutes before the police arrived, and he'd be damned if he wasn't going to give his feet a break before they dumped him in a cell.

Then, legs propped on the desk, toes wriggling gingerly, he slid open the bottom drawer and pulled out a bottle of scotch, took a long drink, swished the liquor around in his mouth, and swallowed. Didn't cough or choke. Took a second drink, and a third, figuring being a drunk wouldn't excuse the assault, but it was a better excuse than hating basketball, by God.

but you don't have to be that way, poor child, don't have to be that way at all.

3

1

With slow studied movements, Trey folded his napkin and set it beside his plate.

"Mr. Falkirk."

He looked out at the boulevard for a long careful moment before turning to Harp. "Who," he said, "the hell are you?"

Harp didn't blink, didn't twitch. Just a small sad smile. "A friend, my dear fellow. A friend."

Trey shook his head. "No, I don't think so. Friends don't bother my neighbors with questions behind my back. Friends don't follow me all over the place, bothering other people about me."

"I would have called, but evidently you don't have a telephone."

"You seem to know everything else, why the hell didn't you know that?"

Harp dismissed the question with a bored gesture.

"You a cop? A detective?"

The smile, still sad, widened for just a second. "No, Mr. Falkirk, I'm neither of those."

"In that case," said Trey as he slid out of the booth. "Thank you for the shirt. I'll pay you back if I ever see you again. Which, I sure hope, I won't."

"But Mr. Falkirk, please—"

Trey cut him off him with a sharp wave and walked away. By the time he was on the sidewalk and had swung left he was marching, fuming, brushing past other pedestrians without a backward glance or pretense of apology. Glad for the heat that settled heavily on his shoulders. Glad for the smell of exhaust and hot tarmac.

He saw nothing but the green hulk of the MGM Grand down the street, concentrating on it, excluding everything else. Not thinking at all. Moving on automatic as he pushed inside, made his way to the back and the monorail station, just outside.

On good days he would talk back to the computerized voice that cautioned him to stay behind the iron-fence barrier until the next train arrived; on good days he would flirt a little with the attendants who worked the gates and once in a while flirted back; on good days he would eavesdrop on conversations, to see who was winning, who was sick and tired of all the heat, who was complaining just to complain.

Today he said nothing, saw nothing, and when the train swept in, he took the first available seat in the nearest car, facing forward, scowling at the kids who piled in after him, followed by beleaguered parents with expressions of permanent apology, themselves on automatic with scolds and instructions.

As the train pulled out, he wondered whose bright idea it had been to turn a gambling city into a family resort, whose dumb idea it had been to run a train between just two stations, whose idea it had been to have him followed.

Watched.

Examined.

By the time the train pulled into the Bally's station, his fuming had boiled over into outright temper, and as soon as he was inside, he stepped quickly out of the passenger flow and leaned against a featureless cream wall. Panting. Ordering himself to calm down, that the day would be a total bust if he let the old man get to him.

It took almost ten minutes and the uneasy glances from a young and nervous security guard before he felt he could move without screaming, without striking out blindly. Then he hurried along a broad shopping concourse to the escalators that led up to the casino, and with a deliberate deep breath let the ritual take over.

It didn't work.

An hour later he gave up, knowing that none of the machines would welcome either him or his money. It was his own fault. He had been wasting half his energy holding a short frayed rein on his temper, but it angered him anyway, and he stalked outside, muttering obscenities just loud enough to make others shy away.

On the next corner he hesitated, then shrugged and went in the Barbary Coast, much smaller, much noisier, much gaudier, and the machines just as unresponsive.

tell him, child, that the dragon is dying

Outside again, tapping an impatient foot at the intersection traffic light, trotting across when the light turned green, swinging right and marching again up the long stretch of low wall and misted gardens that fronted Caesar's Palace.

Okay, jerk, he thought; this isn't getting you anywhere. You keep this up you might as well go home and kick in a wall.

It was tempting, and he realized that the pull he felt along the backs of his hands was the result of keeping them in fists. He snapped his fingers out, flexed them, cracked a couple of knuckles, then shook them like a swimmer before launching into a dive.

A man in a multicolored shepherd's robe stood at the curb in the middle of the block, his long white hair tangled and dark with sweat, his deep-tanned face gleaming with sweat, while sweat dripped from the tip of his pointed chin. He wore a hand-made sandwich board on which had been printed in deep red letters, THE NUMBER OF THE DEAD IS NOW 168,215 AND THE NUMBER OF THE BEAST IS STILL 666.

He carried no cup, made no pronouncements, quoted no Scripture.

He simply stood there in the heat with a reminder of the Sickness for those who had come to the desert to forget.

Despite his mood, Trey stopped and looked at him, waiting for the man's gaze to meet his own. When it did, he nodded to the tally and said, "You print a new one every day?" making sure by his tone that the man understood he wasn't mocking.

"Twice a day," was the answer, the voice coarse.

"It must be a grim job."

"It's the Millennium, my friend, the end of the world. I guess you could say that was pretty grim."

A glance up and down the street, but there was no sign of the old man in the stupid cowboy hat. "You need a donation or something?"

"I manage. But thank you."

Trey turned to leave, suddenly reached into his pocket and pulled out a twenty. He moved closer. "Take it. You'll need a lot more paint."

The man accepted it without comment, just a grateful nod, and his gaze drifted, sending him back into whatever state he used to pass the time away.

A second look at the number of the dead, and Trey moved on, no longer marching, hands in his pockets. Aware now of the sun, the sweat on his back and on the back of his neck beneath his hair.

have you ever wondered why you don't seem to be able to get hurt in Las Vegas?

A twinge in his right shoulder reminded him of the nightstick a cop had used on him in St. Louis. Or maybe it was Austin. Or maybe—he grunted. What difference did it make where it happened? It hadn't happened here.

But lots of things hadn't happened here, so that didn't prove a thing. Like, for example, the Sickness. It pops up in a city, a small town, takes its victims, and moves on. A random sequence he knew from the newspapers drove the scientists and doctors out of their analytical minds. Prediction might mean better preventive action. Like the signs that were posted in every school and church in town, reminding people to get their smallpox inoculation before it was too late. The signs worked, of course, but the vaccine itself didn't always do the job.

So how, he asked himself, did John Harp know about the run of luck he'd been having?

And something answered, over two years is a hell of a long run.

He pushed his hair away from his forehead, and smiled at a little girl prancing alongside her mother, both wearing masks, the little one's with a Mickey Mouse painted across the front, the mother's with a Bugs Bunny. The woman saw him watching and raised her eyebrows in a gesture that told him it was better than looking like you were heading straight for surgery; his own look told her *Hey, whatever works.*

But the sight lifted him, just as the street shepherd had jolted him out of his anger at John Harp, and he walked a little more quickly, more confidently, not really paying attention to where he was until he had crossed the first loop of Caesar's open oval, long front drive, and found himself in front of what Moonbow had called his personal statue.

He chuckled and walked past it—high on a marble base, a gold sculpture of two charging horses pulling a chariot, its driver with one arm raised high, a snapping whip in his hand.

Not quite a mirror of the chip his mother gave him.

As he stepped off the curb onto the second leg of the oval, he looked over his shoulder at the chariot one more time, shook his head, and jumped, arms flailing, when a blaring horn warned him he'd nearly stepped in front of an airport van. The driver mouthed a curse at him as he stepped back hastily and almost tripped over the curb, faces in the van windows staring, not a single one of them friendly.

have you ever wondered

Shaken, feeling more than a little foolish, he decided to pass on Caesar's and make his way farther up, to the Mirage or beyond. By then maybe his heart would have stopped trying to claw its way out of his chest. He shook his hands again, and rubbed his sternum; he licked his lips; rubbed his arms.

rattlesnake

He walked a little faster, realizing he'd blown an awful lot of time, both at the restaurant and at Bally's and the Barbary. If he was going to add to his stash, he'd better . . . he'd better . . . and do what? he asked himself suddenly. When you get what you want, what are you going to do, buy a mansion and hide out until the shepherd's numbers are so large he can't carry them anymore?

cowboy

An impatient swipe at the sweat on his nape, a pass of his forearm across his eyes. Maybe he was still asleep. Maybe he was still in the nightmare. Maybe there's still some coincidence in the world.

have you ever wondered

Maybe.

Maybe I have.

a car that jumped the curb

He didn't care about the heat; he didn't care about the danger.

He looked back, he looked ahead, and with a silent cry, he ran.

2

At the first men's room he could find when he reached the Mirage, he banged into a stall, locked the door behind him, dropped to his knees, and threw up.

Damning the tears, damning Harp, damning the stench, damning the sun.

Rocking on his knees until there was nothing left; rocking on his knees while he mopped his face with toilet paper; flushing the toilet several times, flushing it again even though there was nothing there but water; rocking on his knees, thinking maybe he'd gone crazy.

Sagging to the floor, stretching out his legs, his feet poking under the door, his back against the rim of the bowl. Blinking rapidly enough to make himself dizzy. Working his lips like an old man who can't find the words to speak. Fingers stroking his neck as if he could ease the raw burning in his throat.

Sitting there, panting and sweating, until he heard the restroom door open, heels tap sharply across the tiled floor, and finally, after a long silence, a woman's voice say, in a clear British accent, "Pardon me, Mr. Falkirk, but is there something wrong?"

He couldn't help it; he laughed.

3

"Let me tell you something," he said, "but don't expect me to make any sense."

Beatrice Harp neither flinched nor smiled. She sat sideways on the stool next to his, watching solemnly, studiously as he stroked the slot machine's side again, just to be sure. Then he slipped in a quarter, pulled the arm, and shook his head when twelve quarters rattled out.

"I think your old man's a nut."

Another quarter; nothing this time.

"But I'm not going to ask how you found me, because then I'll have to think you're a nut, too."

"Can you do this all night?" she asked, nodding to the machine. "Make money, I mean."

"Sometimes. Maybe. But I don't."

"Because they'll mark you," she said.

He looked at her, finally nodded.

"Very clever, then. Spread yourself around, I expect, is that right?"

He nodded again, watching a dozen quarters bounce onto the bed the others made.

She wore baggy tan shorts that reached her knees, a loose matching blouse with a small animal stitched in dark red across her right breast. Kneesocks and walking shoes. A tortoiseshell band over her head to hold the hair out of her eyes. Both hands gripped a small purse in her lap.

Bells and music two rows over, some cheers and laughter, while just behind them a couple argued loudly about how much money they'd spent, how much they had left.

"Good Lord, how do you stand it?" she asked when he leaned back a little to ease the strain on his spine.

"I don't hear it."

"Surely."

"No, really. I don't hear it. White noise, you know? How the hell did you find me?"

"I thought you weren't going to ask."

He swiveled around to face her and laughed aloud at the pure mockery of innocence in her expression. She was, he thought, something else again. Barging into the men's room like that, helping him to his feet while he spun in momentary hysteria, fussing him over to the sink so he could rinse his face off with cold water and find a way to breathe without either weeping or laughing again.

At one point, after she'd introduced herself and handed him a fistful of paper towels, he asked if she had ever been a nanny, the way she was treating him, and she'd answered, "I've been with Sir John quite a long time. I think that's enough training, don't you?"

At the time he hadn't been sure if she'd been joking, but the look on her face now, her head slightly tilted, was enough to make him laugh again. "So?" he said.

"Mr. Falkirk," she said earnestly, "Sir John was quite serious when he asked you those questions. Quite serious. He does tend to be a bit obtuse, however, I'll grant you that. He knows it's sometimes a bit maddening, but he prefers it that way. He'd rather you found the answers yourself rather than hand them to you on a silver platter. He believes the results are much more effective that way."

With a wave that told her he was still listening, he turned back to the machine and dropped in another quarter.

"And he's quite right, you know. It truly does not make a whit of difference how he . . . we found you. That we have should be sufficient."

"It isn't," he told her flatly, watching the bars, the stars, the face of a leering clown whirl through their paces.

A dozen women, all of them flirting with the far boundary of middle-age, settled themselves on empty stools to either side, chattering incessantly. Laughs, scolds, a reminder that someone had promised someone else to take pictures of the volcano before they left for home.

Pull the arm, Trey told himself; don't think, just pull the arm.

"Mr. Falkirk."

He raised a finger to tell her to hang on, and Time drifted, the tumblers did their work, and he scooped quarters into a large plastic cup. He knew he was winning too much, but he figured that as long as he only took it one coin at a time there wouldn't be all the fuss, the notoriety, than if he gave the machine its maximum four and hit the jackpot.

"Mr. Falkirk, please."

The couple behind them left, still arguing; the women cornered a waitress and pelted her with orders; chimes and melodies and the ratchet of gears as he pulled the arm down slowly, released it, and watched the tray fill.

"Mr. Falkirk! Please!"

Finally he turned his head.

Beatrice touched his arm. "Someplace more quiet, please, Mr. Falkirk. I can't think here."

A hesitation, a grudging nod, and he scooped the tray clean, mouthed a *thank you* to the machine, and rose stiffly. A jerk of his head for her to follow, and he went to the nearest cashier to change the coins into bills, stuffed the bills into his pocket, and looked around for a moment before leading her out of the casino and into the lobby. It wasn't very large as Las Vegas lobbies go, only ten or twelve yards wide, but at least the voice of the games was effectively muted.

The registration and checkout desk was long and lightly manned. There were no lines at all, just a handful of people talking with the clerks. The stations at the far end were empty, and he folded his arms on the countertop and waited for Beatrice to join him.

"My," she said.

The entire wall behind the counter was one massive aquarium, reefs and shallow caves and freestanding rocks swarmed around by fish whose vivid colors belonged to tropical birds. He watched a baby shark flash through a rock tunnel, and wondered, as he always did, what happened to it when it grew.

"Very restful," she said, placing her purse on the counter.

"I know."

"I take it you come here often."

"Often enough. They help me clear my mind. I kind of follow one around until . . ." He shrugged.

"Yes. Well. Where were we?"

A one-sided smile: "You were about to tell me everything about everything so I'd know it all and wouldn't bug you with any more questions, like, just for a crazy example, just who the hell are you people?"

She looked over her shoulder wistfully at the padded benches against the opposite wall, but when he didn't offer her that comfort, she toyed a little with the thin silver chain attached to her purse and said, "You know, I think I've never seen an angel fish that large before."

He frowned. "Look, Miss Harp—"

"Lady Harp, actually," she said absently. "Sir John is my husband."

"Okay. Lady Harp. I—"

"You can call me Beatrice, though. I don't mind. It's Sir John who likes all the ceremony and pomp."

He checked his hands, watching the fingers twitch because just about now they wanted very badly to find a neck to strangle. When she noticed his agitation, she gripped his upper arm briefly. "I'm sorry. When you've been with Sir John as long as I have, you tend to take up his faults."

"No problem," he said. "But I'm not waiting much longer."

"Nor should you have to," she answered kindly. "But I'm not standing here, if you don't mind. My legs aren't what they used to be."

So saying, she grabbed her purse and walked over to a bench, settled herself with a wiggle and a sigh, pulled a pack of cigarettes out of her purse and held it. Waiting.

Trey figured he had a couple of choices here: he could leave her where she was, grab a cab back to the Excalibur, and go home, the heck with fattening the stash, he could always do it another time; if they wanted him that badly they'd have to follow, and meet him on his own ground. It was, by far, the most tempting option. Ever since he thought he had seen Lil and the horse last night, everything had seemed . . . off-kilter somehow, not the least of which were this woman and her husband. He didn't believe for a minute they weren't some kind of private detective team. What he didn't know was who wanted him.

Which made sticking around not a bad choice either. As long as doing it didn't drive him out of his mind.

She sat with her legs crossed at the knee, foot bouncing impatiently, one hand cupping the elbow of the other arm. She cocked an eyebrow, he made her wait a second longer, then crossed over, sat beside her, pulled out his buck-and-a-half lighter and lit her cigarette.

"Thank you," she said, blowing smoke at the high ceiling.

"Sure."

To their left the lobby narrowed to a corridor that led to restrooms, shops, and, he supposed, offices.

"What in heaven's name is that?" she said, pointing across him to the right.

"The rain forest."

"I beg your pardon?"

"Well, you must have seen it when you came in. It's a rain forest. All different kinds of trees and things, a couple of statues, things like that. It ain't very big, but it's humid as hell in there." He frowned at her. "Come on, you must have seen it."

"Sorry," she said, flicking an ash into the sand of a brushed chrome ash tray cylinder. "I had other things on my mind, as you may remember."

"I remember," he said sharply, "that the only reason I'm still here is that you promised to talk to me."

"Ah," she said. "Yes." Another puff, and she stabbed the cigarette into the sand. "First, I must ask a favor, that you let me speak
until I've done. Sir John is much better at this than I am, he just
ignores anyone who interrupts. I," and she smiled, "tend to get a
bit flustered and lose my place."

"No problem."

"That goes for questions, as well."

A grunt for a laugh. "Lady, you have no idea how many questions
I have. But okay, it's your show. I am, as they say, all ears."

Her eyes closed and opened slowly, then followed the movement
of a stocky woman carrying shopping bags on either arm, not looking
away until she sidled into the ladies' room, using her hip to bump
open the door.

Then Beatrice looked at him, once again her eyes closing and
opening slowly. "That woman. Did you see her?"

"What—"

"Did you see her, Mr. Falkirk?"

"Yeah, yeah, I saw her. So what?"

"If you put your hand on her arm, or took her hand, would you
be able to do what you do with those machines? Would you be able
to contact her . . . what you might call her spirit?"

It was his turn to blink slowly, frowning his puzzlement. "No. I
don't . . . no. Good God, what kind of a question is that?"

"It's the one you have the wrong answer to, Mr. Falkirk."

He shifted uncomfortably, made to rise, and changed his mind.
"That's . . ." He floundered, unable to find the word he needed, because *nuts* was too ordinary, and *insane* wasn't strong enough.

"Listen to me," she insisted quietly, leaning back against the wall,
turning her head to face him. "These are strange days, Mr. Falkirk.
Strange days indeed, as I've no doubt you are already aware."

"Oh, yeah, right," he said, thinking of the street shepherd and
his sign. "The Millennium and stuff, right?" He shook his head at

the notion, wanted to tell her, though, that she was right about the "strange" part. Sitting in the lobby of a hotel that had an actual rain forest inside, a zillion gaming tables and video gambling and slot machines and an attached complex that housed dolphins and white tigers, while after dark, a volcano blew up every fifteen minutes out front.

All while a woman he didn't know tried to tell him he could take Jude's hand and contact her spirit. Whatever that was.

Strange, he decided, wasn't strong enough either.

4

The simple truth of the matter is, Mr. Falkirk, there is no simple truth.

While you've been hiding here in the city, the world's been falling apart. And don't give me that look, you know damn well you've been hiding. It's safe here for you, Mr. Falkirk, you don't get hurt, and you don't think about it because it frightens you.

But the world has been falling apart. I would guess the violence, the death, began just about the time you decided to come back to stay. When that ended—temporarily, I must caution you, only temporarily— it was followed by the famine. There was rain at last, of course, and the blight was defeated, but you can still see it out there . . . if you'd ever bother to leave. Malnutrition and starvation don't vanish overnight. And even if you don't leave, there are still things you can't readily get because it all isn't quite back up to speed, is it?

Do you follow me, Mr. Falkirk? Do you understand?

There is a man, a priest, his name is Casey Chisholm and—ah, I see you've heard the name already. Is that so? And have you then heard of another man, a would-be writer named John Bannock? No, I don't suppose you have. But they are compatriots of yours, Mr.

Falkirk, and sooner or later you're going to have to meet them. Talk to them. And to do that, you're going to have to leave Las Vegas.

You're going to have to leave soon.

That was the third question, Mr. Falkirk. How long do you think this safety in hiding is going to last?

Oh, dear, I'm not doing this very well, am I. Sir John is so much better at this sort of thing. He's quite fond of you, you know, truly he is. But he has so little strength left, you see, that he can't hold one's attention as he used to, through the sheer power of his will. His voice. His words. He's quite weak, Mr. Falkirk, but he refuses to stop until you've been made to see what must be done.

Here. Take this . . . oh, damn, I can never find anything in this blasted purse when I want to. The curse of my . . . ah. Here. Take this. Mr. Falkirk, please, take it. Thank you. I hope you can read my writing, it tends to get cramped when I write fast. Those places there, and there, the ones I've underscored, I think you'll find that's where the Sickness, as you call it, spreads from. Like ripples, I suppose. Easy enough to check on, if you have the time. But you don't, you'll just have to take my word for it.

Look at the dates, Mr. Falkirk. I believe if you cross-check them against—

Mr. Falkirk, where are you going?

Please, don't do this, oh God, I wish Sir John were here.

Mr. Falkirk, tomorrow night, watch the news. Do you hear me, Mr. Falkirk? Watch the news tomorrow night, then look out your window.

It's dying, Mr. Falkirk. For God's sake, your dragon is dying.

4

He stumbled out of the hotel, and people thought he was drunk and side-slipped out of his way.

Ahead, past the overhang under which limousines and taxis and airport vans stopped to pick up and take on, the cone of the volcano rose above lush greenery and palm trees, just a fountain now, water spilling down its sides into pools in which alabaster statues of Chinese lions waded.

He walked down the left arm of the driveway's half-moon arc until he reached the boulevard sidewalk. Holding on to the iron fencing that kept the crowds away from the grassy knoll that was the volcano's base.

He could go left and watch a full-size British frigate sail into a cove where it would do battle with pirates amid explosions of fire and smoke; he could go up a little farther and duck into a yellow submarine restaurant with portholes for windows, where steam shot from pipes and the lights dimmed and the captain shouted, "Dive, dive," and huge screens cycled through films of underwater caverns and sharks on the hunt; he could cross the street and go to the casino in a place that was Venice, complete with canals and gondoliers and every room a suite; he could go down to Paris and visit the Eiffel Tower; he could go back to Caesar's and sit on a bench near the shops and watch the vaulted arch of the painted sky run through the day from dawn to dark and back again in less than an hour; he could go to the place where slot machines huddled under acrobats and high-flyers; he could stop at the hotel where the food court was Greenwich Village, dark grey cobbled walks and flower pots in curtained apartment windows three and four stories above him.

He could.

But the sun was too bright and the traffic too noisy and he had had enough of things that didn't make any sense. Of being a target.

Of let's pretend.

So he walked back up the drive, left hand gliding along the top of the fence, and got in the line of chattering guests who waited for transportation. He said nothing to anyone and met no one's gaze, and when his turn came, he tipped the all-too-cheerful doorman five dollars and got into the cab and deliberately faced straight ahead so he wouldn't see Lady Beatrice standing back in the entrance, clinging to her purse, her face flushed and her eyes filled with frustrated tears.

He did not think.

He concentrated on the street, on the several lanes of traffic, on the way shadows had begun to fill in the gaps and arches and windows and alleys, and he wondered only briefly where the afternoon had gone.

When the taxi dropped him off, he tipped the driver too much, and walked straight through the Excalibur without listening, without seeing, without thinking, until he reached the parking lot and unlocked the pickup's door and sat behind the wheel with the window rolled down to let the stifling heat spill out of the cab with the engine running to get the air-conditioning in gear.

When he could grip the steering wheel without scorching his palms, he said, "For crying out loud, please, get me out of here, okay?" and pulled into the street, drove past the towers and the drawbridge and the moat with the once-a-night dragon, past the sphinx that crouched in front of the black glass pyramid, and in less than a blink, or so it seemed, backed into his driveway and shut the engine down.

He remembered nothing of the drive—no turns, no lights, no traffic—and his hands began to tremble because he could have hit someone or something and not remembered it at all.

When his hands calmed and his stomach stopped jumping, he shook himself and got out, closed the door, and patted the hood. He muttered, "Thanks," and backed away quickly when the truck shuddered once and was still.

He stood in the tiny shower stall and let cool water wash the stench of sweat away. When he was done, when the cool became cold and the cold became pain, he wrapped a towel around his waist and stared in the mirror over the bathroom basin.

Still you, he thought to his reflection, and looked away when his grin seemed too much like a grimace.

He picked up the white shirt Sir John had given him, balled it up, and carried it into the kitchen, where he slammed it into the trash. He closed the blinds in all the rooms. He turned on the air-conditioning by cranking the thermostat down with a single vicious twist of his wrist and listened to it clank and sputter like the struggle of old pipes. Then he sat cross-legged in the middle of the couch, hands loosely folded in his lap, and watched the sunglare around the edges of the windows fade, and turn dark.

*   *   *

The air-conditioning shut off, thermostat setting reached, and the silence was much larger than the rooms in which he lived.

The girls knocked on the door, giggling, then calling out, then muttering, then leaving.

He heard cars drive by.

There were voices raised in shrill argument.

Later, much later, someone else knocked, softly, and he had no idea when whoever it was finally left.

Even later, the crunch of tires rolling slowly over the dirt. No engine sound. The sharp slam of a car door. Tires passing in the opposite direction.

And through it all, when his mind wavered, couldn't stay blank, all he could think was *who the hell are you?*

A stiffness in his neck.

He inhaled slowly, deeply, and let the air out in an explosive sigh so loud it sounded unnervingly like a sob.

His left hand passed over his right arm, the gooseflesh there like fine-grain sandpaper. Gingerly, hissing in, he straightened his legs one at a time, waiting for the inevitable cramps in foot and calf and thigh. When they came, he rubbed them away absently, not really feeling the pain.

Listening, instead, to the silence in the house. In the street. Wondering how late it was but in no hurry to find his watch. A faint glow marked the windows' edges, so the porch lights were on and the moon was probably out and full. Not yet midnight. Far too long till dawn.

Walking stiffly, kicking out a leg to loosen it, swinging an arm in a circle to bring back the circulation, he walked into the bedroom, tossed the towel aside and dressed without bothering to put on a pair of shoes. His bladder, now that he was back among the living, demanded release, and he gave it, and once given, he checked the mirror again and still didn't like what he saw, even after he turned off the light.

Food, then. He hadn't eaten since lunch, and that had been lost in the restroom at the Mirage. The memory of it put the taste of sour bile in his mouth, and he licked his lips constantly as he hurried into the kitchen and flung open the refrigerator door. A cock of his head—a beer, he figured, probably wasn't wise. He grabbed a package of deli American cheese, a small jar of mustard, a head of lettuce. The bread was on the counter, between the sink and a small radio he usually listened to while he ate. As he made himself a sandwich, not too thick, he finally permitted his brain to get to work.

And the first thing he thought, with a self-mocking chuckle while he cut the sandwich in half, corner to corner, was that Lady Beatrice scared the living bejesus out of him. She was very kind, and rather attractive in a nontraditional sort of way, and she had to be a good . . . what, thirty or forty years younger than her husband? Easily; no problem. But while Sir John merely angered him with his mysterious, mystical, bullshit three questions, Beatrice, in her fumbling for a way to explain and confuse him, made them sound too damn real.

As if she knew, *knew,* that he had posed them to himself a long time ago and had decided, rightly or wrongly, he didn't want to know the answers.

He picked up the sandwich, opened his mouth to take a bite, and laughed briefly, deeply in his throat. A sudden vision of his mother, scolding him for eating breakfast at the counter one morning, ordering him to a chair because eating standing up offended her fragile sense of permanence. Even if you are in a hurry, she had told him sternly, there's no cause being rude, announcing it to the world.

"Sure thing, Ma," he whispered, flicked on the radio because he couldn't take the soft sounds of his moving around any longer, and took the plate to the table. Sat. Stared at the pale green radio dial until the station number blurred. Blinked once and shook his head when he realized he was listening to Eula Korrey, somewhere in the middle of what had become, in so short a time, her trademark song.

. . . you ready?

And the chorus, it must have been a million strong, answered a joyful, affirmative *ready!*

are you ready?

Finally he took the first bite, and the song became the background, and it occurred to him that neither Sir John nor Lady Beatrice had asked him that fourth question. He had walked out on both of them before they'd had the chance. Not that it would take a Strip magician to figure out what it would be.

"So tell me, Mr. Falkirk," he said softly, badly mimicking Sir John's accent, "what will happen to you if you ever leave the city, do you suppose?"

No supposing about it.

ready!

The way his luck had run, the next beating he took would be the last one he'd ever have. Thrashed and trashed, just like his sister. End of story. That's all she wrote. Put a fork in him, Ma, this boy's done.

He grunted. Shook his head.

It was, now that he thought about it, a monumentally stupid notion. Obviously, what had begun as a series of unfortunate incidents had evolved over the years into a full-blown superstition, and he sure wasn't the first gambler in the world to have at least one superstition riding hard on his back.

are you ready

Most of the men and women he had come across off and on the Strip had theirs so ingrained they didn't even think about it, hardly knew it existed. It had taken on the strength of a powerful habit; you did it unconsciously until someone pointed it out to you. Maybe you shrugged in embarrassment, maybe you didn't. But you didn't drop it, either; the consequences simply didn't bear thinking about.

Yet neither of the Harps had even suggested his touching each machine to find the right one was a simple superstition. They had accepted it, apparently, as a given. A fact. That without the touch he wouldn't know one machine from another.

are you ready

That made him sit back and frown.

A glance to the back door, another to the front.

The implication was, they didn't think his not wanting to leave Las Vegas was superstition either.

They believed it was true.

"Oh, yeah," he muttered. "Right."

Yet Beatrice had told him he would have to leave, to find one guy he'd never heard of and another whose name he had heard only in passing from a couple of kids who didn't even know what the hell they were doing. And how did the Harps know that Chisholm's name, anyway? Did they know those kids? Did—

"Whoa!" he said, almost shouting. "Whoa!"

That feeling again, the slipping into some kind of weird warp thing, unreality sneaking in behind his back, whispering things in his ear in an unknown language. Panic over something that had no name, no face. A threat without definition.

are you ready, are you ready for a miracle?

He slapped the table hard with a palm, stood so quickly the chair skittered back against the wall, and stomped to the counter, snapped off the radio and turned its face around, pulled the plug from its socket. What he didn't need now, tonight, was that woman's voice in his home.

It grated.

He had no idea why, but it grated.

He grabbed the remains of the sandwich off its plate, muttered a

"Sorry, Ma," and ate as he wandered through the house, sliding fingers along a wall, brushing them over the top of a chair, the surface of a table, turning on a lamp and turning it right back off, slapping the crumbs from his hand against his leg, trying to whistle but his lips and mouth were too dry, returning to the kitchen where he grabbed three bottles out of the fridge and twisted off the cap of one as he marched to the front door, yanked it open, stepped outside, and shivered at the startling, pleasant feel of cool and rough concrete on his bare soles.

Since the temptation to drain the bottle in a couple of swallows was strong, he forced himself to sip.

Since he wanted, very much, to get into the chariot and find one or the other of those . . . whoever, whatever they were, and wring their necks for unspecified crimes against his peace of mind, he forced himself to sit on the top step, set the unopen bottles beside him, and sipped.

Since there was no reason on earth why he should feel the way he did, he concentrated on the taste of the beer, the feel of the glass bottle in his hand, on the feel of the concrete beneath his rump, on the touch of the night breeze on his cheek, and forced himself to keep his mind a blank while he sat there, in the dark, and sipped.

And when the last bottle was empty and he could find no excuse not to go inside and go to bed, he told himself that no nightmare could be as bad as the day he'd just had. At least, in their own bizarre ways, nightmares made sense.

He gripped the post and hauled himself up, swung toward the door, and heard the horse walking slowly up the street behind him.

He swallowed.

He held up a shaking finger as if to say there's no sense turning around, pal, because there ain't nothing there, and you're just spooking yourself so don't bother.

His hand began to tremble and he pulled it quickly to his chest, holding it there tightly, blinking rapidly because he was afraid, not of the horse but of the way his mind wouldn't stop tripping over things that weren't there. He was losing it. After all these years, he was losing it.

He didn't laugh with relief when he finally looked up the street and saw nothing but the night.

Nor was he tempted to look again for tracks, for signs, for hints or indications.

If they were there, he didn't want to know it; if they weren't there, he didn't want to know that either.

All he wanted to know, as he went inside and closed and locked the door behind him . . . all he wanted to know as he stumbled into the bedroom and stretched out on the bed without taking off his clothes . . . no, he thought and clamped his eyes shut.

No, he thought an hour later, staring sleepless at the ceiling.

"Please," he whispered, angry and uncertain and maybe a little scared. "Please, who *are* you?"

A faint buzzing static from the kitchen.

And Eula's voice, singing, and laughing softly.

Part 3

ARE YOU READY FOR A MIRACLE?

1

1

The moment Trey woke up, he knew the day was going to be a bad one. A disaster. The kind of disaster that strongly suggested he not bother to get up, just stay in bed and wait until tomorrow, when things had to get better, they sure couldn't get any worse.

It didn't take much effort to run down the reasons.

Sometime during the night, the air conditioner had evidently decided to take a few hours off. The unit hadn't clicked on when the temperature rose above the thermostat setting, and the house bordered on being uncomfortably warm.

Sometime during the night he had gotten up, undressed, and by the evidence of the bottles lined up on the floor beside the bed, he had finished all the beer in the fridge. He vaguely remembered heading for the bathroom a few times; he didn't remember taking off his clothes at all.

Sometime during the night, someone had exchanged his brain for a pile driver that pounded now in his head, a solid regular pounding that matched the rhythm of his heart. He groaned and rolled onto his side, pulling the thin blanket up over his shoulder, over his head, while he tried to find a way to burrow through the pillow so the agony of sunlight leaking around the blinds wouldn't take his eyes out.

Sometime during the night, the wind had come up, a hard steady blow that had moaned around the house, promising no one would be able to go outside without getting a mouthful of grit, eyes stinging with sand.

Sometime during the night, nightmares had tried to edge their way into his dreams, succeeding just long enough that he didn't get much real sleep and could still feel the breath-holding approach of terrors that were never quite made whole.

He felt like hell, and he felt like a jerk.

The last time he had lost such a battle with his drinking was the day he learned of his sister's murder, and he had realized that he was, at last, without family. Alone. Too old, maybe, to be called an orphan, but he had suspected the awful empty feeling was pretty damn close.

This time . . .

He threw off the blanket and struggled up to sit on the edge of the mattress, shoulders hunched, head down. Moaning, groaning, gingerly massaging his temples in case the gods were listening and needed to know how much agony he was in so they could toss a little pity his way.

Or a new head.

But why should they?

Feeling like hell was one thing; feeling like a jerk was rubbing salt into the wound.

He deserved it, though; no question but that he deserved it.

His mother, when questioned about how and when to bluff, had explained that bluffing, no matter how you looked at it, was a simple matter of lying. The better liar you were, the better bluffer you were.

CHARIOT

All gamblers were liars to one degree or another, and if they had any innate talent at all, they eventually become damn good liars indeed. The hard part, she cautioned, was recognizing how good a liar the other guy was.

The Harps were damn good.

They had run some kind of weird scam on him, and he hadn't seen it coming. First one, then the other. Not a tandem, but a left jab, a right hook. A fast ball, a curve. Run from one into the waiting, practiced arms of the other, and the next thing you know, you can't be sure of anything anymore. Off balance. Floundering. Ready for the final push.

By the time he had gulped some aspirin down with tepid water and had made himself the most bland breakfast he could—butterless toast and milkless cereal—he figured patience was the key here. Patience, until his head stopped exploding and he could think straight; patience, while he waited for them to make their next move.

The only thing that was clear—or as clear as things could get, considering how he felt—was that someone wanted him out of the city. The how and why and wherefore would have to wait until he didn't feel so much like dying just to find a little comfort.

Meanwhile, he whacked the side of the thermostat with the butt of a screwdriver to get it working again, then flopped onto the couch, arm draped over his eyes, and without planning it, fell asleep.

There were no dreams, but he whimpered once and rolled over to face the back of the couch, curled as tightly as possible on the narrow cushions.

There were no dreams, but the part of him that knew he was sleeping wished there was at last a little color in the dark.

163

*   *   *

When he woke, it was with a grunt, as if someone had poked him in the stomach. Blearily he sat up, rubbed his eyes with the heels of his hands, and squinted at the front window, trying to gauge the time by the light around the edges. Still daylight, and he praised himself sarcastically for such a brilliant observation, rubbed his eyes again, and scratched vigorously through his hair to chase the last of the sleep away. Although he felt a stir of hunger, he decided to behave as if this were a normal Saturday, and it was morning, not halfway to whenever.

Shower and shave; strip the bedclothes and replace them with clean sheets; wash the few dishes in the sink; avoid the radio like the plague because it was still unplugged and he still remembered; pick up here and there, and a glance in the bathroom hamper to remind himself that tomorrow he'd have to spend some quality soap time at the coin laundry before his clothes got up and walked away.

Taking his time in case his head decided to get back into construction.

Checking the refrigerator and wincing when he saw all the empty spaces where the beer had been, then grabbing the last can of soda and, with an unconscious deep breath for courage, walking to the front door and pulling it open.

"Sweet . . . Jesus!" he yelped, and jerked his face away from the sunlight, fumbling behind him to snatch up his sunglasses and put them on with one slightly trembling hand before stepping onto the porch and lowering himself, carefully, unsteadily, into the white wood lawn chair that badly needed a fresh coat of paint and something to brace its back legs.

The shadow of the house had already begun to slip toward the street, the day's heat waning. He reckoned it sometime between five and six, but fetching his watch would be cheating. Instead he looked up the street to see who had already left for work, who was waiting for the last minute.

He frowned.

Two doors up, the front bumper and grill of Cable's Oldsmobile poked out from under their carport. That's wrong, he thought. Even if Cable delayed a bit, Steph would be out on the porch, pacing, practicing a step or stride while she fretted. Something's wrong.

Speculation was forestalled when he heard a breathless tuneless whistling and looked to his left, just as Hicaya strolled up the street from the mailbox row. He wore shorts, the glove, and a nylon-net T-shirt. And from the looks of it, he was in no hurry to change into his penguin suit and get down to the Strip.

"Hey," he said as the man walked by the house.

Rick squinted over into the sun. "That you, Trey?"

"I think so. Most of me, anyway. I don't think my head has made up its mind."

Hicaya stuffed a couple of envelopes into his hip pocket, no response to the feeble joke. "Hard times last night, huh?"

He nodded. "How come you're not dressed?"

The man shrugged. "Ain't going in."

"A Saturday night, you're not going in?"

Another shrug, and he started walking again, abruptly veered toward the house, breaking through the invisible hedge. "You know," he said, keeping his voice low and angry, "those fatheads at the hospital down there, down in Boulder, they wanted to . . ." He gestured vaguely with his gloved hand. "Plastic shit, you know what I mean? Replace it with plastic shit filled with wires and shit."

Trey didn't quite know what to say. "You mean they wanted to—"

Hicaya nodded sharply, made a chopping motion with his good hand. "Bastards. Said it'd be good for my mental health. Showed me pictures and everything."

Trey shuddered sympathy at the image, unable to keep from glancing at his own hands. "Damn." He shuddered again. "So what are you going to do?"

Hicaya straightened, scowling. "You have to ask?" He sounded insulted. "No damn doctor's gonna take me apart, stitch me back together like some kind of monster, you know? I told them to shove it." An emphatic nod, and he headed back to the street. "Got other plans, loafer," he said over his shoulder. "Got other plans."

"Like what?" Trey called after him, ignoring the loafer crack, but Hicaya didn't answer. He patted at his hair, touched his rump to be sure the mail was still there, and walked on, slapping lightly at the hood of Cable's car as it drove past at a crawl. Stephanie was behind the wheel, and she stopped when she spotted Trey.

"Hey," she said, smiling broadly, teeth and lips gleaming.

"Hey yourself."

"You going to the casinos tonight?"

He hesitated, wondering, before saying, "I don't think so, kid."

"Oh," with the slightest hint of disappointment.

"Maybe I'll come see you instead."

Her laugh was quick, and coy. "You'll need a telescope, then."

An eyebrow went up, and he leaned forward, forearms on his thighs. "What? You mean you're not going to work? On a Saturday?" He gestured at the car. "I thought—"

She shook her head. "Just heading for the store, that's all. I forgot a couple of things yesterday." The smile became grim. "Cable and I have plans for tonight." She looked back toward her house. "He was let go the other night, Trey." The little girl voice deepened. "Some asshole complained about his . . . you know . . . and they let him go."

"Damn, I'm sorry."

The car began to coast as she faced forward. "I'm not," she said flatly. "Now he'll have to listen to me for a change."

Again he wasn't sure what he was supposed to say, but her

attitude, her posture, made the decision easy—he didn't say anything. He watched until she turned the corner onto the tarmac, wincing when she floored it and the Olds fishtailed a little, nearly sideswiping the mailboxes. When the engine's roar faded, he scratched briefly at his cheek, wondering what had gotten into everybody.

He stiffened for a moment.

No.

Good God, no, not today, too.

Fearfully he looked back at the road, half expecting to see Harp and Beatrice there, and was immensely, almost comically relieved when he saw nothing but the dying cloud of dust Stephanie had left behind.

You're doing it again, pal, he warned as he set the soda down beside the chair; you're spooking yourself.

He reached to his breast pocket for a cigarette, realized he'd left the pack inside, and sighed loudly. Go in? Be strong and wait? "Screw it." He went in, found an unopened pack on the nightstand, and wandered out again.

And stopped.

Starshine was in his chair, draining the can, legs stretched out. Feet bare. Ponytail draped over her shoulder. She let out a monstrous belch when she finished, and Moonbow, on the floor beside her, giggled behind both hands.

"That," he said, "is disgusting."

"Where were you?" Moonbow demanded petulantly. "We knocked, but you wouldn't let us in."

"He was drunk," her sister said without inflection.

Moonbow punched her arm. "Was not."

"I was tired," he told them, moving to the steps, sitting on the slab with his legs crossed, back against the post. "I had a long day."

He could see their faces now, and neither seemed very happy.

Starshine's brow was creased above her sunglasses, and Moonbow looked as if she'd lost her best friend. They were dressed the same, in the same colors, as if they were canary twins—glossy yellow shorts and yellow tops. That's when he knew there was definitely something up, because Starshine would rather die than have to dress like her sister. Their skin gleamed, as if fresh from a hard bath, and their ponytails had been recently brushed, no wind or racing tangles.

"You guys going out?"

Starshine didn't answer, just glared at the soda can.

Moonbow scooted up a bit so she could see around her sister's legs. "You hear about Roger?"

He shook his head, but he was pretty sure he didn't want to know and was going to hear it anyway.

"He was arrested yesterday."

He looked quickly up the street, back at the girls, and pulled off his sunglasses. "He was what? Arrested?"

She nodded, bouncing with the news and trying hard to be cool. "He beat up his boss. In his bare feet."

"Almost killed him," Starshine said, still studying the can.

"He was drunk when they found him."

"He wasn't drunk when he did it, though."

"There was blood all over the place."

"It took ten people to put him down."

Moonbow pushed her sister's knee. "No, it didn't, dope."

"That's what I heard."

"Well, I was there, too, and I didn't hear it."

"Then you weren't listening."

"I was too listening. I heard—"

"Hold it!" Trey said loudly.

The girls jumped as if they'd forgotten he was there, and Starshine finally couldn't help an evil grin. "They brought him home last night. Late. Momma had to help. The jerk could barely stand up."

Trey lifted a palm to shut her up, turned the palm up in silent question—*would one of you mind telling me what's going on?*

They looked at each other, and Moonbow slumped, began picking at her knees.

"Roger," Starshine said, making the name sound like a bad taste in her mouth, "hit his boss over the head with something, okay? I don't know what it was."

"Clipboard," Moonshine whispered.

"Yeah. A clipboard. I don't know why, but he did. A bunch of kids saw it. It was right outside Roger's class. When the cops came, he was sitting at his desk, barefoot, drinking right out of a bottle." Finally she put the can aside and looked straight at him. "He didn't fight or nothing. They took him away, and arrested him." She waved impatiently. "Other way around. But they took him away."

"What about his boss?"

"Went to the hospital. Nineteen dozen stitches in his head."

"Twenty," Moonbow whispered.

"Yeah. Okay. Like twenty, maybe, something like that."

He frowned, stopped frowning, frowned again and said, "This *is* Roger Freneau we're talking about here, right? Professor Roger Freneau? Rog?" He pointed. "Rog who lives up there? That Rog?"

They nodded.

"And . . . and he was let go? The cops brought him home last night?"

They nodded again.

He leaned back and gave them a crooked smile. "This is a joke, right?"

They shook their heads.

"It's got to be a joke, guys, because if he did what you say he did, they wouldn't let him out. That's like . . . I don't know, attempted murder or something."

"With a clipboard?" Moonbow asked.

He couldn't help it; he started to laugh. The idea that one of the world's biggest self-pitying klutzes had beaned his boss with a clipboard, then walked, was too much. It was the best, weirdest thing he'd heard in ages, a classic that cried out for dramatic embellishment each time it was told.

"How . . ." He put a hand to his throat and swallowed until the laughter stopped. "How did he get out?"

"Now that's the weird part," Starshine said, nodding, knees bobbing, feet jiggling. "His boss, I don't know what his name is, what I heard was, his boss didn't do whatever he's supposed to do."

"Press charges," Trey said.

"Yeah," Moonbow said. "He didn't do that."

"Clobbered in front of witnesses, twenty stitches, and he didn't . . . ?"

The girls said it in unison: "Nope."

"It still doesn't make sense. The cops—"

"Some judge let him go," Starshine said, disgust creeping back into her voice. "It was like, I don't know, bail or something."

"Yeah," her sister said, nodding. "There was bail, and somebody gave the money to somebody, and the cops brought him home because he was too drunk to walk. Or ride, I mean. By himself, I mean."

"Well, well," Trey said. "The man has friends in high places, it looks like." Then he saw their expressions, and knew there was something more. "What? You know who it was?"

They nodded.

"And it was . . . ?"

They shook their heads, Moonbow giggling.

He stared at them for a minute, trying to read their faces, then shook his head. "Good grief, don't tell me it was your mother."

"Not hardly," Starshine said, giving him a look that made him lift a hand in an apology he wasn't sure she accepted.

He checked the street, scanning each of the houses, trying to figure out which one of them had the clout, not to mention the money, to get Freneau out in such a short time. Not to mention doing something to prevent the victim from pressing charges. It didn't take long to eliminate the whole block, and he felt really, briefly, incredibly stupid for even suggesting Jude's name.

He was about to give up, when the girls scrambled to their feet and dashed off the porch. "Hey," he called.

"Late," Starshine called back. "See you later maybe."

"But who?"

Their laughter made them stumble, but only when they reached the middle of the street did Moonbow suddenly change direction and race back to him. "Eula," she said, waggling her eyebrows. "Can you believe it, it was Eula."

2

For a while, Trey remained where he was, watching the street, wondering why someone like Eula would help out someone like Rog Freneau. Christian charity aside, it didn't make much sense.

When his legs began to protest, he stood, still leaning against the post, arms folded. He watched Muriel Carmody lumber across the street toward Freneau's house, with what looked like a casserole in her hands. He didn't wonder about that; Muriel would want to know all the details, and wouldn't be satisfied getting them secondhand. She had never been above a little gastronomic bribery. She had tried it on him when he'd first taken the house, and when he hadn't finished the meal—dry mashed potatoes, fresh green beans boiled soggy, and the world's heaviest meat loaf—she had taken it so personally she barely spoke to him now. Hadn't learned anything, either, so he figured it was a fair trade.

She knocked once on Freneau's front door and went in, too far away to see if she was smiling or not. He waited a few seconds, then shrugged and shifted over to the chair. Opened the pack and pulled out a cigarette. Rolled it between his fingers as if it were an expensive cigar, staring at the tip, the filter, while he debated paying a visit on old Roger himself. A look to his right, through all the porches up to Freneau's house, and he changed his mind. Muriel was still there. His gaze drifted across the street, to the house opposite Roger's: Eula's place. Back or not, he wondered, and figured, probably not. He couldn't hear any music, and the house, even at this distance, looked flat out empty.

Just a feeling, but he thought it was empty.

Like the street now—empty, silent, pressed flat under the sky and heat.

He lit the cigarette, blew smoke, and watched it hang there, curling in upon itself, forming a cloud that seemed too lazy to drift away.

Like an old man long retired, he thought then, and smiled briefly. He's sitting on the porch like an old man, waiting for something to happen in a place where hardly anything ever happened. Waiting for a chance to have a word or two with a neighbor, except the neighbors weren't coming around, weren't anxious to fill him in on all the latest gossip.

Even if everyone had been in the street, he'd still feel as if there was no one here.

Funny, that no one had come around to see him earlier, wake him from his afternoon sleep, eager to tell him about old Rog and his . . . Good God, with a *clipboard?*

Funny, that people who depended on the city for a living had decided to give the city a pass on the busiest night of the week, and didn't seem to care that they might lose their jobs for it. Especially Stephanie. For every one of her, there were scores more waiting for her to turn an ankle, break a leg, get the damn Sickness so they could step in and prove they were a Star.

It wasn't like her; and it sure wasn't like Cable to let her do it without a fight.

A glance toward their house, and he figured it must have been one hell of a fight.

Funnier still, that he even thought being out of the loop was odd. Except for the girls, and once in a while Jude, he was always out of the loop, a situation that had never bothered him before because, for the most part, he encouraged it. Had gotten used to it. Which made it odd that he even realized it now.

Whoa, he told himself; you're gonna make yourself dizzy, thinking in circles like that.

What you should do, young man, is get up off your lazy butt, grab your wallet and keys, and do likewise as the statuesque Stephanie— get to the store and replenish the larder. Maybe, though, not so much beer this time. A decisive nod at the practicality of the notion, and the admonition, but it took him ten more minutes before he made to stand. And only then because he couldn't wait any longer for Muriel to leave.

Do it when you get back, he told himself; drop in when you get back, neighbor to neighbor, guy to guy. If she's not gone by then, Roger will bless you for the interruption and no doubt number you among his heirs.

The slam of a car door stopped him.

A taxi down at the T, and Eula already heading up the street.

Still in her green.

He scowled. If he got up now, she'd see him and assume he was leaving because of her, an awkward situation even if they didn't get along. So he picked up the soda can in his right hand, held the cigarette in his left, crossed his legs at the ankles and waited until she was abreast of the house. Moving slowly, that purse held against her stomach with her green-gloved hands folded across it, that green hat shading her face.

In for a penny, he thought.

"Evening, Eula."

Two steps before she stopped, and turned slowly to face him. Then, thick and honey slow: "Evening, Mr. Falkirk."

"Have a good trip?"

"Always do." A polite smile, not showing her teeth. "Always do."

"Where were you this time?"

"Oklahoma. Lovely place, but powerful flat. Nothing but sky out there, Mr. Falkirk, nothing but sky."

Without thinking: "Saved some souls, I hope."

The smile again, chiding. "Not my job, Mr. Falkirk. I leave that to the pastors. I just bring the songs, that's all. Just bring the songs."

He leaned forward, thinking this wasn't going so badly after all. "Speaking of which, can I ask you a question?"

Barely moving, it was as if she had settled herself in a big comfortable chair. "If I can."

Damn, Trey, he thought; what the hell are you doing?

A breeze kicked up out of the south, easy and steady, right to left down the street; not cooling things off, just moving the heat around.

"The other night, going into town, I heard . . . well, I suppose it used to be called a spiritual? I don't know. It was 'Good News,' you know it? Only they did it like, I guess, the kind of music you do. Faster than I'm used to hearing it, that's for sure. I almost didn't recognize it." He put the can down. "The thing is, I don't know who did it and I'd like to get a copy, and I was wondering if you knew it. That version, that is."

She pursed her lips, lifted her face to the sun, squinting a little. "I believe . . . yes, I believe I do know what you're talking about, Mr.

Falkirk." A single shake of her head. "Don't know that I know who, though. Eddie Hawkins? Angels of Mercy?" An apologetic lift of her shoulders. "So many these days, Mr. Falkirk, so many out there that I can't keep them all straight. Best you can do is go to a store, ask around."

He sat back. "Okay, thanks."

She didn't move. Waiting, as if she understood there was something more. Like, *what have you got against me, Eula?* Patient.

Smiling.

He returned the smile, and wished he hadn't said anything. This was more than they'd spoken since the beginning, and he had no idea what to say next, what the protocol was.

"You know," she said, "seems there's been some trouble between us."

Startled, he blinked, and nodded cautiously.

"Why do you think that is, Mr. Falkirk? Why do you think there be trouble between us?"

"Honest?"

One nod.

"I have no idea." He tried a quick laugh. "I don't even know you, Eula. I mean, not really know you, so I haven't a clue."

"Well . . ." Another shift, hardly moving, settling again. "I don't think it's on account of my skin, do you? Don't think it's that. You don't appear to me to be that kind of man."

Soft, now; still honey, but soft. Forcing him to strain in order to hear her.

"You're no singer, Mr. Falkirk, so I don't believe it's professional jealousy, something like that, don't think that's it at all."

A stirring along the street.

He didn't look, and the houses were too far apart for him to see anyone else without turning his head, but he felt a stirring along the street.

"Ain't your gambling. I do disapprove of that sort of activity, but then, so do most of the others, and you don't seem to have a trouble with them like you do with me, so I suppose it isn't that, either." The smile broadened. "And you'd best put that cigarette out quick, it's gonna burn your fingers."

He checked, saw it was true, and let the cigarette drop to the porch where he made to crush it with his heel, remembering just in time that he wasn't wearing any shoes. Instead he used the can to grind it into the concrete. When he looked up again, the smile was gone, and for a moment, just a moment, he felt as if he were back at Madame Song's and it was Harp out there in his cowboy hat, not Eula Korrey, all in green.

Or, an old man sitting on his porch, talking to an old woman standing in the street.

It was just the image he needed, and he grinned. "So where does that take us, Eula? Doesn't seem like we really have anything to fight about, right?"

A little dust devil danced around the empty lot across the street, defying the breeze, tilted as if it were topheavy somehow.

"I wasn't aware, Mr. Falkirk, that we were fighting," she said. "Exactly."

He gave up. He uncrossed his legs, and gave up. This wasn't getting them anywhere. He had hoped, he supposed, that by being polite, being neighborly, he'd be able to clear the air of whatever hung between them. But it occurred to him abruptly that her outloud musings were nothing more than mocking attempts to unearth the problem.

She didn't care.

The realization was both a relief and annoying. It wouldn't be the first time that two people simply didn't like each other, no explanation necessary. What annoyed him, however, was the apparent fact that she understood this as well, and mocked him for the attempt.

"You been talking to that old man, Mr. Falkirk?"

The dust devil grew, still dancing, straight now, almost as tall as a man.

Trey sat up, hands flat on the armrests. "I . . . what?"

"The old man with the dead serpents on his feet. You been talking to him."

This was too much. She had been in Oklahoma, for crying out loud, how did she know about Harp and his wife? It was as if half the world that knew him didn't give a damn, and the other half watched him so closely they even knew what he looked like while he slept. An idea that, however preposterous, momentarily chilled him.

As did the idea that the dust devil, taller now, less transparent, was waiting over there for him to give it the word and it would sweep off the lot and engulf her.

"What he tell you?" she asked, almost sweetly. "If you don't mind an old woman asking, that is."

"I do," he answered flatly, putting a quick hand up alongside his face when the breeze gusted, to keep sand from getting into his eyes.

"No matter. You tell him for me, next time you see him, it's a little too late for miracles, Mr. Falkirk. The kind he's looking for, it's a little too late."

She turned away, faced up the street, ready to leave.

"Tell him yourself," he snapped.

"Oh, no." She looked at him over her shoulder. "He too afraid of me for that."

That got him out of the chair. "What are you talking about? Are all you people crazy?"

The urge to leave the porch, go to the street and face her down gave him two long strides before she looked at him again.

And smiled.

A smile of such sweet malevolence that he grabbed the post with one hand, as much for support as for something solid to hold on to. Something real.

The dust devil collapsed, sand and pebbles pattering to the ground.

He narrowed his eyes against the strengthening breeze as she walked away. Then he blinked once, once again, and told himself quickly it was like seeing that image of Lil on the horse. A mirage. A hallucination. A bizarre trick of the light that made it seem as if the wind didn't touch her at all. Her hat didn't quiver, her coat didn't flutter, no dust at all on any of all that green.

Grabbing the post more tightly he watched her, and saw the girls on their porch, hands at their sides; saw Cable on his porch, without his cap, wearing good slacks and a clean white shirt; saw Hicaya on his porch, gloved hand pressed to his stomach; saw Muriel back on her porch, hands clasped at her waist.

Eula lifted a hand.

Every one of them waved and smiled.

Damn, he thought; God . . . damn.

Bewildered, thinking he ought to be afraid but not knowing of what, he backed slowly to the door, fumbled behind him for the latch, and backed inside, kicking his heel against the doorsill and nearly falling. Another backward step, and he spun around, charged into the kitchen, and skidded to a halt.

Sir John waited for him at the back door.

There was a gun in his hand.

"My dear fellow," he said sadly, "I'm so terribly sorry for all this, but I'm afraid you're going to have to accompany me for a while."

2

The rustle of sand driven through the grass.
  The low hum of the wind slipping around corners.

"Say it," Jude insists from behind the safety of the screen door.

"Don't want to," Moonbow pouts.

"Say it!"

Starshine inhales; it sounds like a whimper.

"Please, girls. For Momma. Say it."

The sisters look at each other, look out at the street, sun full in their eyes.

Jude slaps the doorframe lightly.

Starshine jumps. "Evening, Eula," she says, barely above a whisper.

"Louder," Jude insists.

Moonbow wants to turn around because it sounds like her mother is crying; she doesn't, because if there are tears she doesn't want to see them.

Starshine settles her shoulders. "Evening, Eula."

Moonbow nibbles on her lower lip before: "Evening, Miss Korrey."
Eula looks over, nods, smiles. "You girls sure do look pretty."
"Thank you, Eula," they say together.
Listening to their mother weeping behind them.

Cable feels as if he ought to have his cap in his hand, something to twist, something to keep his fingers busy. Steph, he knows, will be royally pissed she missed the return, but there's nothing he can do about it but hope he says and does the right thing.

Whatever Eula says to those little brats across the street is taken away by the wind, and he waits until she's looking up the street again before he says, "Welcome back, Eula, have a good trip?"

"Indeed I did, Cable," she answers, giving him a smile that makes her cheeks round and full. "A wonderful trip, surely one of the best."

"Glad to hear it."

"Yes," she says, turning her face away. "I know that, Cable. I know."

Ricardo is nervous, for no reason he can think of. He watches Eula make her way toward him, pays no attention to Muriel across the way, who doesn't seem to know how to stand. She shifts constantly, looking like she wants to run inside and hide. That's not his concern. He pats the glove with his good hand, trying to calm its trembling. A quick look left, down his side of the street, past the empty house next to him, to the Olins', where he sees Cable nodding at Eula's back, rocking back and forth like someone waiting for the word that will tell him he can go inside now, it's okay.

The old woman walks slowly, and it makes Rick want to yell at her to hurry up. All that space between houses, it never looked so big before. Maybe . . . maybe he ought to go back to Boulder City.

Maybe he ought to let those doctors do what they want. Maybe he should cross over and stand with Muriel, strength in numbers and all that crap.

He almost does.

He almost moves.

But when he finally finds the courage, it's too late.

She's here.

"*Buenos noches,* Eula," he says with a grin, and winces because he sounds like such a goddamn phony, and he knows she knows it, and it frightens him because he thinks that maybe she'll just keep on going, ignore him for the fool he really is.

"Evening, Ricardo," she says. "You truly do look handsome this evening."

He locks his knees because he knows he'll fall if he doesn't. "Thank you, Eula. You're looking awfully good yourself."

She laughs silently. "You flatter an old woman, but it sure do sound fine."

"Thank you, Eula, but it's the truth."

"You a little older, boy, maybe I come over there and give you a kiss."

She laughs aloud this time, and Rick has never been so scared in his life.

Not fair, Muriel thinks, fussing with her hair, fussing with her blouse, fussing with her waistband; not fair I have to be the last one. She almost weeps with frustration because everything she does to make herself presentable is undone by the wind. She must look like a harridan, like some kind of bum, and she curses under her breath when her eyes begin to water, and she isn't sure if it's the wind or tears.

She holds her breath while Eula talks with Ricardo, not hearing everything, smiling nervously at the way he almost bows to the old woman he's so nervous. She breathes again only when he takes a small step back.

Her turn.

It's her turn, and she doesn't know what to say.

"Welcome home, Eula." It must have been her, but it sure didn't sound like her voice.

"Why, thank you, Muriel, thank you. It's good to be back."

Muriel feels so ungainly, so fat, she wishes the wind would just take her away.

"If you want," she says, gesturing vaguely behind her, "I'll fetch Lillian. I know she wants to—"

"That's all right," Eula says kindly. "Poor child must be weary, all that exercise all the time."

"It does take a lot out of her, yes."

Eula winks. "Not to worry, then, dear. All in good time. All in good time."

Muriel feels there's something else to say, but she doesn't know what it is, and so says the first thing that comes to mind: "If you want something to eat . . ." Another gesture; a shrug. "They don't feed you right on those airplanes, I know that. If you're hungry . . ."

"Well, I do thank you for that, Muriel," Eula says, sounding a little surprised, a lot pleased, "but I have already eaten my fill for today. Very kind of you, though, and I surely do appreciate it."

Muriel nods, blinking furiously at the hair the wind stabs at her eyes. She takes a step back, and watches as Eula continues on up the street, stopping only once more, to look at Freneau's house and shake her head before turning up her own walk.

That's when Muriel remembers what she wanted to say, and realizes that probably it wouldn't have been right anyway. She wanted to ask how Eula had known about Roger's attack and arrest, and what she thinks about it now.

CHARIOT

Too late.

Just as well.

She has a definite feeling Eula didn't want to talk about it; and if she did want to talk about it, Muriel is also pretty sure she didn't want to hear it.

She looks across the street, maybe Ricardo is looking for some company, but he's already gone.

She looks down the street, and all of them are gone.

Oh Lord, she thinks, and hurries inside and locks the door.

The rasp of sand driven through the grass.
The low moan of the wind prowling around the corners.

Jude sits at the kitchen table, choking on her sobs, holding in both unsteady hands a tiny compact that belongs to Starshine, looking in the tiny oval mirror. Her veil has been shoved up onto her hair. She's glad the mirror is too small to show her whole face.

This is wrong, she thinks; this is so wrong.

"Momma?"

The girls stand uncertainly in the doorway, fidgeting, unhappy.

She wipes her face with the back of one hand, wondering why she deserved two daughters like them. They never flinched at her disfiguration, never made jokes, even loving ones, and were badger-fierce in her defense when someone else made a comment. Without them she would have died years ago.

Starshine takes a tentative step into the room. "Momma, maybe you . . . she . . ." She takes a deep breath, lets it and the words out in a rush. "Momma, she isn't one of those miracle people, Momma, she can't do anything, she's just an old lady who sings on the radio, that's all, please don't do this."

Jude looks in the mirror.

A sensible woman, that's what she's supposed to be. A woman who's put up with trials few others have suffered. They have hardened her. They have made her see the world as few others have seen it. They have, in the end, ripped hope to tatters to be taken by the wind.

All because of the vengeful man who fathered her children, who drank, who sampled every drug on the street, who turned his brain into a pit of vipers. Who came at her babies with a blowtorch one night and got Jude instead.

Who stepped in front of a train when he realized what he'd done.

Too late.

Too goddamn late.

According to those who saw it happen, the train and the man, he was laughing when it happened.

She looks in the mirror.

"Momma—"

"Trey," she says suddenly, looking up, their faces a watery blur. "I should talk to Trey." She smiles; she nods. "Yes, I'll talk to Trey, he'll—"

"He's gone," Moonbow says, misery and fury in her monotone.

"What?"

"He went away with that stupid old man. We saw him. They got into a car, I think that woman was there, too."

"He had a suitcase," Starshine adds bitterly.

"He's . . . gone?"

But they always were, when she needed them.

They always were.

She whispers, "He's gone."

"Yes, Momma." Moonbow tries to smile. "But he'll be back real quick, I'll bet." She looks to her sister. "Right? He'll be back soon."

Starshine turns away, heads for the living room without answering.

"He'll be back," Moonbow insists. "Momma, please, he'll be back."

Jude closes the compact so hard the cover cracks, and she tosses it angrily across the room, where it bounces off a cabinet and into the sink.

Then she looks to her youngest. "Eula," she says.

Moonbow frowns. "Momma, Star's right, you know that. That old lady can't help you. You know that, Momma, you know that."

Everything hurts—the scars, the memories, the look on her daughter's face, the fact that Trey has left again.

"Momma?"

Jude sits back, shakes her head slowly. Closes her eyes.

"I have to try, 'bow," she says quietly. "Maybe you don't understand now, but . . . I have to try."

Uncertain, unaccountably uneasy, Cable stands in the bathroom, not sure that what he sees in the mirror is what everyone else sees. The hideous pockmarks. Craters. Discolored flesh. The way some of it pulls down the lower lid of his right eye, just a little. The way it crawls into his hair. A movie monster. A comic-book fiend.

Steph calls it a mask.

Married eight years, she sat beside him through the worst of the Sickness, not caring that he was infectious, crying at him, pleading with him to be one of the few, one of those twenty percent who didn't give up and die. When the fever broke and the crisis passed, he told her he got well because he couldn't stand the nagging anymore, and living was better than dying because if he died, she'd only nag at his grave.

"A mask," she told him. "People will know you're just wearing a mask, they'll see the real guy underneath, you'll see."

They don't.

Most of them, anyway.

They don't.

But Steph, she just keeps on dreaming. The bulldog of dreams. The pit bull of dreams. Grabs on, never lets go, doing enough work for the both of them, which lets him stand in front of the bathroom mirror and look at his face and wonder if there really is anyone else out there who thinks it's a mask.

He sighs, heads for the kitchen, changes his mind and goes to the living room, drops onto the couch so damn big it takes up most of the floorspace, and picks up the remote. He switches on the pre-game baseball show, but doesn't really listen to all the statistics and predictions, only catches a few words of the anchorman solemnly wondering how many seats will be filled in the park. Not many, probably. Too open. Too many people. Too many opportunities for infection, even in those cities the Sickness has already ravaged.

He thinks instead of how pissed Steph will be when she gets home from the store and realizes she's missed Eula's return.

He smiles. Proudly. Remembering how she had taken over yesterday, laying down the law, standing up to his self-pitying temper, thundering at him from the moment she got into the car until they got into bed. Beating him senseless with that damn dream of hers, until he couldn't take it any longer and surrendered.

In a way, he's glad. It's one of those things where he's got nothing to lose, and what the hell, miracles happen. It happened to him once, right? He lived, right? Practically everyone else in the ward died, but he lived, right? So who says miracles can't happen twice to the same guy?

In a way, he's angry. He knows Eula's just a singer, one of those fat old gospel ladies who work up a hell of a gleaming sweat singing to the Lord. She can't do nothing, except kill Steph's dream.

So he makes a decision while the anchorman announces that the Twins haven't yet rebuilt their team, but are determined to get back into the season. He decides that if Eula is the fake he thinks she is, he's going to kill her.

Kill her, because of Stephanie. No way is he gonna let that fat black bitch hurt his Stephanie. No way.

He changes channels.

He listens for the car.

He thinks that after he kills Eula, he's going to kill himself because he just can't stand wearing the mask anymore.

Ricardo pulls off the glove and examines the withered hand.

Nothing.

No change; it's the same.

Oddly, he wishes Trey were around. He didn't much like the guy, a little too weird for his taste, but at least the guy was someone you could talk to. He listened. He really listened. And he's been around the block three or four times, been just about everywhere, seen just about everything, probably done it all more than once.

Not that he'd say anything smart, but Rick figures just saying the words out loud, letting his doubts hang there in the air, would help him decide if he was being a jerk or not.

He laughs a little.

A jerk? Hell, sure he's being a jerk. They were all being jerks. Thinking what they were thinking, and probably not thinking how much the old woman would charge.

Now, Mr. I'm Too Good For A Regular Job Falkirk would probably laugh. Was probably laughing already . . . if he knew. Now there's a real jerk, and Rick wonders what in hell made him think the guy would even talk to him about this. Man has nothing going for him but a streak of luck, and luck doesn't last, and Rick realizes he's trying to fold the bad hand into a fist, but the fingers only twitch and curl and it looks like a claw that's been in salt water too long, and Rick swears and yanks the glove back on.

Bastard, he thinks.

That son-of-a-bitch bastard.

Muriel stands over the stove, stirring a small pan of tomato sauce, her own creation, with a short wooden spoon. She hopes Lillian won't come home before she's finished, but it probably wouldn't matter anyway. The girl wouldn't appreciate it. In the old days she ate pasta like it was going out of style, packing herself with energy, stamina, she claimed, before she went to the hotel to ride in the show.

In the old days Lillian actually called her "Mother."

Without the sneer.

Definitely she'll be angry because she missed Eula, which is all she talks about anymore. Eula, and that awful music, and walking again.

Muriel tastes the sauce, grunts approval, and turns down the heat, wishing she had a gas stove. Like in the old days. Easier to control the heat that way. No guessing. You looked at the flame and you knew what you got.

You looked at her, and you knew what you got.

A bordering on bloated, middle-aged woman stuck with a crippled daughter who was a bastard.

She frowns.

She nods.

Yes. A bastard. Didn't matter the sex, the kid was born without the mother being married, the kid was a bastard.

Sometimes, in more ways than one.

"Now, now, Muriel," she scolds. "Christian charity, remember? Hard times mean hard people. You can't blame her, can you, after all she's been through? Patience is the key. Patience. And a good hot meal."

She wipes her hands on her apron, checks to be sure everything on the burners is cooking the way it ought to, then hurries into the living room, looks out the window, hoping Eula didn't know she'd been lying about Lillian being home, afraid she's missed something important out there.

But there's nothing but blowing sand and dust, and that bum, Trey, is off his porch, didn't even sweep it clean after last night's blow. Once, Eula said in a joke that Falkirk would probably be improved by getting the Sickness. A man like that is nothing but a burden on the rest of the world. Muriel agreed, thinking at the time it wasn't really a joke at all.

She presses her cheek against the glass, the better to see down to the end of the street, but there's no cab there. No Lillian. Some kind of extra therapy, she had said when she'd left that morning. Don't worry about it, it's free.

Like Muriel cares how much she has to pay to get her daughter back on her feet. Although all those bills . . . and all those doctors who tell them over and over again that it isn't ever, ever going to be back the way it was.

Muriel believes it.

Lillian doesn't, not always.

Why, she wonders, sniffing back a tear; why doesn't someone like that bum Falkirk ever get hurt, and someone like Lillian, who lived for those silly shows, get hurt so bad she can't ever ride? Why is that?

She feels a tear slip down her cheek, catch the glass, and slip around her face toward the sill.

Tonight, she thinks.

It's supposed to be tonight. Eula promised it would be the first night she came back, and tonight is it, and that's why everyone was out there, smiling and chatting and . . .

She sighs heavily.

Is it really that bad? Is it really so bad that they have to believe a woman like Eula can make things right?

Lord, is it really that bad?

Roger sits upright, stiff on the edge of the love seat cushion. He's wearing his best suit, his skin glows from the scrubbing he gave it, his hair is about as neat as it's ever going to get, his beard is trimmed to within an inch of its life, his nails are cut, his shoes are polished.

He can't move.

He knows he's supposed to go over there, to thank her for doing what she did, but he can't bring himself to get up. He can't do it because he still hasn't figured out why she did it. All the time she lectures him about his drinking, praising him for his education, scolding him because he's wasting it, and all the time he nods with a smirk and assures her with a lie that not even a rock would believe that he would straighten up and fly right, don't you worry about me, Eula, don't you worry, I'm changing the way I live with the next breath I take.

After, that is, I take this next sip. Just a sip.

So he sits there as the sun keeps drifting toward the mountains, and he tries to figure it out. The trouble is, he also keeps imaging the look on old Art's face when the clipboard slams him to his knees, and that makes him giggle, and he has to scowl at his behavior and start all over.

But it was truly a wonderful sight. Truly. Honestly.

Finally, cheeks red from holding in the laughter, he says, "The hell with it." He'll go over later, when the sun is down and it's not so damn hot. If nothing else, he has to do it out of courtesy. A heartfelt, honest thank you without getting all sentimental and sloppy, a solemn, equally heartfelt appreciation of the debt he's incurred because of what she did, and a promise he'll never—

"Ah, the hell with that, too."

He bends over and takes off his shoes and socks, sighs, and wonders if sticking his feet in a pan of water with some Epsom salts will take care of those damn cuts and scratches. Not so bad as they were yesterday, but it still feels as if he's walking on needles. Not bad looking, though, as feet go, are they? Not hairy, no toe sticking out from the others, no veins popping out, just smooth skin and a little rough around the edges, the way a foot ought to be. Not bad at all.

"Holy Jesus," he says, "I'm already drunk and I haven't even had a drink."

He laughs, falls back, and kicks his feet in the air. Nearly gives himself multiple cramps when someone knocks on the door and scares him half to death.

"Come on in," he yells. "Damn thing's not locked."

The door opens, and he's on his feet as fast as he can get, too late to do anything about the socks, the shoes.

"Eula," he says, feeling like an idiot. "Hey, I was just coming over to see you."

"Were you?" she says, looking pointedly at his bare feet.

He winces. "Well, not like this, no."

She smiles, an indulgent grandmother's smile, and says, "You sure got yourself a mess of trouble, Roger Freneau." A scolding shake of a finger before she pulls off her gloves. "Now you just sit yourself down again, let this old woman see what she can do to give you a hand."

Embarrassed, he sits. "Eula, look, this isn't necessary. I can't let you—"

"Oh, yes you can," she says, bustling in, putting down her purse, taking off her coat.

Kneeling in front of him, grunting, adjusting her weight, embarrassing him even more.

"Eula, please."

She silences him with a look, grasps his left foot by the heel and lifts it. Dark fingers making his skin look fish-belly white. Lifts it higher, forcing him back, chin against his chest, making him feel a pull at the groin, thinking if she lifts it any higher he's going to slide onto the carpet.

"My, my," she says, shaking her head as she examines his sole. "My, you are something else again, boy, something else again."

She blows on it, runs a finger down it, shakes her head and gently lowers the foot until it's flat on the floor. Then, waving off his hastily offered assistance, she pushes and grunts herself to her feet. "Be right back, got something in my house will take care of that." Peers at him. "You all right?"

"Yes, thanks, but you don't—"

He stops because she's ignoring him. She puts on her coat, pulls on her gloves, picks up her purse, and is out the door without looking at him once.

"Boy," he says to the empty room. "Boy."

A self-conscious laugh, a shrug, and he decides to get himself something to drink before she gets back. Soda, not liquor, maybe iced tea or water. But first he's got to use the john, and he sings wordlessly to himself as he walks into the bathroom, shakes his head, turns on the light and gets a look at himself in the mirror over the sink.

"Oh," he says.

Just before he screams.

The hiss of sand piling up against the foundation.
The keening of the wind as it finds cracks in the eaves.

"Fool," Eula whispers as she stands at her window.

3

1

It had occurred to Trey more than once that, since he was still technically, most likely, within the Las Vegas city limits, the gun Sir John held on him probably wouldn't kill him. Maybe it wouldn't even hurt him. But a probably or two and a maybe didn't equal an absolutely, and for all the rattlesnakes, drunken cowboys, and curb-jumping cars he'd faced, he also couldn't see how the old man could miss.

"Do let me know," Harp said amiably, "when you've decided whether to try to disarm me, would that be all right? I rather think you won't, actually, and this bloody weapon is getting heavy."

Trey sat in the front of their rental car, twisted around against the door, the better to watch both of them without getting dizzy. Beatrice had augmented her outfit of the night before with a gauzy white scarf tied loosely around her neck, and she fussed with it constantly as she drove. At, he couldn't help noticing, a considerable rate of speed.

"You don't need that thing," he said to the old man, who sat directly behind him.

"You wouldn't come with me without it, I think."

Trey nodded at the truth of it. "And I won't try anything," he promised. "Even if you miss, your wife will probably run off the road and kill us all."

"I doubt that, Mr. Falkirk. She's quite a good driver."

He hadn't even bothered to ask why the gun, the abduction, the need for a fresh change of clothes in an old suitcase, because in the short time he had known them he knew them too well. Every question would be answered with a riddle, or a quotation, or with a silence that was meant to be an answer in itself. Despite his anger, at himself as well as them, he figured they would get to the point soon enough. No sense in getting frustrated; it was all he could do anyway, just to keep his mind from slipping away to safer pastures.

He hadn't even been angry for very long, a measure, he thought, of how far gone he was. In fact, the only thing that did register as Harp hustled him out the back door and over to the car waiting beyond the T, was how nervous the old man was. He kept looking back over his shoulder, as if expecting to see someone there.

Trey hadn't asked; nerves or not, the gun was steady in his hand, his finger steady on the trigger.

They had left the westbound highway ten minutes ago, Beatrice sweeping onto a single-lane dirt road that seemed to lead directly to the Spring Range. Dust kicked up behind them. The sun bore through the windshield as it reddened in setting, turning the inside, and the desert, a pale and unpleasant shade of blood.

"Don't you think you're overdoing this a bit?" he said, drawing one leg up, grasping it around the ankle. "You . . ." He laughed without a sound. Shook his head. "I said it before, I'll say it again— this is nuts."

"No, Mr. Falkirk," Sir John corrected. "This is a nightmare."

*   *   *

CHARIOT

The dirt road ended, and Beatrice drove on, the car jouncing over
rocks and hummocks while the mountains, splashed here and there
with late spring green, took up more of the sky. She had said not a
word since he'd gotten in, and each attempt he made to get her to
talk had been countered with a silence and a dead-ahead stare. The
old man, too, had not spoken again, and Trey wondered each time
he glanced back just how heavy that gun was. It was in Harp's lap
now, but his finger was still on the trigger, and Trey doubted the
caliber was too small to punch through the back of the seat if he
fired.

What amazed him was that all the bouncing and swaying hadn't
caused the gun to go off before this. More than once his head rapped
against the ceiling or the window glass; more than once he had to
thrust a hand against the padded dashboard to keep from sliding
into the well. Beatrice didn't seem to care that the car might not
last long enough for the trip back. She neither slowed down nor
avoided patches of cactus or scrub; she plowed through it all as if
she were driving a truck.

Then Harp said, "Here," and she spun the wheel, jammed her
foot on the brake, and the car whirled around to face the way they
had come. And stopped.

Metal creaked.

A spinning dust cloud covered them, visibility zero, granules
scratching across the roof like tiny racing claws.

For the first time since leaving the house, Trey felt a little nervous,
less than sure of their intent. He hadn't thought they were out to
harm him; they just wanted to push more of their incomprehensible
agenda.

But now . . .

The dust settled; the sun was still red.

"Red sky at night," Harp said wearily. "But alas, no sailors here."
He gestured with the gun. "Outside, Mr. Falkirk. Please."

Beatrice didn't move. Her hands were still clamped to the steering wheel.

"I'm not going anywhere," Trey snapped, "until you tell me what the hell's going on here."

Harp pulled the trigger.

The explosion was deafening, and Trey wasn't sure but that he actually felt and heard the bullet barely miss his cheek before it pocked a hole in the windshield.

Beatrice didn't even flinch.

"Out," Harp repeated.

A million tough guy movies, a million tough guy books: *you're bluffing, old man; if you really wanted me dead I'd be dead by now.*

Trey swallowed, nodded, and opened his door, slid out, and stepped away from the sedan, hands away from his sides, fingers spread.

Harp followed, closed his door gently, and stood by the rear fender, inhaling slowly, deeply, without once shifting his aim from Trey's heart. He adjusted his hat by tugging at the brim. Then his hand and the gun disappeared into his jacket pocket. His free hand smoothed the lapels, touched the perfectly folded handkerchief tucked into the breast pocket.

"You do understand," he said mildly, "that we're no longer inside the city limits."

Trey did. It was an agitated pair of wings in his stomach, a weight on his shoulders more than the heat that still pressed on the desert and made bleak the mountains' slopes. It was a feeling he thought he had banished more than two years ago, to a place in his dreams where he seldom visited, and when he did, not by choice.

Beatrice left the car, sunglasses but no hat. She stood on the other side of the hood, fingers tucked into her waistband.

"It's amazing, isn't it," Harp said, waving his hand at the browning grass, the scrub, a stunted Joshua tree not far from the car. All that was missing was the bleached skull of a steer. "Because of the sunlight, you can't see anything but the desert. You'd never know a large city was only a few miles from here. Quite an image, don't you think?"

Trey said nothing, and made no plans to overpower the old man, steal the car, and get out of here.

A million movies, a million books, but he was a gambler, not a hero.

And Harp was a hell of a lot tougher than he looked.

2

"Mr. Falkirk," Harp said, "I have bungled this entire affair quite badly, and I must apologize. Had I not been so . . ." A hand fluttered in search of a word.

"Stuffy," Beatrice said.

"Yes. Well. Perhaps. Nevertheless—"

"Pompous."

Harp stiffened, thrust out his chin. "All right. But—"

"Damnably inscrutable."

Trey, struggling to keep a straight face, watched the old man turn his head slowly and stare at his wife, who walked around the car, shaking her head.

"Damnit, John." No *sir* this time. "If you hadn't insisted on playing games with the poor man, we wouldn't be in this awful mess."

"I was merely trying to educate him, my dear. Under the circumstances, not such a bad idea."

"But you wasted all our *time!*" She shook her head, closed her eyes, sagged against the car. "Mr. Falkirk, I'm so sorry. I'm as much at fault as Sir John, and I'm so terribly sorry."

Trey knew something had to be said at this point, but the situation was so ludicrous all he could do was shrug a *no big deal,* and wait. Especially since he didn't know what the deal was.

"She's right, of course," Harp said to him, barely a hint of contrition. "We're both at fault. We have both fumbled our precious time, and now we must hurry."

"Fine," Trey said. "Hurry for what? Where? And don't," he added, suddenly pointing at the old man, "answer me with one of your damn questions. I've been to school, I know the method, and it isn't working, since you and I don't seem to be speaking the same language."

Harp sucked his lips between his teeth, narrowed his eyes, and smiled. Dipped his head in a slight bow. Took his left hand from his pocket, but left the gun behind. Tapped thoughtfully on his chin.

"No," Beatrice scolded quietly. "No time for poses. Just tell him and let's leave before she knows we're here."

"Who?" Trey said. "Eula?"

They looked at him intently; Harp nodded.

"Too late," he told them. "She already knows. In fact, she told me just a while ago to tell you it's too late. Or, too little too late. Something like that."

"Oh, my God," Beatrice whispered, and covered her eyes with one hand.

Patience, Trey cautioned himself when he felt his temper stir; patience. For a while.

Eula was right about one thing, though—they both seemed afraid of her.

Harp took out his handkerchief, took off his hat, and mopped his brow and hairline. His hand trembled.

"It's rather simple, when you look at it the right way," he said as he replaced the hat, tugged again at the brim. A tremble in his voice as well. "Those questions, Mr. Falkirk, were neither frivolous nor were they meant to be provocative. You are able to do the thing you do not because of those spirits that old Indian told you about, but because you are different from anyone else. Special, in a way you yourself have often considered, and discarded because you did not want to be special.

"You cannot be hurt within the boundaries of this city, because you are protected. You are in danger outside the city, because you are not protected. You learned that quite well and rather painfully over the years as a dog learns a simple trick, and whenever you ever questioned the reasons, your only answer, the only safe answer, has been 'just because.'

"You do not ask yourself how long it will last because you do not want to know. I can tell you now, it will not be much longer.

"And you know it is also true that if you ever venture out of the city again for any distance or any reason, if you ever get in trouble again beyond the protection's reach, as you suffered the last time, you . . ." He shrugged helplessly. "You will probably die."

Trey wanted to hit him, he wanted to sit, he wanted to walk away, he wanted to scream.

With little breath left in him he lowered himself into a crouch, resting awkwardly on his heels, balancing on his toes, the fingertips of one hand spread on the ground for support.

"How we know this is not important, but—"

"Yes, it is," he said, looking up, seeing the old man against the distant mountain slope, the white suit ignoring the sun's red light. "What are you, magicians or something? Some kind of psychics? Angels, demons, what?"

Beatrice took off her scarf and wrapped it around her hands, over and over. "We're not supernatural or divine, if that's what you're asking, Mr. Falkirk. We're all too ordinary, I'm afraid. We've just been given something we have to do, and we're not doing it well at all."

"Given by whom? And what the hell does Eula have to do with all this?"

"Trey," said Harp, so forcefully, so gently, that Trey almost lost his balance. "A good gambler is more than a good liar, you know. He is also a good listener. And surely you've been listening to what's happening out here, outside the city, since you've gone to ground."

"How can you help it?" he answered, poking at the ground, flicking dust off his boots. "People killing each other all over the place, people starving, this damn Sickness . . . how the hell can you help not noticing?"

"Death," the old man said. "Famine. Plague." He sighed and shook his head. "As they say these days, perhaps it's time you did the math."

"John," Beatrice cautioned.

His hand raised to stop her. "No, my dear. This time he must do it himself."

Trey scooped up a handful of grey sand, closed his hand, and let the sand escape slowly. "This is Millennium stuff you're talking about, right? Apocalypse, stuff like that. The Four Horsemen, and all that jazz?" He dusted his hand on his knee and stood, disappointed, disgusted. "You know, you two are as bad as that guy on the Strip. Counting the dead to the end of the world." He frowned, not bothering to work on dampening his exasperation or temper anymore. "Not that it makes any difference, but you're right, I have asked myself all those questions, and a hundred more you couldn't even begin to guess. And you're right, I have said 'just because,' because sometimes that's the right answer." A half step toward the car. "I am what I am, which is why I can do what I do. I don't drive myself nuts anymore trying to explain it.

"But that other crap, it's superstition, nothing more. I believe I'm going to get clobbered, so I let my guard down and I get the shit beaten out of me." A mirthless brief laugh as he shook his head. "I've been around too long, seen too much, Mr. Harp. If you're not going to tell me anything, fine. Great. Take me home." Another half step. "That's not a request, Mr. Harp. I mean it. Take me home."

Harp slipped his hand back into the pocket.

Trey wanted to giggle, wanted to throw a punch.

"John," Beatrice said from behind her hand. "For God's sake, he's not listening, get it over with."

"Not listening?" Trey's voice rose. "Not listening? To what? I haven't heard anything but—" He stopped when he saw the gun. "Now look . . ."

Harp jerked his head to the right. "One or two miles that way, Mr. Falkirk, is the edge of the city. There's no sign, but it's there." His voice hardened. "We're not talking about your bloody stupid superstitions. But we are indeed talking about the end of the world."

Trey laughed.

John Harp shot him.

3

He wasn't clear what happened next.

What he did know was that from reading descriptions of bullets entering flesh they usually mentioned a burning sensation. Which, he thought as his leg buckled and he toppled to the ground, was a crock of an understatement, because it felt as if someone had jammed a white hot poker into his left thigh so far that it popped out the other side.

He gripped his leg above the wound and yelled, rolled onto his side, and the world began to shift into shades of white and red. A voice he couldn't understand; the car starting and leaving; sitting up and spotting, a few feet away, a length of thin rubber tubing and a long piece of cloth.

Obscentities he didn't realize he knew dragged him over to the tubing, which he wrapped and tied tightly around the thigh just above the place where the blood . . . he shuddered, gagged—there were holes front and back, and the blood . . .

Jesus, he didn't know what he was doing. He had never taken first aid, had never seen a real gunshot wound, and he didn't know what he was doing, could only shake the dirt off the cloth and wrap and tie it over the thigh and watch it turn pale, then dark red.

And it hurt so much he could barely sit up, and his knee wouldn't bend, and that son-of-a-bitching old man had shot him, had stood there calm as could be and shot him and left him here to die. Bleed to death. Just to prove what, that he was mortally vulnerable outside Las Vegas?

That it was no supersition, that it was real, that he could really die?

He was afraid to let go of his leg, thinking that if he did all the blood would run out. All of it.

He rocked and moaned, bit hard enough on his lower lip to draw blood which, when he tasted it, he spat out as his stomach exploded bile into his throat. He spat that out as well, rocking, moaning, blinking furiously to rid his vision of the tears that blinded him. Realizing he was periously close to hyperventilating and passing out, which would mean . . .

Swallowing hard, licking his lips, he concentrated on breathing as normally as he could. Slowly, tentatively, virtually one finger at a time, he released the grip on his leg, braced his left hand on the ground beside him, and watched the red cloth gleam in the sunset, watched streaks of red sink into his jeans. He almost panicked again, felt his breathing hitch and stutter before slowing to as close to calm as it was ever going to get. Another swallow while he wiped his face, his eyes, and understood that he was, in fact, alone.

Get it over with, she had said.

"Jesus," he whispered. "Jesus."

They had planned it; they had goddamn planned it.

Still rocking, no longer moaning, he looked around and saw nothing but desert, and the sun touching the top of the range far to his right.

Alone.

So what do you do? he asked himself.

He answered, ask a stupid question . . .

If he stayed, waiting for some miracle to provide him with a savior who just happened to be driving around the middle of nowhere, he would probably bleed to death. The tourniquet and the cloth had stemmed but not stopped the flow, and his leg grew increasingly numb . . . except for the pain.

One or two miles that way, Sir John had told him.

Son of a bitch, what choice did he have?

It took several tries, several cries, before he flailed to his feet, neck muscles bulging, sweat drenching him head to foot as he waited for the poker to stop jabbing him and settle into a constant fiery throbbing.

Another cry, less of anguish than of rage, when he took his first step and the injured leg crumpled and he fell and rolled onto his back and cursed the sky no longer sharp and blue.

Screw it, he thought; I'm gonna stay here.

Screw it, he thought, and cursed himself back to standing and, after a few halting tries, discovered that if he sort of dragged the bad leg he could sort of walk-hop without falling, without passing out.

Every step reigniting the fire; every step releasing just a little more blood, he could feel it mingling with the sweat on his leg.

He could feel it slipping down into his boots.

Step and grunt, step and swear.

He felt light-headed, queasy, and furious enough not to let that stop him. It did, however, blur his thinking for a while, until he realized he could wander off in the wrong direction, and latched onto the tracks the car had made. With his left hand holding on to the back of his thigh, he soon slipped into a rhythm, a routine.

Don't look up; don't look to see how far you've gone, how far you have to go.

Step and grunt; step and swear.

Thinking: Harp didn't really want him dead. The bullet had gone exactly where it was supposed to—flesh, no bone—and they wouldn't have left him the tubing and the makeshift bandage. The desert wouldn't do it for them, either. The heat had lessened, it would soon be twilight and relatively, blessedly, cool.

Harp could have shot him in the heart, in the head.

So it was a test, right? See how strong he was, how much pain he could take, how far he could go before his injuries knocked him on his ass, put him down for the count.

Maybe, maybe not, because Beatrice kept talking about a time factor, how little of it there was left.

For what? The end of the world? For the test?

Step and grunt.

It hurt to think.

It hurt to breathe.

He stared at the faint tracks in the gritty sand and how his shadow flowed over them and almost erased them; he stared at the tip of his boot, but that made him dizzy and he focused on the tracks again, for a long time thinking how the pain had finally gone away until he stumbled and cried out and realized he had gotten used to the pain that reacted now to the beat of his heart.

Step and curse.

Left arm swinging forward hard to pull him along.

Left leg every so often taking a little of his weight while it bled into the sand, into his boot.

He glanced up once, and saw nothing but smears of cacti, smears of grass, and squinting didn't help.

CHARIOT

God help him, the fools had miscalculated. They had gone too far toward the mountains, and now he wasn't going to make it. Sooner or later his strength would fail, his will surrender, his blood run out, and sooner or later he was going to drop to his knees, to his stomach, and he was, no doubt about it, going to die.

Jude, he said as she walked beside him, loose dress flowing around her legs, her hips, what do you say we pool our resources and find a place together? I could hit the dragon a little more often, we might be able to get a place big enough for the girls to have their own rooms, what do you say?

She didn't answer, save to look at him, lift the veil and show him what was there, and what wasn't.

So? he said.

She lowered the veil and walked away, shimmering into the desert until, just as he was about to give chase, she raised her arms to the sky and turned into a Joshua tree. Forever rooted in one place.

Jude, he said as she walked beside him, her hair loose and playing tag with the wind, you're not going to believe this, but I've got nearly twenty-five thousand bucks in my stash under the bed. What do you say we grab the girls, get into the chariot, and ditch this place? Find someplace new. Someplace with real streets and real houses. Someplace where the kids will have someone to play with besides a couple of lizards once in a while.

She looked at him, her eyes flat above the veil. Eula, she said, wouldn't like it.

Who cares what Eula thinks?

We do.

Not me.

I didn't say you.

But what difference does it make whether she likes it or not?

Her eyes turned soft, pitying, and she walked away into the desert, spread her arms, spun in a circle, blended into a dust devil that nicked a large clump of pear cactus and fell apart without a sound.

He stopped. Panting. Wiping a sleeve over his face, shoving wet hair off his brow. His back felt the strain of the left leg's partial drag, and he found himself increasing the tilting forward until he was sure he would fall.

No falling allowed.

Once down, he wouldn't get up.

A tremor that began between his shoulder blades worked its way down his arms, and his hands began to shake as if palsied. He stretched his neck, closed his eyes, opened them as wide as he could several times, not entirely sure that the small black dots he saw up there were circling birds or just something in his eye.

He looked at his leg and said, "Aw, Jesus," at the red bandage wrapped around it, at the black-red jeans leg. Flesh, no bone, but that was obviously just a technicality now. He had no idea how much blood he had lost, and did not, would not look behind him to see how much had been left in his wake.

The tremor eased, and he used both arms to swing him forward, his right knee bending so much he could hardly stand, so he braced his right hand just above it and pushed.

Stepped.

Pushed.

Stepped.

Lurching back into the rhythm, head low, lips dry no matter how often he licked them, throat dry no matter how often he swallowed, feeling things inside him contracting against the pain he couldn't help but grow used to.

And count on, because he knew that once it stopped, he was done.

When at last he fell, he cried out softly, catching his weight on his hands, on one knee, lips working.

It felt so good to stop that he didn't try moving, didn't goad himself, didn't scream the danger, didn't give a damn because it felt so damn good.

For a minute, maybe less, maybe more, he watched the sweat drip from his face and hair into the sand, watched the faint quivering of his locked elbows, watched his fingers dig clawlike into the sand as if afraid that if they let go he would float away.

An unconscious shift of his injured leg spiked fire into his spine, and his head snapped up as he gasped, inhaling sharply, holding his breath, waiting for the fire to subside.

He saw them.

He saw the car.

A whimper because they were too distant to see clearly, and might be only wishful thinking. A mirage. A prayer.

A growl when Sir John took off his hat and waved it, signaling their position while Beatrice moved to one side, and he knew they were real.

Come on, he thought; damnit, get over here, give me a hand, can't you see, for God's sake? Can't you see?

Harp waved the hat again and put it on.

They weren't coming. All this time, all these hours, days, they sat in their air-conditioned car and waited, maybe playing a game to see who'd be the first to spot him. It was, he thought sourly, probably the old man.

Several hundred yards, he couldn't crawl all that way, so he lurched back to his feet, snarling, growling, feeling a space in his skull begin to expand, empty space that made his vision unreliable, tilting the world slightly to the left, to the right, and he had to shift his concentration back to the tire tracks before the nausea in his stomach rose into his mouth.

Step and grunt.

I swear I will kill them.

Step and swear.

Him first, then her.

Hearing a voice, urging, pleading, as if he were a marathon runner late to the finish line.

A snarl, teeth bared, shirt half out of his waistband, covered with sand that stuck to the blood, to the sweat. Stumbling, then pausing as he straightened and swayed. He couldn't keep them in focus, and he couldn't keep his head up for more than a few seconds at a time, and he couldn't keep the hot poker in his leg from making him grunt when he tried to take a normal step.

"My dear fellow," Harp said across the distance Trey couldn't begin to measure. "My dear fellow, just a little more. A few more feet." Admiration thickened his voice. "My God, man, don't stop now."

And the horse you rode in on, Trey thought, and considering the conversation, that made him smile, made him break into a choking laugh that ended in simple choking which turned into a low and steady growl when Beatrice moved to help him and Sir John put out a hand to stop her, shaking his head.

"Bastard," Trey said.

Sir John watched, and Trey tried to follow the direction of his

gaze, seeing nothing on the ground that indicated the spot he had
to reach before someone, for God's sake, bothered to give him a
hand. But wherever it was, he knew he had reached it when Beatrice
yanked open the back door and swept the suitcase onto the floor.

"Well done," Harp said.

Trey, with what little strength he had left, took the longest stride
he could and swung at the old man's jaw.

He missed, and momentum kept him in motion. Turning slowly.
Falling. Feeling two pairs of arms grab him and drag him and push-
shove him into the backseat where he was washed with cool air and
the smell of cool leather that almost masked the smell of warm blood
and sweat.

Beatrice ordered her husband behind the wheel, then leaned in
and scrabbled at the bandage, cursing when she couldn't untie the
knot and demanding Sir John grab her knife from her purse. Trey,
his head propped against the far armrest, watched it all with dazed
dispassion—the free-flowing blood when the bandage was cut away,
the boots and socks she tossed to the floorboard, her fingers moving
over his belt buckle, his zipper, then grabbing his jeans and pulling
them off while he yelled and tried to kick her away. Feebly, too
feebly; she brushed his protests aside as if he were a child, climbed
into the back with him, and closed the door behind her.

"Drive, John," she said.

And he did.

4

There was, Trey thought, a lot to be said for drugs sometimes.

Moments after Harp got the car moving, Beatrice began to work
in feverish silence, pulling a number of things from a small black
bag on the floorboard beside her—damp cloths to wash his leg,

more cloth to wash the entrance and exit wounds, a hypodermic she filled from a tiny bottle and stabbed into his thigh without preamble, which invasion he didn't feel at all because the fire was too strong. She neither warned him about pain, nor asked him how he felt. Yet he knew he'd gone pale when he saw the hole for the first time, and the dirt encrusted around it, the grit in the wound itself. Hell, he thought as the car slammed over the desert floor, all this damn trouble and I'm gonna die of the damn infections.

A few seconds later, he felt a welcome lethargy; a few seconds more and the fire was nearly gone.

"Good stuff," he mumbled as she took a thick square of gauze and placed it over the exit wound, taking his hand to hold it in place. Another square for the front, which he held with the other hand.

"It won't last long."

He closed his eyes. "Shit."

"Not to worry," Harp said from the front seat. "You won't need it. Aspirin, though. You will definitely need a bottle or two of aspirin."

"He's lost a lot of blood, John."

"Well, he would, wouldn't he, dear?"

I'm supposed to be mad, Trey thought; why aren't I furious? Why can't I think?

Surgical tape slapdash over the gauze pads.

"That's going to fall off," he complained. Then, when he wasn't sure his thick tongue and swollen lips had pronounced the words clearly enough, he said it again.

"Can you take your shirt off by yourself?" she said by way of an answer. "I'll give you a hand if you can't."

"No thank you," he said stiffly. "You've done enough already." He shoved with his hands until he was propped against the door, then took off his shirt, but not without an effort that made the sweat break over his face again.

At the same time, she pushed his feet aside so she could sit, and when he moaned automatically, she said, "Oh, do stop, Mr. Falkirk, it isn't that bad now."

When he looked, ready now to kill her, the suitcase was at her feet and open. She was right—it didn't hurt all that much anymore, but that didn't mean she had to be so casual about it.

"You'll need these fresh clothes before we get you home."

"What for? To cover the fact you two tried to murder me?"

"You'll need a good wash, too, when you get there." She held out the shirt until, scowling, he snatched it out of her hand and put it on, again struggling, again biting back an anticipated reaction to the fire that didn't quite break into flames this time. "I must confess," she added as she laid a clean pair of jeans primly across his lap, "I do not understand why men wear boxers. Too short to be shorts, long enough to be silly."

"I've said this before, but I don't care," he told her. "You're crazy. No, you're sick."

She snapped the suitcase shut and dropped it into the passenger seat. "John, when are we getting back on the road? I'm getting carsick back here."

"Just ahead, dear," Harp answered, glancing at the rearview mirror. "Just a few minutes."

With his bare left foot pushing against her thigh, his right foot on the floor, Trey manuevered himself into the corner, left hand once again gripping his leg above the wound. "Did I pass your damn test?" he said, shaking his head to clear it, realizing the drug had already begun to wear off.

"Oh," Harp said, looking at him in the mirror, "it wasn't a test. There's no time for tests."

"Then what the hell was it?"

Sunset filled the interior. The blood tint was gone; it was pale gold now, with dust that floated and sometimes sparkled. The ride leveled smooth somewhat; they had reached the dirt road, heading for the highway.

"What do you make it, dear?" Harp asked to the mirror.

Trey demanded at the top of his voice that he keep his goddamn eyes on the goddamn road before he goddamn killed them all.

"Ten minutes? Fifteen?"

Harp nodded thoughtfully. "Yes, I believe that's about right."

I'm invisible, Trey thought, feeling the first familiar stir of hysteria; these people act like I'm invisible.

He tried kicking Beatrice with his bad leg, and succeeded only in nudging her.

She sighed, and pushed a fall of hair away from her face. "All right, Mr. Falkirk, all right." She faced forward, hands in her lap. "To coin an old cliché, desperate times make for desperate measures. It wasn't a test, Mr. Falkirk." She looked at him sideways. "It was proof."

"Oh, right," he said. "Of what? That I can survive the nasty old desert with a couple of holes in me? That I can listen to you two yammer without going insane?"

"No, Mr. Falkirk," she said calmly. "Of this." She reached over and took hold of the gauze patch on the front of his leg. Watching him. Not smiling. Then yanking it free, along with the tape.

He yelled a "Jesus Christ," and grabbed the leg with both hands. "Let me out. Let me the hell out of here, I'll walk back in my underwear, just let me the hell out!"

She snapped her fingers in front of his eyes, and before he could grab her hand, pointed downward. "Proof, Mr. Falkirk. Proof that you are what we say you are."

At first he wasn't sure what she wanted him to see; he was too mad to focus until she snapped her fingers again, and pointed again.

When he saw it, he began to pant.

By all rights, there should have been blood; by all rights there should have been a ragged gap in his flesh; by all rights he should be gasping in agony, but all he felt was the fading sting of the tape's abrupt removal.

He began to shiver.

"When you returned from your last trip," she said, a sympathetic smile in her voice and on her lips, "you were no doubt far too bitter and much too tired to notice how your injuries healed substantially faster than they would have otherwise. I would imagine you healed completely in only a couple of weeks, rather than the month or so it ought to have taken. This," and she poked at the vivid red scar where the bullet had entered his leg, "is rather a special case, I should think. A combination of fear and anger, a determination to be rid of us which, somewhere in that thick skull of yours, you knew wouldn't happen until you could walk.

"Well, you can walk, Mr. Falkirk. You can walk."

"You . . ." Hesitantly he ran a finger around the scar, pushing down, daring the pain. "You did this?"

"No."

"I did this?"

"In a way, yes."

"That protection?"

She nodded, and Sir John whispered, "Good man."

"Yours?"

"I wish it were, Mr. Falkirk. I truly, honestly wish it were." She fussed with her hair, looked out at the window. "If you want someone to thank, Trey, you can thank Eula Korrey. She's the one who's been keeping you alive."

4

1

When sunset turned to bronze and the dragon began to glow, to push against the flow of night, they came to her door one by one, all asking the same question, none of them really believing, none of them really daring not to.

They had no real idea why it was she they had to talk to, only a feeling they'd been nurturing since she first moved to Emerald City. One thought it was the smile and that face. Another, because it felt right; it just felt right. The others thought it had something to do with the music—make a joyful noise and let your heart do the rest.

She received them with a smile wide and white, listened to the question, nodding, humming a little if someone stumbled and couldn't find the right words that didn't sound too foolish. When they were finished, she held out her gloved hands, fragile lace at the cuffs, and assured them they only had to take the first step, understand what would be expected of them in return, and she would do the rest.

"Don't make any difference, child, how you do it. Don't care how you take the path, honey. Like that song back there is saying, out there in the kitchen—walk, talk, sing, shout, it makes no difference how you do it. All you got to do is come on along, drop on in when the sun goes down, we see what we can do.

"Just be sure, though. Be sure in your heart what you ask is what you want. No turning back, you know. Ain't never no turning back.

"Thing is, you got to believe. Don't really matter in what, long as you believe. It's like . . . well, darlin', you never know, you could be on what that song says. My friends and I, we sometimes call it the King's Highway. Ain't always made of gold, ain't always straight. Sometimes it's just a dirt road like the one you just come up on. You take it how you want. You tell me what you want. Then I see what I can do.

"When the sun goes down, y'hear? You come back and see me when the sun goes down."

2

walking

It was the frustration more than anything. Forgetting once in a while that one leg wouldn't bend and the other wouldn't always do what she wanted. The therapy helped, she could see that, but she could also see that Muriel was right, too—it wasn't ever going to get back the way it used to be. Kidding herself for so long had grown into a belief that threatened to shatter every time she visited her old friends in the stables beneath the hotel and saw the horses, saw her friends in their costumes, saw them leading the animals from their stalls to the hall where they'd mount and ride out.

"You're killing yourself, Lillian," Muriel told her a hundred times a month. "You keep going there, you're going to kill yourself." No self-consciousness there about the times she really did try. Just, "You're killing yourself." Another way of saying she was being a damn fool.

The crutches, too, didn't help. People saw her with her forearms braced in those metal cuffs, and assumed a disease had stricken her or something. There had been a time when she'd corrected those dumb enough to ask; now she just grunted and let them believe what they wanted.

She stood at her front door.

She wore brand-new jeans too stiff and clean for honest comfort, a plaid shirt open at the throat, all that thick rich hair yanked back into a hasty ponytail, and despite everything her mind told her about the fall from the precipice of too much dreaming, she had struggled into her riding boots, kept in the back of her closet so Muriel wouldn't find them.

Tonight Muriel didn't say anything, couldn't even come up with a complaint about her choice of clothes.

Lil cleared her throat. "I . . . I guess I'm going," she called, staring at the door.

Muriel, sitting at the kitchen table, staring at her uneaten meal, nodded. "Okay, dear."

"Any last words of wisdom?"

She didn't look around, but she thought she heard her mother trap a sob before it got out. Other than that, there was no answer.

"All right, then." She opened the door. "Guess I'll see you later."

No answer again.

Pushing the screen door open with one crutch, she sidled onto the porch, looked to her left and saw Eula's porch light on, a soft white glow that seemed to glitter in the night's soft warm air. In fact, she realized, it was almost the only light burning anywhere.

The moon was tucked behind an opaque cloud, and she could see only a handful of stars up there.

But the night didn't feel like rain; it just felt dark.

Another look around, and there was no sign of anyone else, so she moved quickly to the steps, jumping when the door slammed behind her. She shook her head at her nerves and descended to the front walk, decided to do it right, and walked to the street. She looked around in case someone wanted to stop her, wondered why no one wanted to stop her from doing this damn fool thing. Not even Trey was down on his porch, drinking his damn beer, looking like he knew everything and everyone else was too stupid to ask so he could tell them.

God, she thought, moistened her lips, and walked as best and straight as she could.

Just another night in Emerald City, going next door to have a few words of pleasant conversation, listen to some music, have a cigarette without Muriel jumping all over her.

Just another night as she made her way up to Eula's door and didn't even have to knock, because Eula was there, waiting, hands folded at her stomach.

"Child!" she said, as if she hadn't seen Lillian in ages. "Come on in, come on in."

She stepped aside to allow Lillian easy entrance, then touched her elbow. "How you feeling, honey?"

Lil shrugged. "Strange, I guess."

Eula laughed, then snapped her fingers a couple of times to the beat of a song that filled the house, the same song she'd played earlier that evening. When she realized what she was doing, she laughed even harder and winked. "Sometimes," she said, "I just get carried away, even when I'm standing still." She walked toward the kitchen. "Now come on here, girl, I got something to show you."

Lil didn't move. "Eula?"

Eula waggled her fingers over her shoulder. "No time for talk, honey. You just follow old Eula, I think she's got just what you want."

There was no furniture in the front room, nothing on the walls, nothing to indicate anyone lived here at all. She had seen it many times, but this was the first time it struck her how plain the old woman lived. What was the word . . . spartan?

"Lillian," Eula said from the kitchen doorway, "you coming, you change your mind?"

I've changed my mind, she thought; this is nuts, and I've changed my mind.

Her arms shifted to turn her around, but instead she moved forward, watching Eula mouth the words to the song, dancing a little in place, grinning and beckoning and laughing and nodding and taking her elbow when she reached the threshold and guiding her around the tiny table in the center of floor.

"Right out there," Eula said. "Right out in back, I got something for you."

"Look, Eula . . ." but there was no stopping the old woman, and she had to admit she was curious. Praying that when she got back home, Muriel wouldn't curl those fat lips and say something like, *I told you so.*

Eula opened the back door.

Lil couldn't see anything out there, and frowned.

"Thing is," Eula said, leaning close, smelling warm, smelling as if the sun's heat radiated from her skin. "Thing is, child, before you go out, I got to know—are you ready?"

"Eula, I don't know what you're talking about."

Eula looked at her sternly. "You do, child. You know exactly what I'm talking about, and I got to know if you're ready. 'Cause if you ain't, we stop right here, we talk a little, you have a smoke, you go on home, get a good night's sleep, wake up in the morning, read the Sunday papers and shake your head at all the bad that's in the world."

Lil felt the tears that instantly filled and stung her eyes. She blinked until they were gone, but the stinging remained. "I don't want to go," she said quietly, "but honest to God, I don't know what you want me to do."

Eula studied her face intently, then snapped a finger against a crutch. "You want them gone? You want that fool knee to bend again? You want to do what you used to?"

"You know I do."

"Answer's simple, then, child. I am distressed at the presence of a man who has no right to be here. No right at all. Does nothing, says nonsense, stirs people up, and makes them miserable." She snapped the crutch again. "You hear me, child? You hear?"

"You're talking about Trey."

"I don't talk his name," Eula said acidly.

"So . . . what? You want me to . . . what?"

Eula's gaze was steady. Hard.

Lil looked out at the night. Then, slowly: "If you give me what I want . . . I have to hurt him." She shook her head to erase the words. "I have to kill him." A laugh, nervous, too loud. "Man, it sounds like you want me to make a deal with the Devil."

"No!" Eula said sharply. "Not the Devil, child. Never the Devil."

Lil took an awkward step back. "Even if I said yes, Eula, look at me. Healthy and in one piece, I'm almost as short as you and I'd never be able to do it. Not alone."

"Won't be," she answered. "Won't be alone."

The song ended.

The house was silent.

Eula took her arm and gently, almost tenderly, pulled her onto the back stoop. She pointed into the yard.

Lil didn't know what she was supposed to be looking at, because there was nothing out there but what was behind everyone else's house—sand and cacti and . . .

Her eyes widened. "Oh my God."

No moonlight, no starlight, but she saw it anyway.

"Oh, my God."

Eula stood so close their arms touched. "Now," she said. "Tell me now, child."

Lil laughed, quickly, deeply in her throat. "My God, for that, I'd say yes."

She couldn't look away, and barely heard Eula murmuring, barely felt it when the old woman eased Lil's grip on the crutches and took them away. Barely felt it when the old woman bent over and ran a palm over her fused knee. Barely felt it when the old woman touched her shoulder.

"Child," Eula whispered. "Child."

Without thinking, Lil took a step. Froze. Looked down, looked at the old woman, then lifted her left leg, which bent easily at the knee.

"Dreaming," she said.

"Walking," Eula countered. "And," she said with a slow, careful smile, "riding."

Pointing to the familiar pinto that stood in the yard, just beyond the direct reach of the kitchen light.

3

talking

Ricardo paced angrily through his house, muttering, shaking his head, pausing each time he reached the bedroom and telling himself to just get the hell undressed, get the hell into bed, and forget he'd ever even heard of that fat old woman. Then, the first thing in the morning, it didn't make any difference whether it was Sunday or not, he'd drag his sorry ass to the hotel, drop to his knees, and beg forgiveness for cutting out like he did, without even having the courtesy to call in sick. And if they took him back, fine; if they didn't, he had no doubt he'd be able to get another job in the city. Men like him, who knew all the right things to say to customers who were pissed off because they didn't get the right table or the right food or the right waiter, men like him were not a dime a dozen.

He had skills.

He would never starve.

"But you can't do that," he said as he reached the living room for the fifth, the dozenth time. "You told her you'd go over, and as long as you're going to do the thing tomorrow, you don't have anything to lose, you jerk, and you'll just make her mad, and you got to live with her as long as she's around, so why not go over, do the polite talk and smile thing, then tell her you have a headache or something, and leave. No problem. She stays happy, you get no guilt, and son of a bitch what the hell am I doing?"

He was on the porch, arms at his sides, bouncing a little on his heels.

For crying out loud, words were his living, right?

"Look," he said, looking around for the moon, "you talk to people every day who think you're crap but put up with you because otherwise they get stuck by the kitchen door, so why can't you just go across the street, talk the way you talk, make her smile, maybe tell her a joke or something, and maybe even go down to the Boulder place on Monday, let them whack off your goddamn hand, it doesn't do you a damn bit of good anyway, at least with some plastic thing you'll be able to tie a tie again from scratch, and son of a bitch what the hell am I doing?"

"I sure don't know," Eula said, chuckling in her doorway, watching Ricardo prowl back and forth on her porch as if he couldn't decide which side to jump off. "But you sure do make a lot of noise doing it."

"Eula, look, I am really sorry, honest, but—"

She waved him silent. "No need, son, no need, just come on in, I got something I need you to do for me."

A look back at his house, his nice safe house, and he followed her inside, back to the kitchen, where he heard the same song he'd heard earlier that evening. Only louder, and seemingly faster.

"See," she said with a heavy, weary sigh, "this old woman, she don't have the strength she used to when she was a girl and could whip any man in Alabama, one hand tied behind her back." Her laugh was infectious, and he laughed along with her. "Age is a bad thing, Ricardo, you know. Good that you get to live so long, bad that you remember the things you could do when you was younger and didn't have so many bones aching all the time."

"Eula," he said, giving her a sideways look and grin, "you're not that old, and you know it. Hell, you could probably arm wrestle me into Utah if you wanted to."

"With that hand," she said, nodding at his glove, "probably so."

He stared at her, shocked into silence, trying to believe she hadn't said what she said. That wasn't like her. Cruelty wasn't like her.

She turned away to the table, and pointed at a can of vegetables and a can opener, slapped at them disgustedly, and sighed loudly. "Used to be, I could do this in a snap. No more. Can't hold both at the same time anymore." She wiggled her fingers in front of her face. "No strength left, you see? They fat, they like sausages, but they got no real strength anymore. But you, you got the age and the strength, and I'm starving in here," she poked playfully at her tummy, "and if I'm gonna eat, I need you to help."

Still smarting at the crack about his hand, he shrugged and pulled the can toward him. "Well, that's easy. I've gotten so that I do a lot without—"

She grabbed his wrist, squeezing until he looked down at her. "No, boy," she said quietly. "Two hands. You got to use two hands."

"That's not funny," he told her, tugging to get free.

"No. It's not."

He didn't know whether to smile or scowl. "C'mon, you're not weak, Eula. I can't . . ." He tugged again; she wouldn't release him. "Eula, please."

"You want something from me," she said.

"I . . ." He looked at the can, at the opener, and couldn't believe it when he felt the tears. "Just once," he whispered. "You know? Just once, that's all." He held the gloved hand up between them. "They want to cut it off, put on a fake one. Wires and springs and things."

"I know," she said, so sympathetically he didn't bother to stop the tears when they fell. "I know." She brushed a thumb over his cheek, wiping away the moisture. "Don't have to be, Ricardo. Don't have to be."

He listened to her talk, felt a crushing pressure in his chest, heard himself ask her what he had to do.

And when she told him, he didn't hesitate. "If you're saying what I think you're saying, hell, a small price to pay. He's a creep anyway." Tears still flowing. "Oh, God, Eula, they want to cut off my hand."

"Not anymore," she said.

She took the withered hand in both of hers, brought it to her lips, and kissed it on the palm.

"You sure, boy?"

He nodded.

She pulled off the glove.

4

singing

Muriel sat in the Boston rocker, unable to think, unable to find the words, unable to do anything but use her feet to push her back and forth. Back and forth. Rocking slowly in the dark, feeling her heart strain.

Maybe a hymn, she thought; that'd be fitting.

She sobbed.

She pressed the heels of her hands into her eyes, and she sobbed.

A tiny voice, but rough and stumbling: "What a friend we have in Jesus . . ."

Her hands dropped away and she looked to the ceiling, chin quivering. Silly, but all she could think of were things she sang when she was a kid. Twenty years, more, since she had been inside a church; she didn't know what they sang anymore.

When she stood, using her forward momentum to help her to her feet, she nearly fell, and clamped a hand hard to her chest to stop her heart from getting out.

Now or never, she told herself; Lillian's gone, you going to wait or are you going to do it right for a change?

There was no hesitation at the front door, none in the street.

"Jesus loves me . . ."

None when she knocked on Eula's door.

". . . this I know."

When the door opened, she couldn't speak, could only sing in a voice she hadn't used in forty years, ". . . for the Bible tells me so."

"Well, now," Eula said, reaching out, taking her hand. "What a sweet song you got there, Miz Carmody. Ain't heard that one in ages. Makes this old heart of mine feel real good." A smile, a wink. "You ready?"

Muriel swallowed, and nodded.

"Good." She took Muriel's hand and pulled her gently inside. "You know, Miz Carmody, I been looking around, I found something in that Oklahoma I think you'll like. Got it in the kitchen, you just come with me."

Muriel followed numbly, not seeing Lillian, not wondering where she was. She would have asked, but on the kitchen threshold she jerked and stopped as if she'd been grabbed from behind.

Eula passed a hand over the table. "You like it? Not fancy, don't go for things like that, but I saw it in this store and I thought of you right away. Hope you don't mind. Hope you don't got anything against taking gifts from a poor stranger."

A simple black dress, with raised black-stitched roses across the breast, and a black leather belt at the waist. A size she hadn't worn, hadn't been able to fit into, in decades.

"Say yes," Eula whispered, "and it's yours."

5

shouting

Stephanie wanted to scream.

It had been bad enough she hadn't been here when Eula finally came home, and Cable, shaking like a leaf, had bellowed at her for an hour, threatening her, stomping around the house, lashing out at everything he passed with a fist, a foot, telling her, screaming at her that he'd been through enough, goddamnit, and he wasn't about to make a damn jackass of himself crawling up the street to some voodoo black lady's séance or whatever the hell she was running up there, just so Stephanie, who couldn't hold a tune in a bucket, could pretend she was finally going to be a goddamn star.

An hour, while she cringed by the front door.

A full hour before he exhausted himself, hoarse, sweating as if it were noon in August, and begging her, practically weeping, not to make him do this thing.

Now he was in the street, throwing punches at the sky, doing his best to yell loud enough to wake the dead but too hoarse to do much more than croak, which only made him angrier.

Eula stepped out beside her, hands clasped in front of her, shaking her head. "My, that boy sure is afraid of something, ain't he?"

Stephanie tried to talk and gulp air at the same time. "He won't . . . he won't . . ."

"Sure he will, child, sure he will. He just needs a little time, that's all. A little time to work off that hate he got there, all that fear."

Cable spotted her then, and Stephanie froze when he pointed a finger, trembling with rage, and marched toward the porch.

"Don't worry," Eula assured her. "He won't hurt me. And he sure won't hurt you none."

At the foot of the steps he glared at each of them in turn, his face dripping perspiration, his eyes wide and insane. "You tell her," he said to Eula. "You tell her this crap isn't going to—"

Eula reached out and touched his face.

Stephanie braced herself for the slap, or the punch; even in bed, she wasn't allowed to touch his face.

Cable stiffened.

And Eula said, "How bad you want that Trey to be gone, not look at your woman the way he do? How bad, Mr. Cable? How bad?"

6

Moonbow stood resolutely beside her sister, and together they formed a barrier at the front door. Their arms were folded over their chests, their faces as hard as they could make them. It had been nearly half an hour since Cable Olin had gone bellowing up the street, more than that since Mrs. Carmody had wandered around, singing to herself so badly they wanted to cover their ears, and couldn't because it was so horribly fascinating. Twice in the past hour, Moonbow had raced down to Trey's, but he still wasn't home. The chariot was still in the carport, but there were no lights on inside, no response to her banging on the door, and the house . . . smelled . . . empty.

He hadn't come back.

Maybe, she had thought, he wasn't ever coming back.

But she didn't believe it. He had promised her, he had promised all of them that he was here to stay. Never again vanishing for weeks or months at a time, coming back in moods so black it made nighttime look like noon. Sometimes coming back like the last time, bruised and cut and wearing a cast.

He promised her a birthday present, a necklace of pearls.

But he wasn't back.

Tonight they were on their own.

"Momma," Starshine said, trying to imitate her mother's most stern voice, "you can't go. We . . . we're not gonna let you."

"That's right, Momma," Moonbow agreed. "You heard what's going on, we can't let you go."

Jude stood in the living room, back in the shadows where the end table lamp didn't quite reach. "I have to," was all she said.

Moonbow felt her sister wavering, and nudged her with a hip, reminding her she had an ally.

"We can't, Momma," Starshine said. "We can't let you do it."

"It isn't right," Moonbow said. "You know it isn't right. You know she can't do anything. If you'd just wait a little while, until Trey—"

"He's not coming back," Jude snapped. "You saw the suitcase, you told me he had a suitcase. He is not coming back."

"How do you know?" Moonbow answered, practically screaming. "You don't know that. You don't!"

"They're all there," Jude said patiently. "I have to be there, too."

"Roger isn't," Starshine said.

They had changed clothes as soon as they'd run back into the house once they'd greeted Eula, and they had huddled on the porch after the sun went down, watching them going up to Eula's one by one. It was spooky. None of them acted right. Muriel singing, Rick talking loud to himself, and Cable the worst with his yelling and screaming and looking like he was going to jump on Steph and beat her up.

But Roger wasn't there, hadn't shown his face.

Starshine took a deep breath. "Momma . . . if she can do what you . . . what you think she can, why doesn't she fix Roger, huh? Why doesn't she get him to stop drinking? If she's so good, she could do that with her eyes closed."

"Listen," Jude said, that patience growing thin enough to raise her voice, "in the first place, you do not tell me what I can and cannot do. I know you're concerned, but this is my decision, not yours." She moved out of the shadows, a long white dress, hair brushed to a shine, eyes glittering wetly above the veil. "And secondly, I cannot read her mind, so I don't know why she hasn't done anything for Roger."

"If she can," Starshine said sullenly.

"Maybe she already has," Jude countered. "Now let me pass, girls. I don't want to be too late. I don't want to miss . . . I don't want to be late."

They didn't move, and Moonbow was afraid her mother would push them both aside, and what would they do then, fight her? Really fight her? A look at her sister's face showed her she was thinking the same thing. And she knew that they wouldn't touch her. They would have to let her pass.

"Momma," Starshine said, "I'll make you a deal. *We'll* make you a deal."

"Yeah," Moonbow agreed. "We'll make you a deal."

Jude shook her head. "No deals, girls. Please move."

"You go to Roger's," Starshine said quickly. "You go to Roger's and see. Just see, okay? You do that for us, and we won't bug you anymore. Just go see him, Momma. Just go see."

"Yeah," Moonbow said, adding a firm nod. "For us, Momma, okay? Do it for us."

Jude put a hand to her brow, briefly covering her eyes. "No more trouble?"

"No, Momma," they answered quietly.

"You'll stay here?"

This time they hesitated, until Starshine finally said, "Yes, Momma. We'll stay here. We'll wait on the porch."

"No trouble," Moonbow said. "We won't cause any trouble, promise."

Jude looked at each of them carefully, weighing the strength and sincerity of their promise. Then, with a decisive nod: "All right. But you stay on the porch? You don't come sneaking after me?"

They agreed, adding a hint of *you don't trust us*? hurt that made Jude laugh without losing the frown they could see above the veil.

"Okay, then."

Moonbow moved first, and Jude walked between them, pushed open the screen door and waited for them on the porch.

The street was dark, except for Eula's place; and silent, except for the music they could hear, so happy, so excited, it made Moonbow want to spit.

"No cheating."

"No, Momma."

Starshine poked her arm. "But you have to come back and tell us first, okay?"

232

"Why, dear," Jude said with that same exaggerated *don't you trust me?* tone they'd used on her, "you think I'd cheat?" Then she took her hands on their shoulders, leaned over, kissed them on the top of the head. "This is important to me," she told them. "I want it to be important to you, too. That's the only reason I'm going to Roger's. Because I want you to want this for me, for yourselves, not just because I want it."

She kissed them again and hurried off, the slap of her sandals soft on the ground.

Once she was out of earshot, Moonbow rapped her sister on the arm. "What'd you do that for?"

Starshine rubbed the arm absently. "To give us time to think of something else."

"But we promised, Star. We promised."

"But if we stall long enough," she said, and looked down the street toward Trey's.

Moonbow understood, but she knew it wouldn't work.

She had seen the suitcase.

She knew Trey was gone, with that funny old man and that frightened woman.

"I just wish . . ." Starshine said.

"Wish what?"

Starshine turned around to show her sister the tears in her eyes. "I just wish that stupid bitch would turn that stupid music down!"

7

Jude walked quickly, drifting rather than angling toward the other side of the street. She was mad at her children for putting her in this position, and mad at herself for letting them do it. If she hadn't needed their support so badly she would have broken the deal without a second's thought. But she wanted them to be on her side. She needed them to understand she wasn't getting any younger, but she was definitely getting more lonely. It was amazing, a miracle, that they accepted her as well as they did, as if her face were the norm and all the others were disfigured. The girls had been that way since the beginning, and sometimes, in bed, Jude wept uncontrollably, soundlessly, because she knew she didn't deserve their strength.

So she would go over to Roger's, have a short talk, report back, and . . . go to Eula's.

The music was loud, and as she cut across Roger's front yard, she wasn't sure but she thought she heard laughter. Was it true, then? Could Eula do it?

She hopped onto the porch, made sure the veil was in place, and knocked on the door.

Yet if Eula really could do it, could do what she never said aloud but strongly implied, why wasn't she famous? Why wasn't she besieged with the crippled and the sick? Why did she stay here, in Emerald City?

She knocked again, harder, and the door swung open, a hinge creaking softly.

Wonderful, she thought; wonderful.

"Roger?"

No lights inside, except for a faint glow to the left, where an arch led to the narrow hallway that separated the front room from the bedroom and bath.

"Hey, Roger, it's Jude."

Freneau had a major crush on her; that had been obvious from the first day they'd met. Since then, it had been almost comical the way he stumbled around her, watched her from a distance like a foundling puppy uncertain about his welcome. She hadn't encouraged him because, aside from his sudden, ridiculous efforts to turn himself into a lush, there was something dark there that made her uneasy. Nothing she could put her finger on, but it was there nonetheless.

She sang, "Roger," and stepped inside.

He could be across the street, of course. He could already be at the party, if party it was. Still, she used the glow to keep her from tripping over furniture and piles of books and a few empty bottles, crossed the empty hall and stood in front of his open bedroom door.

"Roger?"

It smelled funny in here. A long time since a cleaning, and something else, but she couldn't place it. When she heard the groan, she closed her eyes briefly in disgust.

"Damnit, Roger, are you drunk again?"

She marched across the small room to the open bathroom door, looked in, almost didn't see him lying in the tub, only his bare knees showing. Then an arm flopped over the side.

Another moan, and violent coughing. "Jude, help me, huh?"

Common sense ordered her to turn around, go home, but she figured the least she could do was make sure he hadn't fallen while trying to take a shower. Drunk or not, maybe he needed medical attention. He might have cracked his skull on the porcelain, could be bleeding to death in there.

"Roger, how do you do it?" she said. Averting her eyes because the last thing she wanted to see was Roger Freneau naked, she grabbed his hand and pulled. "Did you fall?"

"Help," was all he said, voice rasping.

She pulled again, rolled her eyes as she realized she'd need to take his other hand. Pulling this way, on virtually dead weight, would only slide him around, not sit him up.

Which meant she would have to look.

She did.

"Jude . . . help . . ."

She jumped back so quickly her legs hit the toilet and she sat on it, hard, hands up as if to push the sight away.

His face and upper chest were marked with vivid pink pustules, most of them concentrated around his swollen lips, his puffy eyes, in the hollow of his throat. Thin trails of fresh blood twisted across his face from his brow where he'd been scratching; pus glistened on his chest, on his stomach; a foul darkness to his skin under the eyes and across his temples.

A stench that made her gag.

When his lips parted and she could see the bright color of his tongue, when he croaked, "Jude . . ." she screamed and ran, slipped on a small rug and slammed into the door. Screamed again and battered her way out of the house into the street, thinking that she had to get home, stand for as long as she could take it under a boiling shower, then take the girls and run.

It was here.

The Sickness was finally here.

8

walking

Ricardo, bobbing his head in time to the music, stood on Eula's back stoop, grinning so hard his cheeks began to ache. The kind of ache he would gladly suffer for the rest of his life. When Lil waved, he applauded. With both hands.

talking

*   *   *

"His name is Joker," Lil told him, riding the pinto up to the stoop. Her hair was loose and lovely, her cheeks flushed pink with pleasure. "I used to ride him in the show, remember? I don't how she did it, but it's Joker." She blew him a kiss, and the pinto reared, and Lil and Ricardo laughed.

singing

"If you don't come out of that bathroom now," Stephanie said, laughing and crying simultaneously, "I'm gonna explode!"

Muriel put her hands on her hips, stood on tiptoe, and tried to see lower than her waist. The dress fit perfectly, and Eula had given her a single-strand pearl necklace to complement the black. "Not bad for a broad of fifty-plus, huh?"

"Gorgeous," Stephanie agreed truthfully. "But Muriel, I gotta go!"

"It's the biggest mirror she's got," Muriel complained. "I want to see my legs."

Laughing, Stephanie grabbed her arms and yanked her out, kissed her cheek, shoved her away. "Later," she said, closing the door. "Later."

shouting

Cable stood in the middle of the living room, bellowing the words to the song Eula sang along with him. He didn't give a damn if they were the right words or not; he sang what he felt, what made him feel good and right and whole, what had detonated in his heart when he had seen the look on Steph's face after Eula had run her fingers over his forehead, his eyes, his nose, his cheeks, his chin with the dimple that had attracted Steph to him in the first place, so many years ago.

And oh, *Lord*, but he felt good!

Eula heard the scream and hurried to the door, pulling on her gloves. She stood on the porch, frowning, as she watched Judith Levin race ghostlike down the street, arms waving wildly.

No sense going after her.

That one was lost.

She didn't move when Stephanie joined her, still laughing a little, gasping for air, hands pressed to her chest.

"I don't know what to say," Stephanie said once she had herself under control.

Eula didn't answer.

"I've never seen him so . . . so . . ." A helpless wave for the loss of words.

Eula waited.

Stephanie wouldn't look at her. "I feel so ashamed, you know? because I can't help wondering if you could . . . if you could . . ."

walking talking singing shouting

All Eula said was, "How bad do you want it, girl? How bad do you want it?"

5

The celebration waned as they grew tired, and ignited again when Ricardo asked Muriel to dance with him under the moon, even if there wasn't a moon and the stars weren't anything to shout about either.

Eula heard it, nodded, and made her way around the outside of the house, so they wouldn't see her and grab her and thank her and weep over her and each other.

The air was still, the sky still fogged with thin clouds.

She stood at the corner, out of the light that slipped through the back door and the kitchen window, and waited while the pinto walked over to her, head bobbing, hooves silent. When it reached her, it pushed its muzzle against her chest, and she stroked its brow.

Then, in a single liquid motion that belied her size and age, she swung onto its bare back. Its ears pricked up, it snorted, it pawed the ground.

"That's right," she said. "That's right. It's time."

Part 4

CHARIOT

1

1

Trey stared at the back of Beatrice's head after she crawled into the front seat. Neither had spoken to him, and he couldn't think of anything to say, to them or to himself. There were other things he could do, of course:

He could assume, since it was after sunset, that he was dreaming. But he wasn't.

He could assume that the shock of his injury still lingered in his system, and his mind had decided to retreat until the pain and confusion had sorted themselves out. But there was no pain, only confusion.

He could assume that he was, pure and simple, out of his mind at last, all the bizarre, coincidental events of the past few years catching up to him in a single crushing wave. Overloading him. Tipping him over the edge. Sending him round the bend. Dropping him into the abyss. Lots of ways to put it, and no way to prove it had or hadn't happened. Which, he further assumed, probably meant it hadn't. A lousy string of logic, and oddly comforting.

Whatever the answer, he wasn't going to find it in the back of this car. And the answer was what he needed. Badly.

He had already put on the fresh clothes Sir John had made him bring, the blood-stained ones jammed into the suitcase.

"Where are we going?" he said, wincing at the dull sound of his voice.

"Home, I should imagine, is the best place for you now," Sir John answered solemnly.

It probably was.

Home. A shower. A couple of forty beers. Two or three bottles of the hard stuff. A long night's sleep filled with images of—

"No. Take me to the Strip."

Beatrice shifted so she could see him more easily. "Are you certain that's wise, Mr. Falkirk?"

"I'm not certain of anything," he answered irritably. "Just take me there."

"As you will," Harp said, glancing at him in the rearview mirror.

Not another word until, by accident or design, they were parked in the lot behind the Excalibur. Trey had already put on his boots, after wiping them off with his dirty shirt. The socks he discarded out the window when he felt them stiff with his blood.

Harp said, "We'll wait."

Trey opened his door. "Don't bother."

"Nevertheless," Harp said, and turned the engine off.

Trey was halfway up the carpeted ramp to the casino, pennants overhead, the voice of coins and cards already loud, when he realized he was limping. And realized he didn't have to.

A shudder, a determined roll of his shoulders, and he slipped instantly into the routine, taking the measure of a Saturday night, most of the tables filled and overflowing, the faces he saw flushed with excitement, grim with purpose, anxious with the overwhelming size and choices spread before them.

A party of seven, three with extravagant art deco masks, reminding him of the Japanese he had seen outside Madame Song's, and he veered away.

A woman seated on a padded red bench near Registration, flanked by two children no older than ten, waiting, he suspected by the expression on her face, for the father to come back so she could have her turn; the kids were simply tired and getting cranky.

A man in faded jeans and backward baseball cap standing in the middle of the keno area staring at the huge electronic board on the wall, watching the latest game's numbers light up, a single tear resting on the bulge of a fat cheek.

A middle-age couple talking with a security man in a plain brown suit, the husband resigned, the woman indignant: "Yes, we're from Oklahoma, but we've been here for three days, for God's sake. Damnit, we aren't taking any damn test, and if you make us, we'll sue, isn't that right, William?"

"Vera, I don't think this is the time—"

"Hush, William, these are our rights we talking about here. For God's sake, all I did was cough. Since when has that become a crime I want to know."

Like a fish in the monster aquarium where Beatrice had tried to tell him things, he darted in and out of the slot machine islands, testing, looking for a safe cave.

Hi, and no response.

He avoided the tall ones, the loudest ones, the complex ones, the jackpot ones; he looked for the simplest play, not wanting distractions.

Concentrating, walking, *hi how are you,* until he found one and grabbed the stool and a plastic cup, and sat down, nodding to his neighbor, a young woman who seemed to have forgotten the ciga-

rette dangling from her lips. He took a quarter, slid it in, and pulled
the bandit's arm.

"I'm afraid for him, John."

"No need. He needs to believe."

"You mean he doesn't? After all this, he still doesn't?"

"Yes. He does, but he needs to believe that he does."

"He's a good man, John. I don't want to see him hurt."

"About that I'm afraid we can do nothing. All we can do is be
patient."

"That's not the answer I want to hear."

"Beatrice, my dear, that's the only answer I have."

Take a quarter from the catch-tray, put it in, pull the arm.

Take a quarter from the catch-tray, put it in, pull the arm, wait
for the quarters to stop falling, clattering, each fall a chime.

How do you stand it? Beatrice wanted to know.

White noise, he'd answered; *it's all white noise.*

Before they reached the highway, they told him more about the
priest called Casey and the man called Bannock, and it hadn't taken
him long to follow their drift. Never speaking directly, they managed
to lead him to the idea they had planted earlier, that this was indeed
the Millennium of legend, and it made no difference whether you
believed it or not.

It was here, and They were riding.

Quarter in, pull the arm.

He was told about a preacher, white hair and intense, who believed in what he preached, but only believed so much until Bannock
somehow forced him to believe more, and Trey wondered if it was
the same man he had seen on television last week while searching

for a baseball game, or a movie, or anything to pass the time—unlike the other evangelists, this one was solemn and solemnly earnest; he didn't rant or exhort, and was all the more convincing for it.

Quarter in.

He was told about one teenager who died, and two others who lived, because living and dying are random at the end of the world.

Pull the arm.

And now, Trey supposed, he was supposed to believe that he had been driven back to Las Vegas because he was somehow important to the woman who called herself Eula. His accidents had been real; the results were not. It had taken him a while to figure out the truth—leaving town would kill him, staying here wouldn't.

As if—quarter in—he were being kept on ice—pull the arm—for the party to come.

He scooped the quarters from the tray into the bucket, realized he'd need another, and stuffed the remaining money into his jeans pockets.

And if all this was true—

"I have never been so insulted in my life," a familiar voice said behind him, shattering the white noise. "William, you should have stood up to him."

Trey swiveled around, clipping the man's leg with his knees. "Sorry," he said automatically.

"No problem," the man said.

Trey smiled up at him. "I get intense sometimes."

The man smiled back. "I know how you feel."

"So, what part of Oklahoma are you from?"

"Oklahoma City," William answered. Shook his head morosely. "Not that that's a good place to be from lately."

"William," the woman snapped, and walked away.

William gave Trey a what-can-you-do shrug and followed meekly.

Trey watched until he couldn't see them anymore, swiveled back to his machine, took a quarter, and watched his fingers pinch the coin hard enough to sting. Because if they didn't, he would drop it.

No, he thought. But he knew, just as he knew which machine would welcome him, that if he went back to the house and found the list Beatrice had given him, he would see that each major outbreak of the Sickness coincided with an appearance by Emerald City's gospel singer.

He already knew that her debut had been in Paris.

Quarter in.

Can't be.

Pull the arm.

He didn't believe it. Any of it. None of it. Not a word.

Listen to the falling quarters.

Jude and the girls, and Eula was home.

He stood so fast as he turned that he nearly fell against his neighbor, pulled away from her with a muttered apology, and stared blindly at the plastic bucket filled with his winnings. He touched it. He touched the side; it was real. He touched the coins; so were they.

He looked down and touched his leg where the bullet had gone through.

So was this.

He took the bucket to the Change booth and smiled as he was expected to when the woman commented brightly on his lucky streak tonight. He took the bills she gave him, and became stiff-legged, awkward, as he tried not to run through the casino. A few heads turned in his direction, wondering if he were drunk. He didn't care; not tonight. A wrong turn put him at the main entrance where the recorded voice of Merlin touted the banquet spectacle downstairs.

A moment to get his bearings, and he started for the back, was halfway there when a hand grabbed his arm.

"I thought," said Dodger O'Cleary, "that you were going to take care of that little problem."

2

O'Cleary pulled him unresisting out of the flow, into a niche beside the escalators that led to the shops and restaurants above. The man looked as if he could use a good night's sleep, but Trey was too confused to make a wisecrack.

"So one of our boys," O'Cleary said, keeping his voice low, his expression pleasant, his grip still in place, "is walking around the outside, checking cars and stuff, you wouldn't believe how many jerks we catch trying to use electronics out there to screw up things in here. Anyway—"

"Evening, Dodger," Trey said, equilibrium back. "Nice to see you, too."

"Anyway," O'Cleary repeated, "you'll never guess who he finds sitting out there?"

Trey smiled politely, said nothing.

"A weird old guy in a stupid Western jacket, and a woman young enough to be his granddaughter, for Christ's sake." He sighed loudly to mark the extent of his professional patience. "My guy asks them is everything's okay, and the old man says everything is fine, they're just waiting for a friend." The grip tightened, just a little. "They're not supposed to be here, Trey. Don't I remember telling you that? I'm sure I remember telling you that. They are not supposed to be here."

"It's a free country," Trey told him.

"Not in my casino, it ain't. Now, I don't care if you guys are buddies now or whatever. You told me you'd take care of it, pal, and you didn't."

"So I'm banned, right?"

O'Cleary's face darkened. "Getting close, Trey, getting close."

Trey didn't get it. He hadn't understood before, and now he really didn't get it. What the hell kind of threat were Harp and Beatrice to the Excalibur? Or any other casino in town, for that matter. They were looking for him, they found him. It seemed to him that O'Cleary didn't have a beef.

"I think," he said mildly, "you're overreacting a bit, don't you?"

The grip turned into a vise.

"You don't tell me my business, Trey, I don't tell you yours. Whatever the hell that is."

Trey looked pointedly at the hand on his arm, but O'Cleary didn't move it. "I'm going home, Dodger," he said. "I haven't done anything wrong, and neither have they. You want me banned, that's . . . whatever. I don't really care." His voice deepened. "Just let me go, lay off, okay?"

O'Cleary watched him carefully. "That a threat?"

Trey rolled his eyes. "Jesus, Dodger, what the hell's the matter with you?"

"Maybe," O'Cleary said, glancing at the ceiling, "You ought to come with me."

"Dodger, come on," he said, not getting the security man's attitude, "this is getting ridiculous."

"So now you're calling me ridiculous?" O'Cleary glowered and tugged. "That's it, pal, you're coming with me. There's some people upstairs who want to talk to you."

Trey stood his ground, anger narrowing his eyes. "Let. Go."

An unpleasant tiny smile touched the security man's lips.

"Just give me an excuse, Falkirk. Just give me an excuse." With his free hand he pulled a small walkie-talkie unit from his hip pocket, put it to his lips without taking his gaze from Trey's face. "O'Cleary here. Listen up. There's a car in the lot, license number—"

When Trey yanked his arm free, O'Cleary cursed and reached out to snag it again. Instead, what he caught was Trey's hand, and they stood there as if shaking hands in farewell.

Bewildered by the man's behavior, Trey recalled something Beatrice had said about his touch and the machines, about people, and as O'Cleary's face tightened and darkened because he couldn't budge Trey at all, he thought, *hi, how are you tonight,* because it was the only thing he could think of.

It was enough.

A flash of brilliant white, and all that he could see around them became a photographic negative for less than a second.

It was enough.

No images, no words, no thoughts; he just knew.

"You bastard," he said, not sure if he was shouting or not.

"You goddamn son of a bitch, you work for *her.*"

Sudden bedlam nearby as a dozen slot machines began to spill quarters and trumpet jackpots; people yelling, cheering, applauding; music blaring as customers converged on the clutch of winners, one or two noticing that one or two of the winning machines had no one playing them.

O'Cleary turned to look, gaping, and it was enough to allow Trey to break the grip and, without thinking and without caring, swing his left fist to strike just under the man's jaw. O'Cleary didn't fall, but he yelped and staggered into the rapidly growing crowd, which instantly welcomed him as another celebrant, spinning him around while he bellowed into his walkie-talkie until it was knocked from his hand.

Trey ran.

He used elbows and shoulders to shove his way through those who were trying to get past him to the machines. Ignoring the curses and the alarmed looks. Breaking free, searching the area for a sign of his location, then running again, out of the white noise into a cacophony that nearly deafened him. When he reached the ramp he slowed to a fast walk as one of the resident-tower guards appeared at the bottom.

"You should see it," Trey told him as he passed. "More winners than you can shake a stick at."

"No shit?" the guard said, but Trey was already through the doors and outside, trotting across the pavement to the blacktop, then sprinting for the car. He scrambled into the backseat and said, "Home, I have to get home. All hell's breaking loose."

"Not quite," said Harp dryly, but started the engine and left the parking lot in a hurry.

"What is it?" Beatrice asked anxiously.

"He was stalling me," Trey said, practically bouncing on the seat as if that would make the car go faster. "The son of a bitch was stalling me. Something's wrong at home. This ain't right. Something's wrong." He leaned forward to grab her shoulder. "He was working for her. My friend. He was working for her, did you know that?"

She shook her head quickly. "John?"

Trey slumped back, fighting to slow his breathing, not bothering to try to figure out how he had done what he had done. Nor did he try to guess what was happening in Emerald City. All he knew was that something had gone wrong there, and he had to try to stop it.

"John?" Beatrice said again. "John, you know what will happen if—"

"I know," Harp said calmly. "But the man must get home."

"Oh dear," she said. "Oh, dear."

Headlights flooded the car's interior, washed away and left the dark.

Suddenly Trey scrabbled at his belt buckle, swearing until it parted and he was able to yank his jeans down to his knees. When the next set of headlamps filled the interior, he saw the entry wound, and it was still there, still raw. When he poked it around the edges, he felt needles, distant but there.

He looked up and saw Harp watching him in the rearview mirror. "She took it away. The thing, the protection."

Harp nodded.

"But you don't need it now," Beatrice told him as he pulled his pants back up.

"Me?" He grinned, although he really didn't feel like it.

"Not exactly, but close enough." She looked over her shoulder, and he saw the dampness in her eyes. "Not as strong, of course, but yes, Mr. Falkirk, you're still protected. In a way."

He didn't question her because he knew that now there were no doubts, no more questions. It terrified him, made him shiver with a cold that wasn't there, but he believed it at last; he believed it all.

"I can't kill her," he said, looking for a way to marshal his courage.

"No," Sir John said.

"But I can kind of . . . what? Stall her?"

No answer.

Unconsciously he touched his jeans where the bullet hole was.

"Does she know this?"

"She does now."

"Oh, man, she's gonna be pissed."

"Oh, my dear fellow," Sir John said, laughing, "you have absolutely no idea."

3

Harp turned the headlights off once they reached Emerald City's access road, and slowed the car to a maddening crawl. Trey scooted over to the right side and lowered his window a couple of inches.

The engine's soft grumbling, the crunch of tires over pebble and sand on the crumbling blacktop.

The wind, slow and steady, not much more than a breeze.

In the distance, the houses along the street were squat silhouettes against a bright glow from Eula's place, each more vague the closer to the intersection they were. He couldn't see his own house at all.

For a while he thought he heard music and maybe, although he wasn't sure, the sound of laughter; for a moment he thought he heard the quiet neighing of a horse. But when he strained, he heard nothing but the tires and the wind, and he inhaled with a shudder.

"What time is it?"

Beatrice said quietly, "A few hours before dawn."

He forced a laugh. "Just like a Western." He raised the window, cut off the noise. "So, do you guys have some kind of magical sixgun for me? Because if you do, I sure would like to see it about now."

"No sixguns, Mr. Falkirk," Harp said regretfully. "Or magic wands. Or magic spells."

The car stopped a hundred yards from the intersection.

"Well, that's okay. You guys going to be my sidekicks?"

Neither of the Harps answered.

He sat with his hands folded in his lap. He had already known the answer, but he had to ask anyway. With his hand on the door handle, he closed his eyes briefly, then opened the door and slid out.

What it always comes down to, he thought as he waited for his night vision to find his house; alone, what the hell.

Then he smiled, moved to the passenger door, and rapped a knuckle on the window until Beatrice lowered it. He leaned over and grinned at the dismay he saw on her face, at the unreadable expression on the old man's profile.

"You know," he said, shook his head and chuckled softly. He placed the back of a finger against Beatrice's cheek, and she leaned into it, for a moment, just a little. Then he took the finger away. "You know, you guys still haven't told me who you are. But you know something else? All that stuff you told me, about how you're not divine or supernatural?" He stepped away from the car. "That's the only thing about all this now that I don't believe for a second."

He made his way off the road without looking back, concentrating on keeping away from the cactus and the scrub, his home beginning to define itself in the dark he knew wouldn't last much longer. By the time he reached the back door, he had to remind himself to breathe; once inside, he had to order himself not to turn on any lights.

His previous sense of urgency had gone, leaving behind only expectation, and he wasn't sure if that was a relief or not.

He had no idea what was going on up there at Eula's house, or what had already gone on, but he had a feeling he didn't need to. As he dropped onto the couch and pushed his fingers back through his hair, he also wasn't so sure he actually needed to make a plan, since he had no idea at all what the hell he was going to do.

Or what, exactly, he was supposed to do.

It was all so overwhelming that it all seemed perfectly natural.

Just sitting here wasn't, however, especially when he smelled like he'd just spent several hours hanging around a pig sty. He could always go to bed, work things out once the sun rose, but it didn't take a genius to realize he wouldn't get any sleep. So to keep his brain reasonably on target, he stripped off his clothes and wandered into the bathroom, deliberately avoiding a look in a mirror, and took a shower as hot, then as cold, as he could stand it. Feeling the muscles in back and stomach, arms and legs bunch and relax. Grabbing a peek at his left leg because he just couldn't resist, then scrubbing the faint pink scar as hard as he could, daring it to hurt and cursing mildly when it didn't because he didn't really think it would, but what the hell, it was a shot, right? It was another shot at the old *I'm dreaming* explanation.

By the time he was dry and dressed, several internal systems reminded him that he hadn't eaten for hours, and it wouldn't do to drop from starvation weakness right in the middle of whatever comes next.

Without thinking, he flicked on the kitchen light and made himself a thick sandwich, washed it down with a glass of almost tart orange juice, and decided that maybe he really ought to have a plan after all. For what, he had no idea, and the Harps were obviously halfway to wherever it was that they disappeared to when they weren't busy telling him his life wasn't what he thought it had been.

He went out to the front porch, leaned against the post so that he could look up the street and, because of the night, not be seen, in case anyone was watching.

A soft glow and a soft wind.

His nose wrinkled as he smelled dry dust on the air, and he rubbed a finger across his upper lip, then scratched behind his ear.

You are, he thought, entirely too damn calm.

His stomach didn't agree, and neither did the ice-spiders that strolled up and down his arms, his spine, raising gooseflesh here and there until he hurried inside and dropped back onto the couch.

"Okay," he said to the living room. "Okay."

The chairs, the coffee table, the television on its cheap wood stand were too vague to look at in the dim glow from the kitchen. Highlights on the screen and on smooth wood surfaces gave the illusion they were made of dark glass, and when he turned his head slightly they seemed to shift, slipping toward him, slipping away.

Entirely way too calm, you jerk; entirely way too calm.

Still, the ghostly images drove him back into the kitchen, where he poured another glass of juice and sat at the table, staring at the radio he had unplugged the other night.

Curiously enough, what bothered him, what began to unnerve him and annoy him as he sat with his hands cupped around the glass, wasn't the business with Eula, or what he was supposed to do about it; it was the way he had assumed, back there in the car, that he was, in fact, supposed to do something about it.

No options had been offered.

There were always options.

From a cupboard above the sink he fetched a cheap ashtray, one that had been in some hotel or other until he'd slipped it into his suitcase a couple of lifetimes ago. He put it on the table, walked around the table once, a finger trailing along the surface, then took a pack from the drawer next to the sink, sat, lit a cigarette, and followed the smoke's plume as it made its way toward the ceiling like a sidewinder's ghost.

Options:

He could ignore it all, keep his life simple, add to his stash and . . . He snorted. Sure. Right. Sometimes options weren't options at all.

He could borrow Jude's gun, walk up to Eula's, knock on the door, shoot her right between the eyes, and end it right now. Tempting, but too easy. Much too easy. He had never read the Bible except for excerpts in church, but he had a powerful inclination that someone like her wouldn't be stopped by something so simple.

He could always run, but like the old cliché says, he sure couldn't hide. Besides, running would mean abandoning Jude and the girls. He was perhaps a fool, but he wasn't an idiot.

His gaze shifted absently to the long ash on the cigarette. When he twitched his finger, the ash fell onto the table in two long pieces, like, he thought, a column fallen from some ancient temple.

Which made him think of something else: accepting the premise of Eula's nature had to mean that she wasn't demonic, wasn't satanic, wasn't a creature loosed from the bowels of Hell. Which meant . . . he put the cigarette down, pushed at it with a finger until it fell into the ashtray. Which meant she was, theoretically, one of the Good Guys.

He squeezed his eyes shut, shook his head sharply, and fished another cigarette from the pack and lit it, blew smoke, and decided he wasn't clever enough to handle stuff like that. He was a gambler, not a philosopher; just keep it straight and simple, don't get yourself lost in a Biblical swamp.

Halfway through the second cigarette, it occurred to him that neither Sir John nor Beatrice had actually said he had to fight. They had made a great point of telling him about the others, Chisholm and Bannock and those who were with them, but they'd said nothing, not really, about actually standing up to Eula Korrey. In fact, Beatrice had straight out told him he had to go find these guys, right? Didn't she say that? That he had to go find these guys?

He sat up.

Yet if he did, if he tried . . .

"Son of a bitch."

He looked around the kitchen, hoping something on the counters, in the cupboards, on the floor, in the air, would warn him away from the conclusion he had reached.

"No."

He crushed the cigarette out so furiously it fell apart, tobacco spilling across the table.

"No."

He was halfway out of his chair when someone pounded on the front door, then shoved it open. He tried to move quickly, but his feet tangled with the chair legs, knocking it over sideways, forcing him to grab the table's edge so he wouldn't fall as well. By the time

he was able to stand again, the girls were in the room, yelling at
him. Their eyes were swollen from crying, cheeks flushed with helpless anger. Starshine's hair was loose and wild, strands clinging to
her face; Moonbow's T-shirt was smudged and damp with tears.

"Where were you?" Starshine demanded in a near scream, slapping his chest as hard as she could while grabbing for his arm.

"We thought you'd left," Moonbow yelled, grabbing his other arm.
"Where were you? We thought you'd left."

They couldn't decide which way to pull him, and so practically
tugged him over the table before he could brace himself and yank
himself free. "Stop it!" he snapped. "Damnit, stop it!"

They froze, lips quivering, breath coming in hard hitches.

"What the hell's going on here? And what the hell are you doing
up so early?"

Moonbow tried to answer, couldn't, and Starshine, glaring, teeth
bared, said, "You left. You left us."

"I left," he said tautly. "I'm back. You haven't answered my question."

Moonbow shook her head. "What's the matter, Trey? Don't be
mad. What's the matter?"

His right hand shoved at his hair, while the fingers of his left
tapped stiffly against his leg. Having finally understood what the
Harps expected him to do, he hadn't realized how furious he was
until the girls had charged in, cornering him, accusing him, pushing
him on the defensive. He couldn't take it out on them, they had
nothing to do with it, didn't even know about it, and he held up a
hand to keep them silent until he was able to muster some semblance of calm.

What he wanted to say was, "Look, kids, I've had a really crappy
day, okay? I've been shot, left in the desert to maybe die, sort of
kind of healed myself I think maybe, punched out a guy I thought
was a friend because he's working for a woman who really isn't who

you think she is, and I'm not in the mood for your goddamn kid hysterics."

What he said was, "Tell me."

There was a brief silence before Starshine blurted, "Momma, Trey, it's Momma. There's something real wrong with her. Something bad."

2

1

Trey had too many images and no reliable information as he followed the girls at a run through the house and across the street. He was aware of their footsteps on the dirt, of the still-blowing wind, of the night that hadn't cooled off as much as it should have for this time of year. He was aware of the way his lungs wouldn't work exactly right, causing him to gulp air despite the shape he was in. He was aware of a spreading heat across his face, of a midnight chill in his stomach, of a muffled steady roar in his ears that had nothing to do with the girls' constant desperate chatter, making no sense, only saying that Jude had gone out around eleven and returned shortly afterward, crying, pushing them away, racing into the bedroom and locking the door behind her.

"We saw your light," Starshine said, slapping open the front door.

"We were watching," Moonbow told him, practically shoving him inside.

A few long strides took him to the arch; another took him to the bedroom door, where he knocked and said, "Jude? Jude, it's Trey, you all right?"

The girls stayed back, holding hands, doing their best not to cry. He knocked again. "Jude?"

A voice on the other side, but he couldn't make out the words.

"Jude, I can't hear you. Let me in, okay?"

"Don't touch me!" Jude screamed. "Stay away! Don't touch me!"

Jesus, he thought, and looked over his shoulder. "She tell you anything? Anything at all?"

Moonbow shook her head. "I couldn't understand her. She was . . . she was . . . I couldn't understand her."

"She went to see Eula," Starshine said, fear and anger in her voice. "We made her a deal. She wanted to see Eula, but she had to go see Roger first."

"What? Why, for God's sake?"

Moonbow sank to the floor, crossed her legs, grabbed her knees. "Momma wanted to be better." Her voice quiet, each word an effort. "She said Eula would fix the others, and she wanted to be fixed, too."

Aw, Jesus, he thought; dear God, aw Jesus.

Starshine knelt beside her, an arm around her shoulders. "We made her a deal. We said she could go if she'd see Roger first and find out why he wasn't with *them*. She promised us. She said you'd left again. She promised us." Her face twisted; she swallowed hard. "Where were you, Trey? Why weren't you here?"

He looked back at the door. "Jude, let me in."

She screamed something incomprehensible, and something thumped hard against the door. A shoe, probably; it made him jump.

He straightened, inhaled slowly. "Jude, I'm not kidding. If you don't unlock the door now, I'm going to break it in." The girls made a sound like a whimper, or a stifled scream. "I'll do it, Jude. The kids are scared to death, and I'm telling you, I'm not doing so well out here myself." He leaned closer. "Jude. Please. Unlock the door."

He stared at his feet, at the tiny gap between the door and floorboards, nodding when he heard the lock turn over, wondering if the kids could hear her crying.

"Stay here," he ordered.

They didn't move.

Another deep breath, and he opened the door just wide enough for him to slip in; when he closed it again, he waited until his eyes adjusted to a faint light that slipped past the partially ajar bathroom door. Jude sat in the corner on the other side of the bed, knees drawn to her chest, arms wrapped around her shins.

"Don't touch me," she warned when he stepped around the footboard in order to see her more clearly. "Stay away. Don't touch me."

A gentle question: "What happened, Jude?"

"Don't touch me, please don't touch me."

Left hand on the footboard for balance, he lowered himself into a crouch, balancing on the balls of his feet. "I won't, Jude, I won't. Tell me what happened."

She tried to make herself smaller. "I'm going to die. Don't touch me. I'm going to die."

He blocked most of the bathroom's light; it was like looking at her through dark gauze. "You're not going to die, Jude."

She shook her head. "Yes, I am. I saw him." Her voice rose, near hysteria. "I *touched* him." Her voice fell, near sorrow. "I'm going to die."

"Talk to me, Jude. Man of action, remember? Maybe I can help, but you gotta talk to me."

She raised her head, and her dark eyes held glints of silver. "Roger has the Sickness. I found him. I didn't know." She began to rock, to get excited. "I found him. In his bathtub. His face." She began to bounce a little. "His skin. I didn't see it at first, Trey. I swear to God, I didn't see it at first so I tried to help him out because I thought he'd fallen or was drunk, but he wasn't drunk, he was sick, and oh God, Trey, I touched him. I reached out, and I touched him."

He didn't hesitate. He pushed forward onto his knees, reached out and grabbed for her arms. She cried out and pulled away, slapping at his hands, his arms, his legs. "Don't touch me, you'll die, don't touch me, I'm dying." He batted away the slaps, his head back so she wouldn't accidentally punch him, and this time grabbed her shoulders and yanked her toward him, gathered her to his chest, and held her tightly while she struggled and cried and pleaded with him to let her go because she didn't want him to die, didn't he understand, she didn't want him to die.

One arm around her back, his right hand cupping her head firmly, he waited until whatever terrified her drained her and she couldn't struggle anymore. Weeping instead, and he could feel the tears seep through his shirt, warm on his chest.

He held her.

He rocked her.

When even the tears were too much and she could do nothing but moan softly, he said, "Jude, I'm not going to die."

"Yes," she said.

"No."

"I touched him. You can get it by touching."

"I know." He stroked her hair. "I know you can." He stroked her back. "But I'm not going to die. And you're not going to either."

For five minutes, ten, he rocked and he whispered and when she finally lifted her face, her veil pushed down over her ravaged nose, he looked down at her and said, "I ain't lying, Jude. You're all right now. I ain't lying."

In the dark he could almost imagine that her face was whole.

When she realized the veil was nearly off, she gasped, but he wouldn't let her free to set it back in place.

"Jude."

She rested her forehead against his chest. "I don't want to die. The girls . . . I don't want to die."

"You won't."

She shook her head. "How do you know?"

"Funny you should ask." He looked to the door and suspected the girls were on the other side, trying to eavesdrop, too scared to barge in. "If you got a minute, I got a hell of a story to tell you."

2

There was no light in the desert, but she didn't need any. She rode the pinto in a large circle well away from Emerald City, humming to herself, nodding every once in a while, touching the horse's neck whenever it shied from a shadow.

She had sent the others home after telling them when she expected them back, and not five minutes after the last one had left, she had known.

She had *known.*

Rage had clenched her fists so tightly blood dripped from her palms; fury had made her storm through the house, swinging at anything that got in her way, each punch spilling more blood as a door was slammed off one hinge, as a mirror was shattered into black shards that rippled into shadows that slid into the walls, as the walls trembled and the ceilings bulged and dust fell like fine rain.

She rode to find calm.

She rode to remind herself that those who had gone before her had been stymied as well, that none of it really mattered because she was who she was and it wouldn't happen to her.

Because she *knew*.

She *knew* that nothing the old man and that foolish stupid woman told the gambler would do him any good, knew that their time was short and she was going to make it shorter, knew that she had an army and all he had was children and cripples and old men and stupid women who didn't know enough to know how hard they would die.

The pinto snorted, steam roiling from its nostrils.

"Hush, now," she whispered, caressing its neck and mane. "Hush, now."

It was time to get back.

Time to get ready.

When she reached the boulder that marked the edge of the gambler's world, she read the words he'd scratched into it, and she lifted her face to the stars and she laughed.

3

In the mountains, coyotes howled.

On Lake Mead there were whitecaps.

In the desert, the wind blew, and dust and sand lifted from the ground and formed a cloud.

That waited.

4

When he dreamed before, when he imagined himself a great sports star whose prowess and fine looks were known throughout the world, it was, before, soccer of which he was king.

In soccer hands were a liability unless you were a keeper.

In soccer you were penalized if you used your hands to touch the ball.

Now, drifting through a light sleep in which dreams were a wafer's width beyond his control, he was a gridiron star, a basketball hero, an unbloodied two-fisted heavyweight champion of the world.

Top of the world, Ma; top of the world.

A moan and a grin as he rolled onto his side.

Top of the goddamn world, and all he had to do to stay there was rip a gambler apart.

Lying on top of the sheets, hands folded on her stomach, too astonished, too bewildered, too excited to sleep, Stephanie Olin stared at the darkness with a grin so wide she thought the corners of her mouth would split and tear her cheeks. Cable lay with his back to her, every so often punching his pillow to reform it, drawing his legs up, straightening them out, sighing quietly, grunting as if he found it difficult to breathe.

She touched his bare hip, stroked it, squeezed it lightly, an often-used trick to settle him down when his dreams got the best of him.

This time, however, he wasn't sleeping.

"Honey?"

"Yeah?"

"What's the matter?"

He stirred under her hand, pulling away, and she frowned.

"What is it?"

"I don't know," he said, almost growling. "I don't think I can, Steph. This whole thing . . . I don't think I can do it."

That didn't surprise her. Once he'd stopped examining himself in the mirror just in case it was a trick and he hadn't changed a bit, he had become quiet, almost sullen, and didn't even take the hint when she'd stood at the foot of the bed and gave him a slow strip.

She kept her voice even. "What are you talking about?"

"You know what I mean."

She sat up, suddenly punched his shoulder so hard he flipped onto his back with a curse, automatically reaching for her arm. She hit him again, on the chest, as hard as she could.

"Jesus, Steph!"

"No," she said, leaning over him, grabbing his chin, squeezing his cheeks. "You will not screw this up for me, Cable, you hear me? You screw this up, you bastard, Trey isn't the only one seeing angels in the morning."

He didn't try to break free, didn't try to hit back. "Steph, for God's sake, what's the matter with you?"

"Nothing," she said, barely recognizing her own voice. "Nothing. Not anymore."

She released him with a snap of her wrist, fell back onto her pillow, and wondered why she had put up with him all these years, all his harsh words, the once-in-a-while slap, the snarls and the animal sex. Maybe it had been love once; it wasn't love anymore.

Shape up or ship out, she thought to him angrily; you blow this one, brother, you're on your own, I'm not dragging you to the top with me.

Satisfied, ultimatum given, she smiled and dozed and dreamt of being a star.

*   *   *

"You ever coming to bed?" Muriel called. Not that she cared. It just seemed like the right thing to say.

"No," Lillian called back, laughing. "I'm practicing, okay?"

"You can walk, what's to practice?"

"The feel of it, you old cow. The feel of it."

Not so old, Muriel thought, for the hundredth time running her hands along the new flat of her stomach, over the new firmness of her breasts, along the new curve of her hips; not so old that I have to put with your shit anymore.

"For God's sake, Lil," she yelled, "we gotta be up in a couple of hours!"

"I'm already ready," Lil called back, still laughing, still wandering the living room, the kitchen, the narrow hall. "You have no idea how ready I am."

Muriel sighed, but she smiled. "So what're you gonna use? The gun? I got dibs on the gun."

"Shit no, Mother, I'm gonna ride that son of a bitch down."

Muriel laughed.

Her daughter laughed with her.

"Jesus God Almighty!" Lillian shouted. "Praise Jesus God Almighty!"

"Watch your language," Muriel snapped. "It's Sunday, remember?" A moment later she yelled, "And save your damn strength, you stupid child. You're gonna need it."

The angel, Roger guessed it might have been Jude, left him in the bathtub, and it had taken him over an hour of patient waiting before he could crawl out. God knows how long after that before he could haul himself up to the sink and turn on the water. He figured he drank a gallon, but it didn't do any good. His skin felt fiery and tight, and he could feel the pustules splitting, could feel the liquid burning down his cheeks, his chest, running down his sides from under his arms. He didn't think about what Eula had done to him. He didn't think about how long he had to live. All he wanted to do was stop the fire inside and out; all he wanted to do was do something right for a change before it was too late. Calling the cops wasn't an option. What would he tell them? That an old black bitch had cast a spell or something on him? That the world-famous gospel singer and lovable old woman was really some kind of witch or demon? Even if he held a Bible in both hands they wouldn't believe him. Not after what he'd done today. Hell, once they got a look at him they'd figure he was raving because of the fever, because of the Sickness, because he was dying.

He staggered, stumbled, fell into the living room and crawled toward the open cardboard box he kept handy beside the couch. If he got there soon enough, if he could open one of the bottles inside, he might be able to drink the pain away, or at least keep it at arm's length. Either way, it would be enough. Either way, he'd find the strength to make it outside. And once there, he'd make his way down to Jude's and show her what happened to angels who left the sick and lame behind.

3

1

Trey stood with his back to the room, staring through the slats in the blinds. He saw nothing out there; he was too busy listening to the breathing behind him. Jude and the girls sat on the couch, and once he had finished they hadn't said a word. He knew, however, that Jude believed him. She had to, or she wouldn't have planned on going to see Eula. The kids, on the other hand, hadn't given him a clue, and halfway through his story he had turned to the window so he wouldn't see their faces, shimmering in the faint light drifting from bedroom and kitchen. Starshine clearly skeptical, Moonbow clearly afraid.

Belief or not, putting it all together aloud had convinced him of one thing—he had no intention of taking on Eula Korrey. He was a guy, nothing more; he wasn't a superman or superhuman. Just a guy with a weird talent, and that definitely did not include taking on part of the end of the world.

Finally he said, "The sun's almost here."

Across the street he could just make out the outline of Stephanie's house, the front windows taking shape as if the building were waking up, getting ready to open its eyes.

"You're gonna leave," Starshine said, flat and accusing.

"Not alone if I can help it," he answered.

Jude cleared her throat with a quick harsh cough. "If . . . if we go with you, where will we go?"

"As far away as we can get before she knows we're gone."

"And when she does?"

"I don't know."

"The girls, Trey."

He put his back to the window, saw them looking at him. Jude's eyes were invisible above the veil, Starshine's were narrow, Moonbow's were wide and shining. They were all holding hands, and he did his best not to grin when he understood they weren't questioning the truth of the story; they wanted to know how he planned to protect them.

He glanced down at his feet, shook his head, looked up again. "Listen, this isn't something my mother prepared me for, you have to understand that." A hand brushed nervously across his chest. "I guess this kind of thing isn't in the Mother's Handbook."

"No," Jude said, voice telling him she was smiling. "If it is, I missed that page."

"So what I'm saying is . . . what I . . ." His fingers brushed his shirt again, and stopped when they felt the gold chip inside. A weak wavering smile that folded into a frown when he pulled it out and stared at it, turning it over, turning it back. A sound in his throat, a laugh stillborn. "No." He slipped it back under his shirt. "No, that's too much even for this." He patted his chest and brushed the absurdity away, then checked over his shoulder. "I'm going to get the truck. You've got that long to throw some things into a suitcase."

Moonbow pushed off the couch and looked at her sister, who didn't move until Jude nudged her. Then she too stood, but instead of following Moonbow into the bedroom, she crossed the room and stood in front of him. She's too old, he thought; much too old for a child her age.

"You know you're gonna get hurt if we go," she said, arms stiff at her sides, lips barely moving.

"I've been hurt before, Star."

"We could use the gun."

"Honey," Jude said from the couch.

He leaned over and, before she could move, cupped a cheek with his hand, gratitude for her concern. "We'll need the gun for someone it'll hurt. I don't think she's it."

"But—"

"No, Star, we have to go." He pulled his hand down the cheek and away, and poked her shoulder. "Now git. There's not much time."

She nodded and ran from the room.

Trey blew out slowly. "This wasn't exactly how I planned to sweep you and the girls off your feet, you know."

Jude nodded. "I know."

He wanted to say something else, something clever, something to mark this time in memory, but there were no words, only a sad shrug before he headed for the door. When she didn't stop him, didn't offer words of her own, he went to the porch and checked the street. It was empty, but he could see the houses now, brightening, growing out of the dark as the dark drained away.

Not much time, and he ran to the house, to the bedroom where he pulled the metal strongbox from under the bed. Tucking it under his arm, he walked quickly up the hall and into the kitchen, saw nothing he needed, and checked the living room.

Nothing.

He had nothing to take with him.

He grabbed his jacket, the keys, and closed the door and locked it, more out of habit than a belief that he would ever return. Once done, he felt strange, free and confined at the same time, but he refused to think about it as he crossed the porch and stepped down under the carport. He tossed the strongbox and the jacket into the gap behind the seats and, keeping a watch on the street, he bent down to climb in, and whacked his brow against the frame.

"Damn," he muttered, standing again, swaying a little as he rubbed the injured spot and checking his fingers to be sure there was no blood, positive he had hit the edge hard enough to break the skin. This time he braced a palm against the frame, but this time he didn't get in because he knew he'd hit his head because the frame was too low. Getting into a vehicle was virtually automatic; you knew how high it was, how low you had to duck to get in without taking half your head off.

The gap between house and truck was too narrow to crouch comfortably in so he moved to the front, stood back a step, and saw all four tires bulging and flat to the ground. He only checked the right front, running his hand around the rubber until he found the gash. The others would be the same.

Running footsteps, and the girls raced by him to open the passenger door.

Hushed whispers: "Put them in the back."

"We'll get squished, 'bow. There's not enough room. We'll stick them in the bed."

"But they'll bounce out!"

"He's got rope there, remember? We'll tie them down."

Trey put a hand on the hood to help him to his feet, then leaned against it, head down as though packed with lead.

"I can't tie ropes, you jerk."

"I can, you dip."

Softer footsteps, scuffing over the ground, and a hand on his spine. "Something wrong?"

He was too weary to nod. "The tires." He pushed upright and turned to her. "The goddamn tires are slashed."

Jude stepped to one side and squinted into the half-light, one hand at her throat. "Who?"

He gestured vaguely up the street. "Who the hell knows?" He punched the air. "Who the hell cares, it's done."

A squeal, and Moonbow skidded around the truck. "Trey, the tires!"

"I know." He sniffed, put his hands on his hips, lifted his face to the sky. "I know."

"What're we gonna do?"

Starshine joined them, swinging her arms nervously. "We can take Cable's car, maybe. Or Ricardo's."

"You have keys?" Moonbow asked her derisively.

"No."

"Oh. So you can hot-wire a car, huh?"

"Very funny, dip, very funny."

"Well, you're the one who said—"

"Stop it," Trey said, so firmly and quietly they backed off quickly, then eased around him to stand beside their mother. When Starshine started to ask a question, he added, "Hush. I need to think."

As he watched the morning's soft blue nudge the dark west, he wondered why they had gone to all this trouble. Eula knew what would happen to him if he left town, so why didn't she just let him go? Keeping him here served no purpose, made no sense. Unless . . .

He walked slowly down the drive to the street and looked south, toward her house.

Unless she couldn't let him go. Unless she couldn't take the chance that he'd survive long enough to join up with those two other men. What might happen then he had no idea, couldn't even begin to guess, but it was clear, now, that simply keeping him safe so she could keep an eye on him was no longer one of her options.

The notion that he, somehow, was a threat almost made him laugh aloud. He was a gambler, for crying out loud. Worse, he played the slots, quarter in, pull the arm, what the hell kind of gambling was that?

A morning breeze slipped through his hair, across his face; warm, and promising heat.

A tiny dust devil tottered drunkenly through the empty lot across the street.

"Keys," Jude said.

He frowned. "What?"

"Give me your keys, I'll go inside and call a cab."

Without waiting for an answer, Moonbow raced over and snatched them from his pocket, ran to the door and was inside before he could tell her it was a stupid idea, he didn't think Eula would wait that long. But the look Jude gave him, the expression on Starshine's face, kept him quiet. They were grasping for the straws that would build them a way out, and he wasn't about to stop them. He didn't have the heart. He didn't have the courage.

Starshine wandered down the length of the pickup, examining the tires, searching for a miracle. Jude stayed where she was, hands clasped in front of her, a small travel bag at her feet.

"She's going to be angry, you know," he said, loud enough for her to hear, hopefully not loud enough for Starshine.

"I know."

"I should have left when I had the chance. Bring you into this . . ." He shook his head.

"Karma," she said.

"Bullshit," he told her. And grinned when she made a gesture and a sound that told him he hadn't learned a thing after all this time, that she wasn't as off the wall as he believed.

But she was, and that was one of the reasons why he loved her.

Well, damn, he thought as he looked away, suddenly embarrassed; this is a hell of a time to figure that out, you jerk.

Then Starshine called his name just as her sister left the house. The look on Moonbow's face told him all he needed to know about the time it would take for a cab to fetch them, but he smiled anyway and hurried to the backyard when Starshine called him again.

"Look," and she pointed toward the mountains, shading her eyes against a slow steady wind that had kicked out of the breeze.

"What?" Moonbow demanded. "I don't see anything. What are you talking about?"

Trey saw it without help.

It seemed at first to be nothing more than a morning haze that blurred the distant range and the desert floor. But there was no water out there, no man-made lake or natural stream.

It wasn't a haze; it was a cloud.

Although it was still several miles away, Jude touched the girls' shoulders to pull them back, then turned them and pushed them toward the street. "Inside," he heard her tell them. "We have to get inside."

He didn't move.

A long time ago, he had been on the banks of Lake Superior, watching a thunderstorm make its way toward him from the west. Black clouds gliding effortlessly across the blue turned the land and water beneath them to hazy midnight, and he could feel the storm's cold wind, see the rain making its way over the water. He had been so fascinated by the sight that it had taken a crackling bolt of lightning to make him sprint for the nearest shelter before he was drenched.

The storm, as intense and violent as it turned out to be, didn't last as long as its approach. At least in his memory, where the clouds and the rain took their own sweet time. The better, he had thought then, to scare him half to death before it crushed him.

Here, the sky didn't change from its gentle early blue, and the wind wasn't cold, and there was no rain.

Only sand, and dust, and bits and pieces of brittle grass and dead cactus and whatever else it found lying loose on the stark desert floor. Only browns and tans and an occasional black stripe, darker in its huge long center, throwing twisting pale tendrils of itself at the rising sun and the land around it.

The storm on Lake Superior had a beauty about it, dark and powerful; this storm had no beauty at all, just the browns and the tans and the swirling black stripes and bands he knew would vanish when it was close enough and became a solid grinding fog.

The way it moved, its direction and speed, told him it would bypass the development a good distance to the south, and probably wouldn't even reach the city. Tempting, then, to consider it an omen of some kind, but he couldn't figure out what it might mean, so he returned to the street, rubbed his chest, and started walking.

Jude called from his front door.

He didn't look back. He wanted to know where everyone was, and he figured getting them up this early would give him some advantage in case they had aligned themselves with Eula, the only conclusion he could reach after hearing about the festivities Jude hadn't attended last night. Not that he was all that concerned. The only one who might give him serious trouble was Cable, who was bigger and heavier and definitely meaner.

Unless, he realized as he stepped onto the Olins' porch, they all brought their guns.

He froze.

You are, he thought, just too stupid to live.

A snap of his fingers, and he ran back to Jude, still waiting on the porch. He said, "Your gun," and she pulled it out from behind her back, a small nickel-plate revolver she told him was already loaded.

"I was hoping," she said, smiling and scolding at the same time. "The storm's not coming this way. How long for the cab?"

"They told me an hour," Moonbow answered from the doorway, saw the gun in his hand, and turned so pale he feared she would pass out. Jude saw the reaction and wrapped her arms around her, hugging her tightly while her frown told him to get on with it, you're wasting time you don't have anymore.

A nod, and he ran easily, a lope, not going full-out because he didn't want to be winded when he reached Steph's house.

Once there, he took a few seconds to convince himself that this was something he really had to do. "Preemptive strike" was a phrase he remembered from the news, but however apt now, who-ever used it didn't know that he had never pointed a gun at anyone in his life. When he had to protect himself, it was always with his fists.

It would be easy to say he would use it if he had to; he just hoped he wouldn't have to prove it.

He tried the door, found it unlocked, and slipped inside before he could talk himself out of it. Moving swiftly over the carpet toward the bedroom, whose door was open. There was no one inside. No one in the bathroom, no one in the kitchen. He didn't realize how tense he was until he was outside again, and his legs felt as if they were about to turn to water.

He grunted, breathed deeply, blew it all out in a rush, and trotted up to Hicaya's place, then over to Lil and Muriel's.

Empty; both empty.

He was well aware now that they were undoubtedly at Eula's, watching him, scorning his pitiful attempts to unearth them. Playing hero. Action hero. Probably taking bets on who would be the one to get him, if they didn't die laughing first.

And the more he imagined it, the angrier he became. The more he understood how managed, how manipulated his life had been, how little control he had actually had over the past few years, the less he tried to manage his temper.

He strode across the street, checking to be sure there was a round under the hammer, then holding the pistol down at his side. His face felt made of stone. His gaze centered on the old woman's door, seeing nothing else, hearing nothing at all, not bothering to question what earthly good this would do because questions, now, were irrelevant. If it was true that he had a purpose unknown to him before, then he was going to do his damnedest to make sure that purpose was fulfilled.

One way or another.

The door was unlocked, but he didn't open it.

Rage was one thing; suicide was something else.

And a voice behind him said, "Don't bother, they're not there."

2

He spun and dropped into a crouch, revolver at the ready until he saw Roger Freneau in the middle of the street. The man wore only boxer shorts, and he seemed to be having a difficult time standing. Streaks of blood mixed with pus covered his face and chest, was matted in his beard and hair; his left leg was swollen to near twice its normal size from groin to knee. One eye was dark purple and puffed shut, the other squinted hard as if it couldn't see clearly.

"Jesus, Rog," Trey said, standing, not wanting to stare and unable to look away.

"No sweat."

Neither of them moved.

Trey used his empty hand to gesture toward Freneau's house. "Get back inside, I'll call 9-1-1."

Freneau coughed, spat, a laugh that made him sound like an ancient raven. "Too late, man, too late. I pissed her off. Big time. My old boss, Davis, he's got nothing on her." He staggered sideways, belched, coughed, and spat blood at the ground. "Got to find my angel, though. She wouldn't help me, you know?" He turned by pivoting on his swollen leg. "Got to show her what happens when you don't do what's right."

He lurched forward, and Trey came down off the porch.

"Rog, where are they?"

Roger, his shoulders hunched, slowly swiveled his head around. "Who?"

Trey nodded once at Ricardo's house, at Muriel's, pointing with his chin.

"Oh. Them." He gestured toward the end of the street and the desert beyond. "Out there." Then he pointed the other way. "I'm going this way. Got to find the angel."

"No, Rog." He took a step. "Get back inside, okay? You're too—"

"Shit on that," Roger snapped, swollen tongue trying to lick his chapped and bloody lips. "I'm dying, you jackass, or are you too stupid to figure that out? But I'm not dying until I find her and show her what the hell she's done."

A gust of hot wind shoved him sideways, and he almost went to his knees.

"No, Rog," Trey said again. "I can't let you do that. She didn't do anything, you know that. It was Eula."

Freneau turned clumsily, tried to walk backward and fell hard on his rump, legs straight, arms braced on the ground to keep him from going all the way down. He cried out, the raven again, and struggled to stand. "Help me, man. I got to . . . help me, man."

Trey shook his head. He was fairly confident he wouldn't catch the Sickness if he wrestled Freneau back into his house, but the way it looked now, Roger would probably put up a fight. There'd be a cut or two, a scratch, and he didn't know just how far his protection would take him. Yet he couldn't leave him in the street, either.

"Look," he said, moving closer, seeing tears spill from the man's one good eye. "Look, I'm going to get a sheet or something, and I'm going to pull you inside and get you some help. Like the movie says, we can do this the easy way or the hard way, your choice, Rog. Your choice."

The wind blew dust over the raw eruptions on Freneau's skin, and the man whimpered, lifted a beseeching hand and let it drop when the arm proved too heavy.

"I made her mad," he said in a desolate whisper. "I didn't thank her, and I made her mad." He lowered his head. "I don't want to die, Trey. Jesus, I don't want to die."

Helpless, and angrier at Eula for it, he looked down the street for inspiration, for help, and noticed Jude hurrying toward them. He lifted a hand to stop her, wave her back, but she ignored him, and Roger twisted around awkwardly, spat blood, and grinned.

A growling, sandpaper voice: "My angel, there's my angel, the little—"

"Enough!"

Roger looked at him, his smile revealing teeth turning black. "What, hero, you gonna shoot me? You gonna shoot the dying man?"

Trey hesitated only a moment. "If you try to touch her . . . yeah, I will."

Ragged mocking laughter made him take an angry step forward, not realizing he had raised the gun until Roger laughed again and twisted around to face Jude, who faltered when she was close enough to see him clearly, veered away but didn't stop.

"Jude," Trey said, "go back."

She shook her head and pointed, jabbing at the air until he turned around.

"My God."

He had been wrong, really wrong; while he'd been playing hero, the sandstorm had reached Emerald City.

3

Despite the wind that grabbed at their clothes, tore at their hair, the cloud of sand and debris moved slowly, impossibly slowly. Rolling and cresting high above the rooftops like a dead-sea wave. Faint at the forefront as it moved right to left, more like thin smoke as it reached the half dozen empty homes that lay at the street's upper end beyond Freneau's and Eula's. Dimming them, fading them, eventually obscuring them entirely.

Puffs of it passed overhead, torn off by the wind, and he ducked and twisted away, protecting his eyes, unable to understand how it could move in such slow motion yet still dig at his skin, scrape and burn it.

A window shattered.

A handful of tiles rattled off a roof.

"Trey!"

The way ahead was dun and grey and tan and black.

"Trey!"

Mesmerized, fascinated, he backed off one careful step at a time, his free hand in front of his eyes as though to block a glaring light and he needed to see through it to what lay beyond.

Jude grabbed his arm. "Trey!"

Her dress was splotched with dust, the veil rippling against the contours of her face.

"We'll be all right," he said, raising his voice above the wind. He swept his arm eastward. "It's going that way." He looked at Freneau, who tried frantically to stand, his one eye wide with terror. "We have to help him, Jude. We can't leave him here."

She yanked down on his arm, grabbed his hair and forced him to face the storm.

The cloud had stopped, a maelstrom wall that defied the wind, growing visibly thicker, visibly taller, visibly darker.

More windows shattered, and somewhere inside was the rend and scream of tortured wood just before gunshot sounds indicated a porch torn apart.

She begged him to hurry, to get back to the house where they could hide with the girls until it passed; Roger begged him not to leave, not to leave him in the open, then pulled his good leg under him and lunged, grabbing for Jude's ankle, cackling and coughing, smearing the ground with yellow-streaked blood.

She screamed, and danced and kicked out of his reach, screamed again as finally panic took her and she ran a few blind steps toward the cloud before Trey hooked her waist with an arm and turned her effortlessly around. Disgusted at the sight of Roger's ravaged body, disgusted at himself for hesitating to help, he shoved Jude toward home, assuring her he'd be with her in a minute, he had to find something he could use to drag the man inside.

Roger lunged at them again.

Jude bolted, this time in the right direction.

"Bitch!" Freneau screamed after her. "Goddamn angel, get your ass back here, you gotta see what you—" He choked, spasmed, rolled onto his back while his heels pounded the ground. Froth bubbled between his lips. Fresh lesions broke over his face, and Trey couldn't help thinking he looked as if he'd been blasted with shotgun shells packed with needles.

Something stung and burned the back of his neck, and he looked quickly to the storm, groaned because the cloud-wall had begun to move his way, its thinner, lighter outer edge catching him with debris. And no longer silent as sand hissed and scratched along walls and roofs, while twigs and pebbles hammered tiles and glass.

Constant noise that sounded too much like rasping laughter.

Instinctively he backed up, trotted a few paces after Jude before he remembered Roger, cursed himself and turned back.

Stopped.

Damn, he thought; this is . . . damn.

Movement inside the cloud, dark grey ghosts passing through it toward him. Indistinct and indistinguishable, rippling as if they were submerged in muddy water.

He had no doubt what they were. Who they were. What they wanted. Still, he made one more move toward the stricken professor, and immediately changed his mind when Roger rolled again, this time to his hands and knees and snarled, teeth bared, growling what might have been words as he crawled toward him, reaching.

The ghost-figures grew, and grew nearer.

"Damnit, Rog," he said helplessly, took another look at the cloud, and ran. Thinking the only way he was going to get any of them out of this was by taking the pickup, even if he had to drive it on the rims, the only way he could outrun the sandstorm—if that's what it was, and he wasn't about to take any bets. Sandstorms don't change directions as if they're being steered; sandstorms don't stop and wait; sandstorms don't shelter ghosts in the center of their hearts.

As he sprinted past Hicaya's house, Jude and the girls on his own porch, urging him on, waving, shouting, he glanced to his right and stumbled in surprise, and slowed. Frowned. Shook his head and decided to stop asking himself stupid questions, like how the storm could keep moving east toward the city as if it were perfectly normal, yet leave part of itself behind. A check left between houses and he saw it there as well, just as he'd seen it before.

An answer suggested itself as he picked up speed again—cam-ouflage. The part of the storm that followed behind him was using the whole storm to hide it from whoever else might be watching. A traffic helicopter, maybe, dispatched as soon as the storm had been spotted, seeing nothing unusual below except the damn storm itself.

His side and legs protested, the wind swirled around him, nearly blinding him, nearly choking him, and he couldn't push any longer. He slowed while Jude screamed at him not to; he stopped while the girls shrieked at him to move it.

The hell with it, he thought, and long before he reached the house, he turned around to face *them*.

Walking out of the cloud, untouched by sand and wind as Eula had been the afternoon of her return. They were confident. Smiling; actually smiling. Each carrying a thick-knobbed club at their sides, swinging them easily, as if they weighed nothing.

On the right was Cable with his everpresent cap, and a face smooth and clean, Stephanie beside him, shortening her stride to keep in step; on the left was Rick Hicaya, waving with the hand that used to wear a glove, and . . . Muriel? Despite all that he had seen, all that he had been through, he could scarcely believe that slender woman in shirt and snug jeans was Muriel Carmody, looking like a model.

Only the figure in the center held no surprises.

Lillian on a pinto, riding bareback and laughing, sliding off, leaping on, sitting backward, facing forward.

Showing off.

Behind them, still veiled by the roiling cloud, another figure he assumed was Eula. Riding what looked to be a horse much bigger than the pinto. As if she were herding them, encouraging them, and reminding them of whatever promises she had made to turn them against him.

It didn't take more than a second glance at them all to understand exactly what those promises had been.

He ran again, not as fast this time, putting another hundred yards between them before he had to slow down.

"Oh, God, Trey," Starshine called, and over his shoulder he saw what she had seen—Roger crawling down the street, still trying to get to Jude. He must have known who and what was at his back, but it didn't seem to matter. He crawled, he clawed at the ground, he finally looked at them and Trey could hear him laughing. Could see him stop. Could see him lift a hand that started out as a greeting and ended up as a plea when the others stopped while Lillian rode on, circling the fallen man, swinging the club playfully at his head, blowing him a kiss before riding up on her own front yard, turning around, and charging.

Moonbow screamed with her sister; Jude took them hastily in her arms and held their faces against her as Lillian and her mount methodically, gleefully, trampled Roger to death.

4

Trey watched; he couldn't help it.

He had stumbled mostly backward until he was home, stayed in the street, breathing hard, a hand pressed to his side, and watched.

He watched Lillian balance on the horse's back, spread her arms wide, and bow; he watched her sit and watched the horse bow; he watched the others for any signs of remorse and saw only broad smiles that reminded him of sharks.

Still a hundred yards up the street, feeling only a hand's breadth away.

"Get inside," he said tightly. "Jude, get the girls inside."

"Trey—"

The wind prowled down the street.

"Don't argue. Please. Just do it."

The temperature began to rise, already warm, climbing toward hot.

"Trey, I can't."

He saw her at the door, saw the key in the lock, and saw her strain to turn it over, saw her shoulders slump in failure.

"It closed," Moonbow told him. "I saw it. It just closed, all by itself."

"So break the window."

The cloud finally engulfed Eula's house, stretched across and swallowed Roger's as well, swirling closer to his neighbors as they stood in a line, watching him watching them. Swinging their clubs. Shifting their weight. Lillian paraded in front of them, putting her horse through its paces while spinning the club over her head in taunting slow circles.

He heard Jude grunt as she lifted the lawn chair, heard her grunt louder when she swung it against the window, and he braced himself for the crash, looked over when he didn't hear it.

She tried again, this time succeeding only in snapping off the back legs and splitting the back.

Starshine and Moonbow clutched each other tightly, huddled against the door, faces buried on each other's shoulder.

"They can't," Jude said, pleading, stepping to the edge of the porch, dragging the chair with her. A look to the girls, to her friends up the street. "They wouldn't."

He knew what she meant, and he knew that as long as he was still here, Eula's people would kill them all, children or not. But he had a gun and they had none, and even though he wasn't a practiced shot, if he aimed and fired quickly, too quickly for them to scatter, surely he'd be able to even the odds a little. Surely one bullet would find its mark.

Even one out of the way would be better than nothing.

He flexed his fingers around the revolver's grip. Without looking, he said, "When I start shooting, you and the girls run."

"What? Where?"

"Jude, come on, it's the only chance we have."

"Momma, no," Starshine begged.

"Head for the highway. Get on the access road, you'll be able to run faster, and head for the highway."

"Momma?" Moonbow, crying.

"I'll try to get that damn horse or Lillian first." A no-other-choice shrug that Hicaya mimicked, provoking the others to laugh. "With all the commotion, you should have a pretty good head start."

"They have guns too," Starshine reminded him, her voice struggling to sound brave. "Why don't they have them now? Why are they carrying those other things?"

He didn't know; right now he didn't care. The longer they argued, the less chance any of them had of getting out of this alive. So he said, "Ready," swung the revolver up, aimed at the pinto, and pulled the trigger.

Nothing happened.

He tried again, and a third time, stared stupidly at the gun with the same awful empty feeling he had when an elevator dropped too fast. No safety to flick on or off, maybe the bullets were duds, but the odds against all them being that way were too high for credence.

Hell, he thought, and let his arm drop; oh, hell.

Eula again; it had to be. Which was why they all had their weapons and all he had was a useless chunk of metal.

The cloud shifted, bulged, seemed to nudge Lillian and the others forward, keeping their line, swinging their clubs. No longer smiling. A pack of arrogant hyenas moving in for the kill. Swaggering and slow.

Trey flipped the gun over to hold it by the barrel, thinking he might be able to get in one good blow before he was taken down. Better yet . . . if *he* charged *them,* took them off-guard with a suicide move, Jude and the girls still might have a chance for at least one of them to get away.

His left hand absently, automatically, patted his chest, rubbed it, and froze when it felt the comforting lump beneath his shirt. His pulse quickened, and slowed; images and ideas tripped over each other; a distant vague hope surged . . . and remained.

Yes, Mr. Falkirk, you're still protected, in a way.

Me? he had asked, and she had answered, *not exactly, but close enough.*

God, he wished he had more time. Just a few minutes, enough so he could stop worrying about them and think clearly for a change. Think about how Eula would have kept him here, in a virtual cocoon, while she went about her business, spreading gospel music and the Sickness, all in one breath, had not the Harps came along and told him things the old woman didn't want him to know. She could have driven him out, then, easily, and let the outside world do its work, but she hadn't, and he suspected anger had somehow gotten the best of her.

Anger, and the arrogance he saw in the others.

In the way Cable waved to him while holding his club in front of his face; in the way Lillian kept the horse prancing, dancing sideways, dancing back, head bobbing and tail high and arched; in the way Ricardo feinted a charge, and dropped back, feinted again, and dropped back, the look on his face as dark as the dark glove he used to wear; in the way Muriel and Stephanie strutted.

In the way the shadow rider in the cloud refused to come out.

"Trey," Jude whispered loudly, "someone's coming."

"I can see them."

And she said, "No, not there."

5

Eula's people stopped, and the pinto reared, came down hard and pawed at the ground, throwing dirt behind it that the wind caught and spun away.

A finger tapped Trey's left arm, and Sir John said, "My dear fellow, I'm terribly sorry I'm so late, but that damn car broke down and we had to walk the whole way."

Trey looked at him without expression, too startled to speak, and saw Lady Beatrice trudging around the corner. She gave him a half-hearted wave which he acknowledged with a wary nod.

"Why?" he said, returning his attention to Cable and the others.

Harp took off his hat, touched at his hair, and put it on again. "A certain responsibility, my boy. You either understand it, or you don't."

Lillian swung her mount around and headed into the sand-cloud, abruptly reversed direction, and returned to her front position, gesticulating angrily; he could hear her voice, but not the words.

"Any minute now," Sir John remarked. "Blasted wind."

Trey tried to keep an eye on Lillian while at the same time watching Jude and the girls hurry toward Beatrice. He wondered how far away the car was; he wondered if it would make a difference. "You know, Sir John, no offense, but you're a little old for this."

"Curious. That's precisely what my dear wife said not an hour ago."

Trey couldn't hold back a quick laugh, which felt so good he did it again, because for the duration of that laugh he almost believed the odds had actually been lowered. Until he looked at Harp's face and saw the strain there, and the checked fear, and the unmistakable age.

"I am quite all right, Mr. Falkirk," Harp said, keeping his gaze steady and straight ahead. "You are the one you need to concern yourself about. This is all going to move quite fast once it begins."

"No kidding. And how do you propose we take on five angry people with clubs, one horse, and Eula back there? My gun doesn't work."

"Perhaps not," he said. "But this one does." And he pulled out his own, the one he had used against Trey.

"Son of a bitch."

"Once again, not quite."

"So what am I supposed to do?"

"The chariot, my boy. Use the chariot. That's what it's for."

"That doesn't work either."

Harp shook his head in dismay, while Lillian trotted the horse back and forth across the street. Building up speed. Building up resolve.

Sand and dirt scratching across walls; a window exploding deep within the cloud; a beautiful bright blue sky and a full warm sun.

Harp grabbed Trey's arm, rapped a knuckle against his chest where the gold chip lay, then pushed him toward the pickup. "Use it, Mr. Falkirk. There's no time left. You must *use* it."

He was right.

Cable apparently couldn't stand the waiting any longer, couldn't stand seeing the quarry just ahead, helpless in conversation with an old man in silver snakeskin boots. He looked back into the cloud, made a sharp *the hell with it* gesture, and broke into a run. Keeping the club low. Glaring, grinning, gaining speed with each step. The others hesitated until he was a good fifty yards ahead, but when they ran as well, they weren't nearly as fast, weren't by their attitudes nearly as confident. Someone, Trey figured, had noticed the old man's gun.

"Go!" Harp ordered, lifted his chin, and waited.

Trey had no idea what to do, how he was going to get the pickup to work effectively without any tires. But whatever it was, he had to do it, and do it *now*, because Cable had reached his own house and Trey could see the twisted smile, the anticipation as he raised his club.

Oh, God, he thought, and slammed his palms onto the hood.

"Please," he said urgently. "I need you, old buddy. Will it be all right? Can we—"

Harp stood sideways, straightened his arm, aimed, and fired.

The retort echoed in the wind.

Cable took the bullet in his heart, took two more steps, and dropped, the club skidding and bouncing along the ground until it stopped at the mouth of Trey's drive.

There was no key in the ignition, but the black pickup shuddered.

Sprinting ahead of the others, Stephanie screamed, inhuman, enraged, and Harp waited patiently until she reached her husband before he aimed, and fired, and dropped her on Cable's back.

The pickup shuddered, and Trey didn't dare lift his hands, or look over his shoulder.

We need you, he thought desperately; I know this isn't right, but we can't wait much longer.

Another shot, he heard Harp say, "Damn," and assumed the man had missed. Two more in quick succession, followed by a woman's shriek, a man's groan, the sound of two bodies hitting the ground.

Then hoofbeats, a shot, and a long silence in the moaning wind.

Trey couldn't help it, he turned with one hand still on the hood and saw Lillian swing her club like a mallet as she passed on Harp's left, catching him in chest and chin, the pinto's haunch catching him as well and spinning him around as he fell.

Trey shouted.

He heard Beatrice scream.

He saw Lillian race up the street toward the cloud, crying out her triumph as she twisted around on the horse's back and rode facing the animal's tail. Grinning. Grinning madly. Pointing at him as if to say, *you're next.*

Beatrice reached the old man before he did, kneeling, cradling his head in her lap, her hands cupping his cheeks. He stood at their side, trying to shield him from the sun and the wind, the dust clouding the air. There wasn't much blood, and there was too much; the way he tried to breathe betrayed the collapse of ribs and lungs.

Harp peered up at him, turning his head slightly in a futile attempt to see better. "She was right, you know." A quivering smile at his wife. "She's always right."

"John," he said, swallowing hard, and heard the hoofbeats, thunder on the wind.

He reached down and grabbed the gun from Harp's hand, turned and fired in the same motion, blasting Lillian from the pinto's back. The horse reared, shaking its head wildly, then ran over her body and vanished into the cloud still moving toward them.

Damn, he thought, staring dumbly at the gun; damn, I did it.

A weak scrabbling at his leg, and he knelt, not daring even a glimpse of Beatrice's face if he wanted to keep his own composure.

"You know now," Harp said, gulping air for each word.

Trey looked at the chariot, quivering as the engine raced, standing on four full tires.

He nodded, passing a thumb over the chip, the talisman.

The old man shuddered, closed his eyes, opened them again. "I don't know where they are, those men you must meet. I don't . . . know if—"

"Hush, John," Beatrice said, stroking his brow with one finger.

"My hat."

"Here," and she placed it on his chest.

He grabbed it with both hands, sighed and smiled. "My indulgence. Even now, she grants me my small indulgence."

Trey searched for Jude and found her, standing in the street with her daughters. White dress. White veil. Small and fragile against the sky.

Behind him, the steady scrape and claw of the wind.

No time; no time left.

"John," he said apologetically, shifting to stand.

"Quite all right, Mr. Falkirk, quite all right. We understand. Leave now and you'll be fine."

"No," Trey said. "I, uh . . . I wanted to thank you."

Harp worked his lips, widened his eyes, pulled the white straw cowboy hat closer to his chin. "Oh, my dear fellow," he said. And closed his eyes. And died.

6

Trey touched the hat, touched the back of Beatrice's hand, and rocked up to his feet.

You can do it, you know, he said to all his doubts; you can get them into the truck and get the hell out, bury Sir John and take your chances trying to find those men.

But when he looked down at the old man's body, looked into Beatrice's eyes, he knew that wasn't going to happen.

Options.

Choices.

Do one, and Eula carries on, and the man on the boulevard keeps adding new numbers until the sandwich board is too small, until he runs out of fresh paint.

Do the other . . .

"Mr. Falkirk," Beatrice said, "I can't read your mind, but I know what you're thinking."

He nodded.

No more time.

"Can she take my place? Can Jude do it for me? Whatever it is?"

"Yes, Mr. Falkirk, I believe she can. If she will."

"You'll . . . you'll . . ."

"Yes. Any way I can."

He nodded.

No more time.

He trotted down the street, the girls racing toward him and hugging him, weeping silently, almost knocking him over. As if they knew. He lifted his head, and Jude came closer, tentative, unwilling.

"Listen to Lady Beatrice," he told her, "and don't forget the strongbox. You'll need it, every dime." He took the gold casino chip from around his neck, squeezed and rubbed it once for luck, and before she could stop him, he placed it around hers.

And before she could stop him, he lifted the veil and kissed her.

"No," Moonbow whispered when he pulled gently away.

"She'll kill you if I don't," he said.

"I don't care," she answered, and Starshine said, "Me neither."

"Well, I do," he said, and heard the wind and smiled. "Good news," he told them as he turned away. "Damn chariot's a-comin'."

4

Trey grabbed the girls' suitcases from the back and dropped them onto the porch, took the strongbox and set it next to them, got behind the wheel and whispered, "What do you say? Can we go?"

A brief tremor rocked the truck, and he pulled into the street, faced the cloud and gunned the engine, just as the cloud billowed and the wind howled and the sand raked across the windshield and tried to scour the black from the hood.

He took his foot off the brake.

He saw the dark rider inside wheel and race away.

Funny, he thought as he rode the chariot in after her; funny how it is sometimes

when you finally think you've got it all figured out, and you finally think you've got yourself pretty well set for the rest of your life, not all that exciting but not all that dull either, and something comes along and someone comes along and the next thing you know you're driving blind in a freak sandstorm, holding the steering wheel so tight your fingers want to cramp, tempted to use the wipers even though you know they won't help, habit making you turn the radio on but there's nothing there but static, and the scratch and scrape and claw of whatever it is you're in trying to get in with you.

You don't know, not really, how fast you're going because the speedometer doesn't work, and you can't see very far because the headlamps only turn the sandstorm cloud a light shade of hell, and the dark rider ahead of you is only that much darker, a shifting rippling shimmering shape that's only vaguely human.

And you can't tell if you're still on the street because the truck's bouncing and slamming and skidding and dropping and it's all you can do just to keep in your seat.

All you can do just to follow that dark rider, who keeps looking back over her shoulder, probably wondering where it all went wrong, probably trying to figure out how something like this can happen to someone like her, especially when it's someone like you riding hard on her tail.

Funny, but you know there isn't a prayer you can kill her with; you knew that from the start, once you understood what the start was.

But that's all right, because in the here and now, it doesn't matter.

What matters is that John Harp is dead, because of her, because of you, and if you want to keep the others alive, then you do what you do, and hope it's the right thing.

You hope that Jude will find that preacher, maybe he can do something for her; you hope that Beatrice will stick with them, maybe she's stronger than she thinks; you hope with a laugh you didn't think you had in you that this damn truck doesn't run out of gas before . . . whatever . . . whenever . . . however it ends.

Keeping on her tail, swerving when she swerves, speeding up, slowing down, your head and spine aching, your eyes beginning to burn, the screech and howl outside the cab maddening until you turn it into familiar white noise.

Then it's quiet.

Too quiet.

The engine's muffled grumbling, and don't ask how but the hoof-beats outside, an odd combination that somehow finds the same rhythm.

Funny, how it is sometimes

but when the right front tire climbed and slid off a half-hidden rock the storm wouldn't let him see, tilted and almost tipped the chariot over, he allowed himself a smile, not much humor there, but a smile.

He knew right where she was headed, and he didn't think she did.

For a moment, grunting in exasperation as he wrestled the steering wheel over and swung a little wide to her left, he felt a minor eruption of hope that he might get out of this in one piece.

Or, if not in one piece, being alive would do as well.

All he had to do, all she had to was keep checking on him the way she did, no doubt not understanding why he wasn't directly behind her now and . . . he laughed aloud, slapped the wheel, slapped his thigh when she veered sharply to her left and placed herself directly in his figurative crosshairs.

Not long now, then.

No matter what the hell she was, it had been evident from the start that her vision in this cloud wasn't much better than his. An advantage, because now he was leading her from behind.

All he needed was a little luck, and without thinking he touched his chest, and snatched his hand away when it found nothing there but flesh and bone. No big deal. He could do it anyway.

The problem was the timing.

With visibility like a man who refused to wear his thick glasses, he had to rely on memory and instinct to tell him when to make his move.

Soon, he hoped; soon, before the regret he began to feel tainted his judgment and poked a hole in his resolve.

There it was.

A darker patch of dark unmoved by the wind, its edges blurred by blowing sand.

She hadn't spotted it yet, too busy checking on him, so he half rose from his seat and stomped on the accelerator and the chariot hesitated and charged, and he leaned forward as best he could so he could stare at her and hope she could see his eyes, see his taut mirthless smile, recognize his nod when she did finally see him.

Suddenly she whipped her head around, and he knew that she saw it, the boulder he had marked to mark the boundary of his haven, and he couldn't resist a joyful laugh because it was too late for her to swerve around it, too high for her mount to jump it, but just far enough away that she could stop before she hit it.

She did, but it was too late when she realized she was trapped.

"Thank you, old buddy," he whispered.

The chariot roared and left the ground, and the last thing he saw was Eula's startled laughing face before the world turned white.

Red.

Empty.

5

Standing beside a car on the shoulder of a highway, two women waiting for someone to stop and help, two young girls who were women too soon.

They had heard the distant explosion, but none of them turned to look. And none of them wept; that would come later.

"Where are we going?" Jude asked, unable to keep her hand off the chip Trey had placed around her neck.

"I'm not quite sure," Lady Beatrice answered. "Sir John . . ." She faltered, and Jude stroked her arm. "Sir John never really told me." A shaky laugh. "Wouldn't you know it. Something about the sea, though. I remember something about the sea." A gesture east. "That way."

Enforced silence as an eighteen-wheeler blasted past them.

"I've never seen the sea," Moonbow said quietly.

"Me neither," said Starshine.

"An adventure, then," Beatrice told her. "We'll make it an adventure."

"No, thanks," Starshine said. "I had enough of that."

Beatrice grinned, and the girls grinned back.

While Jude finally allowed herself to look back toward Emerald City. The sandstorm had passed; there was no smoke in the sky. A flutter in her chest when a black pickup slowed but didn't stop.

He was gone.

Face it, Jude, he's gone, and it's going to take a while.

Still, knowing it was fruitless, knowing the pain it would cause when she lay in her bed again and felt the dark around her, she couldn't help wondering if Trey had known, really known, how she felt.

He had kissed her, so maybe he had.

Regret was foolish, she knew that, and knew it was inevitable as well.

And when she turned around and saw the towers of Excalibur rise above the interstate and the overpasses and the trucks and the warehouses, she couldn't help thinking that a queen couldn't do better than have a man like him.

6

The dragon lay in the middle of the desert. Sleeping. Always sleeping.
   Until tonight.
   When the dragon stirred.